BK1

WEBER, S. KAY

A TERRI SPRINGE CULINARY MYSTERY

DOUBLE TRUFFLE

	DATE DUE		
7-16-10			

$15.00

from Author

618610

Double Truffle

A Terri Springe Culinary Mystery
(with recipes)

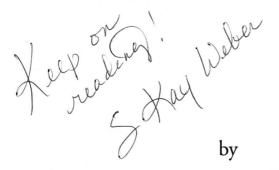

Keep on reading!
S. Kay Weber

by

S. Kay Weber

authorHOUSE®

AuthorHouse™
1663 Liberty Drive, Suite 200
Bloomington, IN 47403
www.authorhouse.com
Phone: 1-800-839-8640

AuthorHouse™ UK Ltd.
500 Avebury Boulevard
Central Milton Keynes, MK9 2BE
www.authorhouse.co.uk
Phone: 08001974150

This book is a work of fiction. People, places, events, and situations are the product of the author's imagination. Any resemblance to actual persons, living or dead, or historical events, is purely coincidental.

First published by AuthorHouse   8/21/2007

ISBN: 978-1-4343-2477-1 (sc)
ISBN: 978-1-4343-2478-8 (hc)

Library of Congress Control Number: 2007905004

Printed in the United States of America
Bloomington, Indiana

This book is printed on acid-free paper.

Dedication

This book is dedicated to my Mom.

I love you, now, always, and forever.

Acknowledgments

The author would like to acknowledge the help and or inspiration, of the following people.

My family, of course, first and foremost, especially my beautiful daughters.

I would also like to thank Eric Mathews, without whose help, I would never have survived my last few years in the restaurant business. Also, thank you Eric, for coming up with a great title! Talk about inspiration.

I would also like to acknowledge my co-workers, as always for your support and enthusiasm.

I would especially like to thank my wonderful editor, Bev Grenawalt. Thank you Bev, for your hard work, patience, and enthusiasm for the story.

I also want to mention, once again, Pete Neitz, of the Boston Redevelopment Authority. He's my hook-up, in Boston, where something interesting *always* seems to be happening.

I also want to thank all the wonderful people in my home town, who read 'Spaghetti with Murder' and expressed so many positive feelings about my writing style and the great characters, that have come out of my vivid imagination.

Last, but certainly not the least, I must thank my wonderful, young friend, Sergio Paz. As he works here in the U.S., he has helped me to understand the plight of immigrants, from Guatemala, as well as other lands. He has expressed, with enthusiasm, his love for his homeland, and his family, especially his sister Michelle and his brother Jose, whom I had the privilege to meet, on their visits here. The fact that, there just happens to be, a large population of Guatemalans, in the city of Boston, is pure coincidence.

Not everything that can be counted, counts.

Not everything that counts can be counted.

- Albert Einstein

Chapter One

Terri Springe was dreaming and it was a good one. She was dreaming she was with Captain Rico Mathews. He was wearing his policeman's uniform, of course, and they were in Paris. They were standing beneath the Eiffel Tower. Rico was handing her a perfect, pink rose. Terri accepted the rose with a beautifully French-manicured hand. Her white silk dress, was blowing in the soft breezes. Her soft shoulder length, silky brown hair, was fluttering about her face. She carefully pulled it back in dramatic, slow motion. Rico was smiling at Terri as she was taking in the delicate scent of the rose. He was leaning toward her for a romantic, gentle kiss, and......., and,.......*suddenly, she sneezed!* Not a delicate, little, cute, feminine sneeze. *Oh no!* It was a horrible, tremendously *huge* sneeze and Rico was running away! *Stop!* Terri called after him but Rico was gone, gone, gone away, forever.

Terri suddenly woke up only to find Maria, one of her poofy, Ragdoll cats in her face. She was tickling Terri's nose with her kitty whiskers. Turning on the light, Terri grabbed a box of tissues and continued to sneeze. Maria made an immediate and hasty retreat. "*Crap!* I'm getting a stupid cold," Terri said out loud to Maria, who was looking at her from the door. And she was hardly in Paris, enjoying a soft summer breeze with the man of her dreams. Just the opposite, it would seem. It was January. She was in Boston in her cozy apartment. The weather was what one would expect on a New England winter morning. Terri got out of her warm bed, shivered, and looked outside, only to discover it was snowing, *again.* Great, just great. Amusing, how, at the beginning of winter everyone wanted it to snow, like around the holidays or whatever. It really got old fast, however, when all the excitement was over and the decorations were getting just plain droopy and sad.

Terri certainly couldn't complain about the holiday season. Not this year. She and her business partner and friend, Brianna Severson, had been unbelievably busy. They had put together and sold, countless sandwich and snack trays, for parties and gatherings of every imaginable sort. Whether it be office meetings, book clubs, even quilting and yarning groups.

Everyone wanted lunches, munchies or finger foods. The girls had made trays with meats and cheeses, or fruits and veggies, along with dips, crackers, and breads. Whatever the customer or occasion called for, Terri and Brianna aimed to please. The party trays were always beautifully presented and made with the freshest and finest quality foods available. Once word got around, Terri and Brianna could barely keep up. So, along with their regular schedule of meal delivery, the party and snack trays had gone over like gang-busters. Terri found herself, once again, thinking about hiring *another* assistant, maybe two. Terri's buddy, Angie Perry, had helped out wherever and whenever she could. But she already had a full-time job being a police officer and Terri's best friend to boot!

Terri decided then she might as well get up. She slipped into her fuzzy, pink slippers and warm cream-colored robe, then padded out of her room. She took a peek into the 'guest' bedroom in her apartment, which was Brianna's room for the time being. She was still sound asleep with Louie, Maria's brother, tucked under her arm. Louie opened his eyes and looked lazily at Terri and closed them again. *What a couple of bums!* She didn't blame them. It was the perfect morning to sleep in. Terri, with the cold coming on, was ready to crawl back in bed herself. She was up now, however, and needed coffee, as soon as possible. Coffee now, tea later for the sore throat she could also feel coming on. Terri would spend the rest of the day doing as little as possible. It was Saturday, after all. They didn't have a lot planned for the next couple of weeks after the busy holidays.

New Year's Eve had been particularly lucrative for 'Terri's Table' because of the addition of party trays to the business. Speaking of the business, Terri had wanted to change the name, trying to include Brianna in it somehow. However, Brianna would have none of that. 'People are used to the name,' Brianna had said. 'The business was already established and it had a nice, short ring to it.' So 'Terri's Table' it continued to be.

Never mind that Brianna's father, David Severson, had financially backed up Terri and Brianna almost immediately as they set up the business. Terri, of course, had every intention of seeing to it that David got back every penny. The way the business was going though, his investment would be paid back in no time. Not that David Severson needed the money mind you. He was already an incredibly wealthy and fortunately, like his daughter, a very generous and grounded person. David was also overwhelmingly grateful to Terri for everything she had done for his daughter, Brianna. On the other hand, David knew a good business opportunity when he saw one. Thus, he didn't hesitate to support Terri and Brianna in whatever they needed to set up a modern kitchen and specialty foods shop.

Before meeting up with Brianna, due to some *very* bizarre circumstances surrounding an, *also* very, strange murder, Terri had cooked four meals a week for six families. This she had done out of the kitchen of a local supper club at which she was employed at the time. After Terri hired young Brianna, however, that changed very quickly. Brianna wasn't just smart, ambitious, and hard-working. She was, *on her own,* much to Terri's shock and disbelief, also unbelievably, terribly rich! It was Brianna who had originally offered to set up the business. That fact, had absolutely nothing to do with the start of the their friendship. On the contrary.

When Terri had first met Brianna, she had been an incredibly confused, unhappy, young woman with an alcoholic, emotionally ill, *also* very unhappy, controlling mother. In an effort to extricate herself from her mother's damaging clutches, Brianna had accepted Terri's offer to be her assistant. It was *after* this, that Brianna had revealed her financial situation to Terri. She was an extremely, wealthy young woman, much of her money having come from a trust fund set up by her grandparents. She was also unusually well-grounded and practical. This fact being only because she had been virtually raised by a loving housekeeper, along with the cook, at the family home. Brianna didn't want *the spoiled rich kid life*. She had no use for shopping, partying, and other foolish pursuits. She had watched with disgust, as her mother and her many free-loading friends, had done all these things. Brianna wanted none of that. She wanted *good* experiences. She wanted *learning* experiences. She enjoyed Terri and Angie's company and she loved to cook. For Terri, the day Brianna came into her life, continued to stand out as a banner day. Brianna's mother Elizabeth, was currently and *hopefully,* on her way to recovery at the best rehab center, David's money could buy. In the meantime, Brianna had moved on with her life in a *much* healthier fashion.

Brianna was also taking several classes at Boston University, all of which she had passed in her first semester with flying colors. Terri was so proud of her young assistant, she felt almost like Brianna was her own daughter. Being only 31 years old, however, Terri looked upon the 18, soon to be 19, year old Brianna as more of a little sister. Terri's younger brother and two younger sisters were elsewhere and didn't need Terri anymore. Being the oldest in the family of four children had been difficult at times, causing Terri to have unusually strong maternal instincts which, of course, drove her younger siblings crazy.

The empty nest syndrome had hit Terri's mother, Emily Springe, especially hard. Terri's father, Harvey, always had something to do and none of their children were very far away. Terri had noticed though, when she had been home during the holidays, that her mother was finally getting involved in more outside activities. This was a huge relief to Terri who always felt pressure from Emily to 'come home for a visit.' At least she didn't feel like they were languishing away at their home on the coast up in Maine. Terri loved going home *occasionally* but her real life was here now, in Boston.

Terri had moved to Boston almost six years ago to be near her best pal, Angie, and start a business. With her savings and Angie's connections, she had done just that, along with furnishing her apartment. She had also taken marketing and cooking classes, the latest she and Brianna were attending together. They had both decided to become pastry chefs, along with their other culinary skills. Terri realized this meant expanding the business even more. But some clients had been making elaborate dessert requests and Terri was extremely limited in this area. She had tried to keep the business as organized and simple as possible, to prevent any unnecessary complications with her customers.

Which brought Terri to her latest problem. Major annoyance was more like it. Terri had always tried very hard, *not* to get emotionally involved or over-wrought in any way, shape or form with any of her customers. This was one of the many reasons, why she had chosen not to be a caterer. She did not have the patience for it. One customer in particular, however, was more difficult than most to ignore. Logan Adams-Buckley was *almost impossible* to ignore. She saw to that, anytime anyone was around. *Especially* if her handsome husband, Alex, also happened to be in the same room.

Logan herself, was a mere 35 years old and, of course, very pretty and fashionable. Angie's opinion was, using one of their favorite movie lines, *"She's like a biscuit older than we are."* Also, the name Logan seemed unusual to Terri. She just couldn't help, but connect it to a mutant in a popular series of

comic books and movies. The first thing Terri had wondered
was if it even was her *real name*. Something about it just didn't
seem to fit. One way or another, Logan Adams-Buckley had
been difficult to deal with from day one of their business
relationship. She always managed to find a new way to come
up with a problem or complaint. *So*, as hard as Terri and
Brianna had tried to ignore the woman, they could not.

She was married to the very handsome Alex Buckley, who
was 61 and counting, and like Brianna's father, very, very
wealthy. Brianna was not impressed, however. Having dealt
with her mother and the people she had kept around her in
those party years, Brianna knew a phony when she saw one
a mile away.

"I am not sure how much more of her I can take," Brianna
had remarked one day, as they left the Buckley home. She and
Terri had dropped off some party trays for a *soiree*, Logan's
word for the parties and gatherings she was constantly putting
on. No matter how annoying Logan was about herself, her
clothes, her jewelry, or her demands, the worst was the way
she treated the mild-mannered Alex. Oh, it wasn't that she was
unkind, critical, or even a nag with her husband. Quite the
opposite, actually. She crawled all over him! When the girls
dropped off the food she had ordered, Logan always insisted
that she be there to supervise and comment. She always
had poor Alex in tow and was kissing him, touching him, or
grabbing him, in some embarrassing way. She also constantly
baited Terri and Brianna, trying to get them to comment, on
'how handsome her husband was' or 'was she not just the
luckiest girl in the world to have caught such a gorgeous,
fantastic guy?' Worse yet, and this would always be directed
at Terri, 'didn't she wish that Alex was her husband?' Terri
always commented in some noncommittal way but Logan
never took the hint. She and Brianna would barely make it out
of there with their wits. It was beyond insufferable.

The biggest drawback, unfortunately, was how they had
gotten this woman as a client in the first place. Logan was a
first cousin of Will Collins, Angie's partner on the police force.

Will was not just a good police officer and partner to Angie. He was a genuinely nice person, which made it difficult to believe that he and the awful Logan, were related in any way, shape or form. Oh, and Logan was her *middle* name. Will had told them. Her first name was Kathryn. She had been named for her grandparents and had started using her middle name in her teenage years because she thought it sounded cooler than her real first name. For some reason though, in Will's eyes, she *was* pretty cool. Well, he was obviously blinded by her charm because around Will, she was a totally different person.

Also, Will had just gotten through a difficult divorce and they had all sympathized, as he had been devastated. However, when his cousin had moved to town with her rich husband and settled into a huge mansion in Beacon Hill, Logan had gotten in touch with Will.

And as if all of these things weren't enough, there were Alex's two children from his previous marriage. His first wife, who had also been much younger, had died and left behind two young children, a boy and girl. Logan had been their nanny. The rest, as they say, is history.

"God, the P.D.A.! Heaven help us!" Brianna had gone on as they were driving away from the Buckley *mansion. P.D.A. Public displays of affection*, a big fat no-no, as far as Terri, Brianna, and Angie were concerned. Whatever people did in private was their own business, but in front of other people, it was embarrassing and unacceptable.

Terri just plain did not know what to do. It was a conundrum of massive proportions. They did not want to hurt the clueless Will. Also, Logan spent a ton of money, buying specialty foods most people just would not put into their daily diet. Terri had always preferred to prepare wholesome, good old-fashioned meals, most of the recipes from her mother's own kitchen. Meatloaf, beef roasts, fried chicken, chicken breasts, sliced pork loin, casseroles, stroganoffs, soups and stews, along with fresh vegetables, potatoes and gravies, were normally on the menus she and Brianna, delivered to a dozen families each week. All of her customers appreciated Terri and Brianna's delicious meals, conveniently delivered to their doors and put into their refrigerators or freezers. Except for Logan and Alex Buckley, of course. Logan's preferences included gourmet foods, expensive fish and seafood, or any other extravagance she may have read about in a magazine or saw on a cooking show. Terri and Brianna patiently tried to fill her indulgences. Terri had the feeling, Alex Buckley would have preferred a decent meatloaf dinner once in awhile. Logan, on the other hand, would have none of that. Apparently, her years as a nanny had been rather bitter ones. She certainly had a chip on her shoulder for some reason.

Which led back to *the other* problem. The children, 10-year old Jenni and 11-year old Benjamin, *absolutely loved* Logan. Their mother, who had been gravely ill with pancreatic cancer, had hired Logan in the first place to help with the children. Logan truly *did care* for the children and they were well-behaved, polite, and friendly. They also had become quite attached to their 'cousin Will' *and* a surprised Brianna. Terri cared for Jenni and Benjamin very much herself and did not know what to do. Needless to say, it was a mess.

Speaking of messes, Terri had been mulling this all over in her mind as she looked out at the thickening snowstorm. Finally going into the bathroom, she looked in the mirror. *Yikes!* What a sight she was! Pillow hair to the extreme, along with a red nose, looked back at her. Terri knew she would not be leaving the apartment today and probably not even tomorrow. They had a long week coming up and it was the perfect time to get some much needed rest. It would also be a day to put miss, *pain-in-the-ass,* Logan Adams-Buckley, out of her mind for awhile.

This having been decided, Terri washed her face, rinsed out her mouth with warm salt water, and went to the kitchen to make coffee. The sudden ringing of the land line interrupted her thoughts. She decided to let the machine take it since it was the business phone and she didn't feel like talking to anyone. Even Captain Rico Mathews, Angie's boss and Terri's *sort of* boyfriend, had her cell phone number now. She waited for the answering machine to pick up, listened to her own voice, and then the caller.

"Terri Springeeeee...." Terri heard the greeting and the caller stressing the silent e. "Grrrrrr......," she said out loud to the phone, and then tensed when she heard who it was. "This is Logan-Adams Buckley calling. I am putting on another *soiree* next weekend and need some specialty foods. This is an extremely important event, Terri. You *must* call me back as soon as you get this message. I'll be waiting by the phone." This was followed by a sharp click.

Chapter Two

Suddenly, Brianna came tearing out of her room with a freaked-out Louie at her heals. Her silky, dark brown hair, which she had cut to shoulder length last fall, was standing up on end with static electricity. Brianna's big, brown eyes were wild. Louie, on the other hand, immediately calmed down and meandered to the litter box and then his bowl. *Typical,* thought Terri, as she watched the pair with amusement.

"Oh, my God!" Brianna shrieked. "Did I just hear Logan's voice? Where is she? Tell me I was having a nightmare. Cool," she said then, as easily distracted as the cat, "it's snowing again."

Terri didn't answer immediately, just went to the phone and hit the message button. Logan's voice filtered out of the speakers. Terri filled her coffee cup and Brianna followed suit.

"Geez," said Brianna. "I mean, what the hell? It's freakin' Saturday! Are you getting a cold Terri?" She finally looked at her boss and surmised the situation at hand. "You look like crap. Are you calling that puke back, by the way?"

"One crisis at a time please," Terri begged as she sipped her coffee, put her cup down, and then started to sneeze. Grabbing a box of tissues off of the coffee table, she blew her nose in dramatic fashion and flopped onto the sofa. Brianna joined Terri with her own cup of coffee.

"Well, that answers the first question," said Brianna, trying to be sympathetic but then went on. "Oh, and hey, don't give your germs to me."

"Thank you for your support!" Terri said, as she finished blowing her nose, got up to deposit the tissues into the garbage, and wash her hands. One thing Terri had learned about colds and flu over the years was, wash, wash, wash, as most germs were spread from the hands. Going back into the living room, she flopped back onto the sofa next to Brianna and went on.

"To comment on your next question, I would rather have the bubonic plague, then call that woman back right now. I am tired, crabby, and as for your observation on my appearance, I have already looked in the mirror and *I feel exactly the way that I look!*" She finished in grumpy fashion and sniffled.

"I think you covered everything," said Brianna as she got up from the sofa and headed back to the kitchen for more coffee. She came back out and looked at her poor, miserable boss. "That being the case, I will fix you a nice breakfast. How about waffles with blueberries, your favorite?" Terri nodded gratefully and started to sneeze again.

Brianna went into the bathroom and, after taking care of her morning routine, came out with a strong cold pill for Terri. They had stocked up before winter, on essentials for the cold and flu season. Terri's young, wonderful assistant presented the cold tablet, on a silver tray, with a glass of 100%, Florida orange juice. She also refilled Terri's coffee cup, adding cream and a bit of sugar. Accepting it all with a quiet, "Oh, thank you so much!" Terri then snuggled herself into the sofa with a *blankie*. Louie and Maria, who were not afraid of *people germs*, both cuddled with Terri.

Suddenly, the phone rang again. "Don't you dare move!" Brianna said firmly, "I will take care of it, and *yes,* I will be careful. Just leave it to me!"

She looked at the caller I.D. "Oh yeah, it's her. Stay quiet and calm," Brianna cautioned Terri before she picked up the phone.

"Wait!" Terri had a quick thought. "Put it on speaker phone." She grinned as she pulled the *blankie* up to her chin and snuffled.

"Oh, you are sooooo….. bad." Brianna shook a finger at her boss, pushed *speaker* and the talk button. "Terri's Table, this is Brianna, how may I help you?" She said all in one, *trying to sound polite,* breath.

"Well, this is Logan *Adams-Buckley* here," Logan said sharply. "I am sorry but I must speak with Terri. It is an extremely urgent matter." Terri *so* rolled her eyes at this, as Logan's definition of *urgent* was, of course, completely different from everyone else. Brianna smoothly moved along with the conversation, ignoring Logan's demanding attitude.

"Terri is unavailable right now, Mrs. Buckley. May I take a message?" Brianna was trying *not* to sound condescending but it wasn't easy.

"Brianna," said Logan, losing patience fast, "I really need to speak with Terri. It is a matter of the utmost importance. I'm sure you understand." Terri wrinkled her nose at this and Logan went on, trying charm as a last resort. "Could you perhaps give me Terri's cell phone number, Brianna, so that I can contact her personally? I seem to have lost it."

"Once again, Mrs. Buckley," Brianna *pretended* to sound patient and professional, "Terri is unavailable, as I just told you. Also, there is no possible way you could have *lost* Terri's cell phone number because you didn't have it in the first place. We have a *very* strict policy about our clients having *only* the business phone number. Terri is *extremely* jealous of her privacy. If you will please just simply call back on Monday morning after 9:00, during regular business hours, we will be more than happy to take care of your order at that time."

"You know, young lady," Logan was really going in for the kill now, "I have a half a mind to call my Cousin Will and let him know that I am *not* happy with your attitude….."

Terry covered her mouth to keep from laughing uproariously and stifled another sneeze. Brianna smoothly interrupted the, by this time, *very put out Mrs. Adams-Buckley.*

"Well, you go ahead and do that Mrs. *Adams*-Buckley," Brianna said with finality. "I know your cousin Will pretty well. I seriously doubt he is going to arrest us in the middle of a snowstorm, for telling a client that we only do business on business days, during business hours. Have a good day and thanks for calling Terri's Table." At that, she shut off the phone and unplugged the damn thing! "Boy, she certainly has half a mind all right," Brianna said then and started laughing.

Terri was on the sofa giggling and sneezing at the same time. "Oh, my God, Brianna, that was unbelievable. What are we going to do with this woman? This is so horrible! Man, I hate being sick." Terri sunk further into the sofa and clutched her blanket. "*Jealous of my privacy, huh?* Where did you come up with that one, Sweetie?"

"Oh, did you like that? My mother used to say that, when she was plastered and didn't want anyone to figure it out. 'Brianna', she would say, please tell the servants, I do not want to see anyone. You know how jealous I am of my privacy!' Please follow this with a heavy sigh." Brianna imitated her mother to the best of her ability once again, with great effort. Terri felt a little bad but then Angie came through the door, fortunately, breaking the awkward moment.

"Whew! Whoa, it's a blizzard out!" Angie shook and stomped off as much snow as she could, onto the large rug that Terri kept in front of the door for the blizzard season. She still made a pretty big mess though, as she peeled off the top layer and took off her boots. "Lead me to the coffee!" Then she looked at Terri and said, "Man, are you sick Terri? You look like shit." Terri stuck her tongue out at her best friend and blew her nose without answering. "Hey, keep your germs to yourself!" Angie finished and headed to the kitchen to get her coffee.

"That's what I told her, as a matter of fact, only with a slightly different adjective," Brianna said, still laughing. "Oh, and listen to this, Angie." She played back Logan's first message and Angie nearly spit out her coffee.

13

"Oh, you have got to be kidding me. That woman is beyond belief! Please tell me you *did not* call her back, Terri," Angie pleaded with her sick buddy. Angie had not believed, or at least could not imagine, just what Logan Buckley was like until she had accompanied Terri to the Buckley home one day. She had come out of the house shaking her head and saying, "What the hell?" They were *all* equally mystified with Logan and her weird idiosyncrasies.

"Oh, *she* called back," Terri said, as she blew her nose for, what felt like, the millionth time. "Brianna took care of her. Logan threatened to call the police."

Now Angie rolled *her eyes*. "Again? How many times do we have to tell this woman, that her *Cousin Will*, is not going to arrest *you* for not catering to *her* every whim? Want me to arrest *her* for being an idiot?"

"Nay," said Terri weakly, "but how about breakfast?"

Brianna stuck her head out of the kitchen. "I'm making waffles, Angie. One or two? Blueberries or strawberries? Frozen though, of course, it being winter."

"Two or three and blueberries are fine. I know that's what Terri is having." Angie plopped down next to her friend, germs or no germs, and looked at her seriously. "I mean, really," she asked, "what are you going to do about Logan?"

"Well," Terri started but it hurt her head to think about it. The cold pill was beginning to take affect, so that helped a little. "It would be nice if there were not so many *other* people involved when dealing with this *one person*. I can't seem to sort it out without thinking about other people getting hurt."

Brianna was frying bacon in the kitchen and mixing up batter for the waffles. Terri had a brand new waffle iron, picked up at a yard sale last summer. Obviously an abandoned wedding gift, they used it often in the winter. Angie got up then to render assistance.

"I'll help Brianna while you rest. It's probably better if you *do not* think about Logan for awhile and just concentrate on getting better. K.?" Angie said as she tucked the blanket around Terri's neck and went into the kitchen to help with breakfast.

Angie and Brianna put waffles and bacon, with warm syrup, more juice, along with warm blueberries and sauce on a tray. Then to top it all off, the inevitable, fantastic, *nothing like it,* whipped cream in a can.

Terri felt pampered but wasn't able to eat much. She just felt way too lousy. Angie and Brianna both polished off two delicious, crispy waffles, along with several pieces of smoky bacon and had a blast with the canned whipped cream. Terri shook her head and wondered if any of them would ever grow up. What the hell? Why bother when they were having so much fun?

Right now, though, fun was not the word for how Terri was feeling. Breakfast over, Angie and Brianna sent Terri back to bed with a fresh bottle of water and her tissues. They shooed the puzzled cats out of Terri's room so she would not be disturbed, and cleaned up the dishes. Angie was on her way to work at the local precinct by noon. The police department would have to deal with fender-benders, tow trucks, and tickets to the max in this snowstorm. Angie's partner, Will, would be picking her up shortly. Brianna would spend the day doing paperwork for the business. She would also sweep and shovel snow off of the steps, going down the outside of their apartment *and* in front of their business down the block the best she could, even though it would pile up again!

Terri, tucked into bed with her box of tissues and bottle of cold water for her sore throat, couldn't stop thinking about the bizarre Logan *Adams*-Buckley. There go my weird instincts again, thought Terri as she suddenly felt a chill. I must have a fever, she realized. Why do I feel so weird?

Something was very wrong, in the Buckley home. They were missing something about this woman. She was not just selfish and super affectionate to her husband. *She was up to something!* Go to sleep Terri, she chided herself. They would figure it out later. Terri couldn't do anything if she didn't get enough rest.

Terri didn't realize it, as she finally drifted off to sleep but she was going to need all the rest she could get.

Chapter Three

By Monday morning Terri was feeling a little better. At least she could leave the apartment and try to get some work done. Her nose wasn't as red and the sneezing had gotten down to a minimum. Her throat was still a little sore, though, and she sounded like a croaking frog when she tried to talk. She also knew she would have to summon up the strength to deal with the ever-obnoxious Logan.

So, when Terri and Brianna went down to 'Terri's Table' (Kitchen and Specialty Foods Shop), at 8:45, turned on the lights and saw the answering machine flashing a dozen messages, she knew she was in for it.

"Oh sheez," said Brianna, "wanna place any bets that *most* of those messages are probably *psycho* Logan?" Terri threw the keys and her bag onto the table next to the phone and hit the button. Once again, there was Logan's voice.

"No bet!" said Terri, as Brianna shook her head at her boss. "You gotta give her one thing. She's persistent!"

Logan was beside herself it seemed, that she had yet to get a hold of Terri. They had kept the phone at the apartment unplugged for the rest of the weekend. They had watched a football play-off game. *Not* the Patriots this year, unfortunately. Terri had tried to rest as much as she could. Brianna took care of the cooking and housework. The snow had finally let up and clean-up crews were plowing and shoveling. Pretty typical in January, in Boston, in the winter of 2006. They were used to the snow but by this time, already looking forward to spring. For now, however, they had a lot of orders for Super Bowl Party trays and sandwiches. That would be in two weeks, two weeks from yesterday, to be exact. Logan, however, seemed to need their *immediate* attention.

"Terri," Logan's voice floated out of the machine, sounding like she was going into cardiac arrest at the very least. "You must get back to me as soon as possible. I just can't imagine where you have been for the last two days. I......." Terri stopped listening to Logan's annoying voice and moved on to the next message. Logan again, and again, one more time, *and again!*

Finally, on the sixth message, one of Terri's suppliers was calling to say, that her order for jams and jellies would be a day late because of the storm.

The next message was Terri's butcher, Jack. 'Had they decided yet, what cold cuts and cheeses they would need for the Super Bowl and how much?'

Two more messages from Logan and a couple more people calling to find out if they could still place orders for the Super Bowl.

"You have to call her back, Terri," Brianna said, " 'cause she is not going to stop. Also, look at it this way. She probably will want stuff that will cost lots of money. With just one of her orders you can make a payment on the loan and that always makes you….." She was interrupted by the phone. *Guess who?* Terri took a deep breath, snatched up the cordless phone, sat down at the desk, picked up a pen, and hit the talk button.

"Terri's Table," she said, trying to sound as polite and normal as possible, despite her scratchy throat. "How may I help you?"

"May I speak with Terry, *please*," Logan Adams-Buckley *did not* sound polite or even just anxious. She sounded *just plain nuts!*

"This *is* Terri, Logan." Terri tried as hard as she could to clear her throat and not just tell Logan off. She was just about at the end of her rope with this person and it didn't get any better.

"What the hell is wrong with you Terri? I have been trying to get a hold of you for days! Do you have any idea how important this is? I am not above choosing someone else to do my business with you know......" Logan finally took a breath so Terri could jump in.

"Logan!" Terri pretty much yelled at her and heard a sharp intake of breath from her foe. "Stop! You are free to take your business elsewhere, *if you so choose.* But I have had a terrible cold for the last couple of days. I still have it, as a matter of fact, and I am in no mood to put up with any more shenanigans from you! Now, do you wish to place an order or do you not?" Terri had *finally* figured out how to handle Logan. She waited then to see if it had worked. It had!

"I am sorry, Terri," Logan said then. "I guess I get a little carried away with myself sometimes. I had no idea you were ill. Brianna just said you were unavailable."

"Same difference!" Terri said then, still angry. "We are under no obligation to say *why* we are unavailable. That should have been enough for you. It would have been enough for me. If Brianna told you I was unavailable, that should have been the end of it. We do have many other customers and clients you know. Yes, you do spend a lot of money," Terri had heard this from Logan numerous times, "but for now, Brianna and I are the only ones doing all the work. We have many orders for the Super Bowl to prepare for in the next couple of weeks. Is that, perhaps, what you are calling about?"

Terri still had a pen in her hand and was tapping it impatiently on the table when Logan, after a pause, finally spoke again.

"What's the Super Bowl?" Logan asked innocently and Terri, *literally dropped the phone!*

"Oh, for Pete's sake....." Terri was the one who was beside herself at this point. She wasn't even sure what had just happened. Was this just another one of Logan's little trick questions? Terri decided to ignore it and go for broke.

Brianna looked at Terri with surprise and raised her eyebrows in question form. Terri shook her head and went on.

"O.K. Logan," Terri began, gritting her teeth, and after taking a drink of water, she went on. "What is on your mind? Do you have an order or do you not?"

"I have," Logan said back to her old, bossy self. "I have a *huge order*. I am having another *soiree* this weekend."

Terri gritted her teeth some more at the word *soiree* and powered up the computer. Brianna was next to her waiting to see what was up. She still didn't know about the Super Bowl question and Terri couldn't wait to tell her. Logan launched into her latest spending spree of foolishness.

"This is a very important event. Everything must be the best, must be perfect and *money is no object!*" Another one of Logan's favorite sayings, as she went on. "I want truffles, lots of truffles, the best you can get! I want beluga caviar, lobster, shrimp, and smoked salmon! My husband's family is going to be in town and I want to impress them." Logan finished with a flourish.

Show them up, is more like it, Terri thought. She quickly brought up her favorite vendor of gourmet foods and put *black truffles,* into the search engine to quote the clueless Logan some prices. Brianna's eyes went all buggy, as she saw what was coming up. Terri also wrote *beluga caviar* on the pad in front of her, making Brianna shake her head and throw up her hands.

"Logan," Terri tried to keep some control, "I know how fond you are of saying 'money is no object,' however, *the best truffles* are a ridiculous amount of money. Do you even know what truffles are?" Terri needed to make sure that she was getting this straight. Did Logan mean actual *truffles, as in, found underground at the foot of a tree,* or a box of chocolates? Logan, on the other hand, confirmed Terri's worst concerns.

"Yes, I know what *truffles* are! They're uh....." Logan struggled for a word, "....a mushroom, of some sort." She came up with that much and then went on. "Truffles are the latest thing for very wealthy people. I can't afford to be left out of the loop, you understand." Logan finished *her* perfectly logical explanation for all this insanity. Terri could just picture her waving her hands around with a hoity-toity flourish and pursing her lips at her victory in this battle.

Terri gritted her teeth, yet some more as Brianna watched her, mystified. At this rate she wouldn't have any teeth left. Terri finally realized that she would have to humor Logan. She still felt hesitant, however, about getting involved in such a costly venture.

"O.K. Logan, fine," Terri gave in a little. "You have *some* idea what you are talking about. Technically, truffles are a *tuber* but they are also considered a fungus. They grow underground, at the foot of certain oak trees in *France and Italy.* They are impossible to cultivate and difficult to find. Thus, they are very expensive and in high demand. *However,* since you fall into that wealthy class of people that you mentioned and are ready to spend the money, let's go for it." Terri sighed and went on.

"I do, however, have a few more questions for you, if you don't mind. If you are going to spend such an exorbitant amount of money, what *exactly* do you want? What kind of truffles, black or white? French or Italian? Do you want truffle butter, oil, vinegar? Do you have any idea how you are going to prepare them, or in your case, have them prepared? Do you have some particular dishes or recipes in mind? Are you getting the picture or not? If you are going to spend the money, you had better understand what you are getting yourself into." Terri tried the best she could to intimidate this woman, but to no avail.

"When I say money is no object, I mean it!" Logan was not to be deterred from her latest indulgence. "My husband's family is very important to him and we want the best for them. They will be staying here at the mansion for the weekend. I will need to bring in more help, which I hope Jasmine is able to assist me with, and I hope you have time to order these items. Now you must realize why I was concerned with getting a hold of you as soon as possible." She finished her latest tirade with what she thought was the upper hand.

"It would have made no difference if you had spoken to me on Saturday, Logan," Terri informed her. "I do not place orders on the weekends, so please keep that in mind for the future. Business days are business days. It's that simple. Today is Monday. Despite the weather, I have suppliers reliable enough to get whatever I need for my customers in a day or two. So, unless you are planning a *soiree* for tonight, we should have no problem getting what you need. Now, let me tell you what the cost of some of the items might be." Terri was scrolling through the list of truffle types and prices.

"I told you, cost is not an issue," said Logan, only slightly deflated.

"Just listen to the costs anyway, O.K.?" Terri was not about to be put off by this person, get herself into an expensive situation, only to have Logan change her mind.

"Fine," said Logan sounding huffy, "but I doubt that any cost you can quote me will be a problem."

Terri shook her head at Brianna in disgust and scrolled down to the bottom of the list of truffles. "French Fresh Black Winter, "Perigord" Truffles, 1 lb., is listed at the cost of $2,160.00. Do you still think you need the most expensive of this item Logan?" Terri waited for Logan to reply. Had she finally gotten through to her? Not yet, it would seem.

"That sounds fine," Logan seemed a little humbled but not deterred. "Oh, and since you mentioned preparations, will you be able to instruct Jasmine on how to prepare them, perhaps coming up with some recipes? I will compensate you, of course. Obviously, cooking is not my forte." She laughed then but Terri was not amused. *Ah ha!* So, there *was* a catch! Logan had *no* idea what she was doing. However, since Terri seemed to have lost control at this point, she finally just gave up trying to get it.

"That's fine, Logan, but I am telling you this only once," Terri said then, firmly, *very firmly*. "There is no way I am ordering the things you have mentioned, only to have you back out. Do you think discussing this with your husband would perhaps be a better plan, than to just dive in? As I told you, I can get these items in a day. Also, please keep in mind that shipping and handling costs will be high. Wouldn't you like to think about it?" Terri really was trying to be fair without being unkind, thus giving Logan one last chance.

"No," said Logan, "*I do not want to think about it.* It's what I really want." She simply went on then with her expensive demands. "Now, what about the caviar? Do you have some costs on that too, or do you understand what I am saying to you?"

"As a matter of fact, I do have a cost on the caviar since you mentioned it." Terri wasn't quite ready to back down either. "The *most expensive* Beluga Caviar listed here is, 1 kg at $5,280.00. How do you feel about that?" Terri asked a bit smugly, thinking she may have *finally* shocked the snooty Mrs. Adams-Buckley.

Logan hesitated but only for a moment. "Done," she decided, not to be defeated. Was her pride getting in the way now? Or was she truly certifiably insane? She went on and then really blew Terri away. "I'll tell you what," she said, "so you can rest easy. You place the order and figure out your costs with it. I will send Ignacio over with a check. How does that sound?"

"Fine, Logan." Terri finally acquiesced, admitting defeat. "I will do that. Oh, and while you're at it, how about Goose Foie Gras, Liver Pate, *with Truffles?* A bargain at $630.00 for 35.2 oz.! Would you like me to add that to your order or have we gone far enough with this expensive undertaking?"

After only another brief pause, Logan agreed. "That sounds just fine, Terri. Order all the foods we talked about, along with 2 dozen lobsters, 20 lbs. of fresh, jumbo shrimp, and 2 large smoked salmon. Along with my regular order of cheeses and spreads, with the appropriate crackers and breads to go with. Let me know *the damages* and I will send Ignacio over with a check. I am going to assume you will *not* question any more of my requests in the future?" She just couldn't help but end on a *snotty* note!

Terri, not to ever be completely undone, agreed cheerfully. "No problem, Logan. I can also look up some recipes on the internet for you and have them ready when Ignacio gets here with the check. Anything you want, since you are so fond of saying *money is no object.* I will put in the order and get back to you with the final amount in a few minutes. Stand by." She shut off the phone and dropped it back on to the base.

"You have got to be shitten' me!" Brianna finally came out of her shock and spoke as she watched Terri place Logan's *order.* "This is so ridiculous! Even my mother never went this over-the-top! What in the hell is this chick up to?"

"I don't know. This is beyond belief, even for Logan as a general rule. It's like she has gone completely out of control," Terri commented as she quickly added up the *sizable damages* in order to call Logan back as soon as possible. "But in this weather I better get a check pretty fast. There is no damn way I am taking a loss on this crazy woman's over-the-top demands. If she wants to send Ignacio over with a check, the sooner the better. I really should have the money before I place the order. That would be difficult without having all the shipping and handling costs in front of me, however. Along with our costs, this is pretty nuts."

"Yeah, and poor Ignacio and Jasmine," Brianna sighed, thinking of Annette, her old housekeeper, and Louise, the cook. Those two wonderful ladies, who had taken such good care of her as she was growing up, had gone through some terrible years with her mother.

Jasmine and Ignacio were the two people Logan ordered around the mansion. Jasmine, along with her daughter Nadia, cooked, cleaned, did laundry, and helped look after Jenni and Benjamin. Ignacio did outside work and ran various errands, which included taking the children to school or wherever. Logan treated them all quite badly, from what Terri and Brianna had seen on their weekly meal deliveries. They never seemed to be able to do anything right, the way Logan acted towards them. Terri suspected they may even be in the country illegally and were afraid to do anything *but* put up with Logan. She kept her suspicions to herself, however, not wanting to get involved in a situation where several people could get hurt.

It had become terribly apparent from the beginning, that Jenni and Benjamin were the most vulnerable of all. Terri and Brianna had already taken the two youngsters on several outings and they were a joy to be with. A couple of weeks ago, Benjamin had called and proudly asked the girls to go to a Celtics game, providing excellent tickets acquired by his father. Along with *cousin* Will and Angie, of course, they had an absolute blast! They saw a fantastic game, the Celtics beating Charlotte, by a score of 109-106. They had yelled and screamed until they were all hoarse and laughing, enjoying one another's company immensely. Terri and Brianna were both very fond of Benjamin and Jenni. Will, of course, was very close to them, just as if they were part of his own family.

Why had they allowed it to get this far? Terri wondered, as she came up with an outrageous amount of money for this incredibly indulgent affair. She immediately called Logan back with the total, still hoping she might change her mind. No such thing! Catching only the slightest hesitation in Logan's voice, she told Terri she would send Ignacio over right away with the check. Terri and Brianna were making their meals for Monday afternoon delivery when Ignacio came into the shop.

"Senora sends check," Ignacio said simply, as he handed Terri the sealed white envelope.

"Muchos gracias, Ignacio," Terri said warmly to the handsome, polite, young man. "Please, sit down to have a cup of coffee and some soup." Terri knew better than to *ask* Ignacio if he wanted anything. She knew he would shyly refuse. He was freezing and shivering on this January morning, however. Brianna firmly sat him down at one of their *tasting tables* and they put the steaming hot food and drink in front of him.

"Oh, gracias Senoritas, gracias," Ignacio said gratefully as he sipped hot coffee and picked up the soup spoon. He took a generous scoop of the thick, hot chicken and dumpling soup in front of him, then crumbled crackers into his bowl. "Is delicious! You good cooks," he said. The girls beamed as they watched him eat. The soup really was wonderful and nutritious. It was brimming with generous chunks of chicken, potatoes, carrots, celery, onions and fluffy dumplings, all in a savory chicken broth. Terri and Brianna had made a huge quantity and would be delivering family sized portions to all of their customers. It was the perfect *cold weather* food. In the meantime, Ignacio ate with grateful enthusiasm and eventually stopped shivering as the coffee and soup slowly warmed him.

Terri refilled his coffee cup and offered him more crackers. The bowl was empty in no time and Brianna refilled it, *twice*. Finally replete, Ignacio refused any more refills. It was a long drive back, so they filled a Styrofoam cup for him with cappuccino *for the road*. Terri also gave Ignacio several pages of recipes for breakfast items, desserts, and main courses that all included truffles, to give to Jasmine with instructions on how to prepare the truffles and add them to other ingredients. It wasn't until Ignacio had left, cup in hand, that Terri opened the envelope. It contained *not just* the cost of the supplies. Along with the first check, was a *second* check to cover a generous tip!

"Holy Moses!" said Brianna, as she and Terri examined the checks. "That even seems like a lot of money to me."

"It would seem like a lot of money *to anyone*," Terri said, frustrated and disgusted by the situation. "Enough to feed quite a few victims of Hurricane Katrina and then some. This is crazy but it has to go to the bank so I can pay for these items as quickly as the computer can send it. I'd better make the trek. Can you finish the stew? I'll be back in a few minutes." Terri was getting into her coat and boots. "I may as well take the truck since it will have to be warmed up anyway."

Brianna assured Terri she could put the finishing touches on the meals for the week, and start getting them ready to go before she got back. Terri walked out the front door and looked across the street. She got another one of her sudden odd chills, and not just from the cold, as she noticed a car across from their shop. It seemed as if it had been there for awhile. Then suddenly, the car quickly pulled away from the curb. Just on an impulse, Terri took notice of the license plate. Turned out later, *she was glad she did!*

Chapter Four

When Terri got back to the shop, she wasn't surprised or alarmed for that matter, to see a police car parked right in front. Assuming it was Angie and partner Will, she went through the door with a greeting for her friends. It wasn't Angie and Will, however. *No, that would have been too easy!* It was Rico and *his partner,* Tabitha Hughes. It took all the control Terri could muster to keep the smile plastered on her face.

"Oh, hey guys!" Terri said, trying to sound casual and normal, even though she felt immediately annoyed. "Nice weather we're having, huh?"

It wasn't that she *didn't like* Tabitha Hughes. She was fine. Fresh out of the police academy, she was enthusiastic, smart as a whip, and very small for a cop. At least Terri felt that way. She always felt *huge* around Tabitha. Rico proffered a friendly wave for a greeting and complimented Terri, as always, on the coffee. They had brought their own donuts and some pastries for Terri and Brianna.

"How nice, you two. Thank you but I sure don't need the sweets." Terri tried to be gracious as she took off her coat and boots and tried to smooth down her hair. She didn't even want to imagine how lousy she looked. She still had the cold, her hair was a mess, and she hadn't bothered with a whole lot of make-up. Brianna looked at Terri sympathetically. Tabitha gave her a friendly smile. Tabitha, of course, looked perfect with her smooth blond hair pulled over her ears under her police cap. She wasn't wearing any make-up but she didn't need any. With her long lashes and perfect skin, her cheeks just pink enough from the winter weather, Tabitha couldn't have looked any cuter.

*Grrrrr......*thought Terri, and then decided not to worry about what she looked like. *What was the difference, anyway?* Either Rico took her as she was or forget it. Terri hadn't even yet figured out if Tabitha was a rival for Rico's affections or not, and Angie didn't have a clue. Rico treated everyone the same. Even though he and Terri were *sort of dating,* their relationship was still on a pretty casual basis. Terri had given up trying to get through to Rico and had just let things go on as they were. She just hadn't figured on someone like Tabitha coming into the equation. Terri had never gotten any negative vibes from her though, so she probably shouldn't look for trouble. Then she remembered the car that had been parked across the street from the shop and mentioned it to Rico.

"You got the license plates?" Making the assumption, he took another sip of coffee and a bite of donut. Terri handed him a slip of paper and Rico nodded his approval.

"I wrote it down when I got to the truck so I wouldn't forget. Probably nothing. Just me being paranoid, *again.*" Terri laughed and then saw Rico's reaction. "What is it?" The look on Rico's face was more than a bit strange, making Terri feel slightly alarmed.

"I don't think I would be breaking any laws here, Terri, by telling you this is an F.B.I. license plate." Rico handed the piece of paper to Tabitha and she nodded in agreement.

"Absolutely," Tabitha said, and then noticed Terri's shocked face. "Terri," she asked, "do you have any idea why F.B.I. agents might be watching your shop?"

Terri felt even more annoyed as suddenly Tabitha was questioning her, and she looked to Rico for help. Seeing none forthcoming, she swallowed and lied through her teeth.

"I have absolutely no idea why anyone would be watching this shop." Terri strained to sound convincing. "Hey, we aren't the only place on this block you guys. They could have been there for something completely different that had nothing to do with my place."

Rico looked at Terri suspiciously and tucked the piece of paper into his pocket. Terri resisted the urge to ask for it back. Their break over, Rico and Tabitha finished their coffee and took off into the snow for parts unknown.

"What in the hell was that all about?" Brianna jumped on Terri the second the police car was out of sight. "I could tell you were lying and I think Rico could too. What's going on, Terri? Please, let me in on what you are thinking!"

Brianna grabbed Terri's shoulders and shook her a little. Terri suddenly had a sneezing attack and grabbed for a box of tissues. She had sort of been in a little bit of shock. She didn't want to think what she was thinking.

"I'll tell you in a second, Bri. Could you please put on some water and make some tea? I have to think for a couple of minutes...waaaachooo!"

That is, if she could ever stop sneezing. Maybe she was allergic to Tabitha, along with this lousy cold. Doubtful. She was definitely not happy though, with Tabitha suddenly giving her the third degree. Who in the hell did she think she was, anyway?

Terri wanted to yell at her, *"Hey you little shit, I saw him first!"* Much good that would do. Another day of making a total dork out of myself. That's just great! Terri thought, once again feeling sorry for herself. She grabbed more tissues and tried to figure out what to tell Brianna. Her feelings were pretty mixed up right now. She could just be getting paranoid. Still, the F.B.I. guys were definitely watching her shop, so something must be going on.

Brianna brewed a pot of strong English tea. She set a tray with pretty cups and saucers, added biscuits, cream, sugar, honey and lemon, and placed it all in front of Terri, along with the pastries. Terri looked at them with distaste, however.

Suddenly, she didn't want to see another pastry for the rest of her life.

"O.K., I made the tea. Here it is. You have stopped sneezing. Tell me what's happening here." Brianna waited for Terri to spill the beans as they both fixed themselves cups of the strong, hot tea. Terri added honey and lemon and took a careful sip before speaking.

"I think the F.B.I. was here because Ignacio came into the shop," Terri said, finally putting her fear into words. "I think he and Jasmine, and I suppose Nadia too, could be illegal aliens. You've seen and heard in the news about this immigration problem."

"Oh, c'mon," said Brianna, as she carefully put down her delicate tea cup. "Why in the world would the F.B.I. waste their time on small potatoes like Logan Buckley's hired help? That's crazy! I mean, I'm sorry Terri. I'm not saying you're crazy. It's just that the immigration issue *is so huge*! Reports say that thousands of people are managing to enter this country illegally, *every day!* Why would the F.B.I. waste time on one person, or two? Surely these people have better things to do. Damn it!" Brianna started laughing then, realizing what she had just said.

"Don't call me Shirley," Terri quipped, grinning, always trying to keep her sense of humor and jumping at the chance. Then she sobered again as she sipped her tea and crunched on a delicate biscuit. She was trying to mull it all over and figure out, if there was a connection, or if she really was crazy, or paranoid, *or both!*

"Maybe," Terri continued to puzzle over the weirdness of it all, "it has something to do with Logan and Alex. *Maybe* they, the F.B.I. that is, could be looking for a way to discredit them. You know how it is when someone is a big corporate hot-shot like Alex. The Buckleys may even be keeping Jasmine and Ignacio and treating them like slaves." Brianna looked at Terri and raised an eyebrow. "C'mon, you hear stories like that all of the time. They're in this country illegally and so they have no choice but to pretty much sell themselves into

slavery to keep from being sent back." Terri shook her head
and sipped her tea.

"Ooooh-kaaaay!" Brianna had listened and was mystified
by the possibilities too. "Well, do we even know what country
these people are from? There's an awful lot of Latin American
countries. Is it against the law for *anyone* from *any* of these
countries, to come here to live and work without all the
government complications?"

"I don't know," Terri said, confused as ever. "As you
already stated, we don't even know what country they are
from. Until we find out, there's not much we can do."

Brianna put more tea into Terri's cup and then her own.
She picked up a biscuit and waited for her boss to go on. Terri
shrugged and was about to say they had better get going on
their meal deliveries, when the door opened again and another
police officer blew in on the cold.

"What's up?" Angie looked at her two friends sitting at a
table drinking tea, when they should be working. Terri and
Brianna both looked at Angie, prompting her to pay closer
attention. "Whoa, *what is up?* Shouldn't you two be packing
the truck?"

"Yes, as a matter of fact, we should be. Pastry?" Terri
asked nonchalantly offering Angie the plate of flaky treats.
"Where is Will, by-the-way?"

"Doing paperwork *on our break*, imagine that?" Angie filled
a coffee cup, added cream, plopped down on a chair, and took
a pastry off of the plate. "O.K., so tell me *what is going on*," she
finally said, starting to lose patience.

Terri opened her mouth to begin explaining when the
phone rang, giving Angie another couple of minutes to wait.
Terri sipped her tea and munched on another biscuit as Angie
drank her coffee with a flaky, raspberry pastry. Brianna
answered the phone and wrote down delivery information,
coincidentally, for some of Logan's expensive food items.

Phone call finished, Brianna sat back down. She and
Terri began to relay to Angie what had happened. Logan's
outrageous demands, Ignacio coming into the shop, the car

and what Rico had said. Angie listened carefully and looked at Terri. "You wrote down the license, of course?" Terri nodded.

"Yeah, and Rico took the piece of paper. He and his little partner, *Tabitha Hughes!*" Terri finished, in very cranky fashion.

"Meow!" Angie said and waited for Terri to calm down.

"O.K.," Terri said, instantly ashamed of herself. "I'm done with my fit now. I *remembered* what was on the license plate anyway." She told Angie and her friend nodded, agreeing with Rico and Tabitha.

"F.B.I. alright. Mmmm......verrrrrry interesting!" Angie grinned, and Terri and Brianna both came back.

"But shtupid!" All three of them said this in unison.

"Man, we are so pathetic," Angie said laughing. "The weird things we picked up from our *Baby Boomer* parents! O.K., c'mon you two. I'll use the rest of *my* break to help you pack up your truck. Then I have to go back and pick up Will. We'll talk about all this nonsense later." She snagged another pastry, someone had to eat them after all, and they each grabbed a stack of containers.

By the time they got all the dinners delivered, Terri was so exhausted, that Brianna firmly told her to go back to bed. She would clean up the remaining dirty dishes, from their meal preparations and be back up to the apartment to make supper by 4:00 or so. Terri gratefully agreed and trudged up the stairs. She stamped her feet outside of the door and literally fell into the apartment. Louie and Maria greeted her joyfully as she peeled off her winter clothes.

"What have you guys been up to, huh?" Terri asked them as she took off her boots and sighed. It was good to be home. She was wiped-out from the cold, the snow, Logan and her demands. She just wanted to take a hot shower and crawl into bed. Instead she filled Louie and Maria's bowls, gave them fresh water, and took chicken breasts out of the freezer for supper. She also found broccoli, made sure there was cream of chicken soup on hand, along with curry and mayo. When

Brianna got back to the apartment, she would make, Quik Chicken Curry Divan. With it, they would have homemade macaroni and cheese. The ultimate comfort food dinner, they called it. Angie would be over for supper and they would watch 24. No more 'Monday Night Football', unfortunately, *ever again*! At least not on ABC anyway, which totally sucked! How would they go on? Terri wondered dramatically. By switching to ESPN, apparently. So much for tradition. Anyway, they had Jack Bauer to muddle them through and keep Monday nights interesting.

Terri and Angie practically went 'into mourning' when football was over. Then baseball started pretty quick as winter mercifully wound down. It was the couple of months in between that were tough. They always took in a Celtic's game or two, though, which were always fun. Football and baseball took precedence, however.

Finally, Terri couldn't stand up anymore and *literally* flopped onto the sofa. She turned the T.V. on low for noise. Louie and Maria, always ready for a nap, settled in with her.

Brianna walked in the door at about 4:30 and found Terri fast asleep. Maria and Louie hopped off the sofa and raced to the door. Terri didn't move an eyelash.

"Shhhh.....," Brianna said to the excited pair as she reached down to pat them both. She took off her coat and boots and quietly moved around the apartment so as not to wake Terri any sooner than she had to. Brianna knew Angie would be *blowing* in soon too. She started to prepare the chicken breasts and boil the macaroni for their dinner. She blanched pieces of broccoli, drained the macaroni, turned the chicken which was cooking in the microwave, and opened the cream of chicken soup.

Brianna was shredding medium cheddar cheese for the sauce with the chicken and broccoli when Angie came in, interestingly enough, carrying her overnight bag. Something had told Angie not to rush in with her usual noisy greeting, however. She watched Terri sleep for a few seconds and then joined Brianna in the kitchen.

"Geez, I hate to think we have to wake her up," Angie said quietly and Brianna agreed.

"Terri's so exhausted, I think she could sleep there all night," Brianna said as she mixed the sauce for the chicken divan. Angie opened a can of cheddar cheese soup and blended it with the white sauce that Brianna had already prepared. A few minutes later they placed the deliciously creamy chicken and broccoli dish, along with the old-fashioned, homemade macaroni and cheese, into the 350 degree oven. In about 45 minutes they would have the perfect, hot, winter evening meal.

Angie grabbed a glass of wine. Brianna filled the teapot, to brew herbal tea for herself and Terri. They stood and looked at their sick friend, sound asleep on the sofa. Suddenly, Terri opened her eyes and jumped, startled to see the two of them standing there.

"Man, you guys," Terri protested as she stretched, and Maria jumped up on the couch for attention. "How long have you two been standing there?"

"About two seconds," Angie said as she plopped down next to her. "Supper is in the oven. How are you feeling?"

"I don't know. A little better, I guess," Terri said as she sat up and yawned. Her hair was flat on one side and her cheek was red from sleeping on it. Angie and Brianna made no comment about her appearance this time however, as Terri went on. "I'm glad to be awake. I felt like I was ready to die there for awhile. No such luck I see."

"Yeah, once again, you're not getting off that easy. Besides, you don't want to miss our favorite 'comfort food' supper after Brianna and I worked so hard," Angie said firmly. With a satisfied sigh, she snuggled into the comfy sofa with her glass of wine and a warm *kitty* throw. It was good to be out of the snow and the cold, in the pleasant, cozy apartment.

"Oh, and it smells wonderful, thanks," Terri said gratefully, as Brianna came into the living room with a tray holding tea things. Brianna poured and Terri as usual, added honey and lemon to her cup. Angie sipped her wine. But nothing could beat a hot cup of tea in this weather, especially when you were nursing a lousy cold.

"Mmmm......, Brianna, this is wonderful," Terri commended her brilliant, young assistant, as she sipped the soothing, hot drink, and leaned back on the sofa. "What kind is it? It feels really good on my throat."

"As a matter of fact, this tea is exactly for that purpose, your cold and sore throat I mean. It is called 'Winter Night Cold Soother.' I stopped in to Amber and Kellie's shop before I came up here and asked for something *specifically* for your cold symptoms. Kellie recommended this one."Brianna handed Terri the pretty, as always, elaborately decorated box filled with fragrant tea bags.

Kellie and Amber Hennesey owned the health food store right next to Terri and Brianna's shop. They were cousins and had many wonderful things in *their* shop. Herbal teas, obviously, vitamins and other dietary supplements, gift items such as pretty frames, jewelry boxes, small plants, and knick knacks, filled the shelves of their beautiful store. They ran a brisk business and, of course, now made a habit of coming over to Terri and Brianna's place, for coffee or cappuccino, particularly in this cold weather. The two shops complimented one another perfectly and everyone was satisfied with the arrangement.

Also, Terri and Angie often took Amber and Kellie with them to Red Sox or Patriot games. They always had a great time. Even last year's World Series was pretty awesome. Kellie's parents lived in Chicago and the White Sox finally broke *their* 'curse.' Terri did not believe in curses but it was O.K. with her, and even Angie, that the White Sox finally took the series. They were all pretty excited and happy with the results. The most important thing for all of them was the genuine *love of the game.* The fact that they patronized one another's shops didn't hurt either. Thus, the wonderful tea Terri was sipping was right next door.

"More, please," said Terri as she proffered her cup. "This is wonderful. I approve, and I think I may even be hungry." Her appetite had been almost nonexistent since the cold had hit her like a ton of bricks! She had eaten only a small bowl of the chicken-dumpling soup for lunch, with a couple of saltines. Mostly, she had just tried to drown herself and the nasty virus, with water for her scratchy throat and 7-Up, which always helped her stomach. Speaking of which, she suddenly put down her delicate cup, jumped up, and ran for the bathroom. Brianna and Angie looked at each other and grinned, waiting for Terri to look in the mirror.

She came out and glared at the two of them laughing at her. Of course, she had thrown some water on her face and brushed her hair.

"Thanks a lot you two!" Terri said, trying to sound mad. "You could have at least told me how goofy I looked!" She plopped back down on the couch and socked Angie, something she had done often in their years of friendship. One unwritten rule was, never touch a police officer when they are in uniform! When Angie was in plain clothes, however, she was fair game.

"Man, what a spoiled sport!" Angie said, laughing. "Well worth the punch too. C'mon, who cares how you look anyway? It's just us. It's not like we took a picture or anything. Speaking of which, why is there never a damn camera around when you need one?" Angie was enjoying herself immensely, at Terri's expense, of course. "Anyway, where's your sense of humor?"

"Yeah, but still....." Terri started a comeback.

"Whoa," said Brianna, "Terri 'but stilled' you Angie, so you're done. So is our supper, by the way. Let's eat!"

The creamy curry, soup, cheese, and mayo sauce, covered with breadcrumbs and bright red paprika over the chicken and broccoli, was bubbling. The *meltie* cheesy, mac' and cheese, hot and comforting, also covered with paprika, was ready to go with the main dish. Both of these mouth-watering recipes were pretty, as well as delicious. Terri and Brianna's clients loved them, so they usually made both every three weeks or so in the winter. For now, the three friends loaded up their plates and sat down to watch yet another, literally *explosive* episode of *24*, it being only the third hour in the season so far!

As Terri started eating, she noticed something out of the corner of her eye by the door. It was Angie's over night bag.

"Hey, Ang," she said as she took a bite of the delicious chicken and rolled her eyes with pleasure. "Oh, this is absolutely wonderful! Truly, a can't miss dish. O.K., what was I saying?" Terri suddenly felt just a bit light headed, pretty normal for her, actually. "Oh yeah, Ang, what's with the over night bag?"

"Oh, that!" Angie said, her mouth full of mac' and cheese. "Uh yeah, I've got no heat in my apartment. So mind if I bunk here?"

"'Course not," said Terri. "What's up with your building this time?"

"No idea. I called the Super and he's supposed to be coming over but I wasn't going to stick around and freeze my butt off. I just hope everyone else in my building has somewhere to go. It was already pretty cold at my place. I was going to tell you when I got here but you were asleep, and when you woke up you looked so funny, I forgot." Angie finished her tale and kept eating.

"Yeah, thanks again for that," Terri said, kicking at her. As they watched Jack Bauer going through another miserable day to save the world, Terri pondered. "You know, how I know, that this is not real?" No answer from her friends forthcoming, she went on. "Jack Bauer probably should have been dead, like two seasons ago! He's like, Indiana Jones or James Bond or whoever. You cannot kill these guys!" She chewed another piece of the tender chicken thoughtfully and took a sip of wine.

"Absolutely, absolutely," Angie agreed, "keeps the fantasy alive. Everybody loves a hero. Besides, don't forget the most important part. Kiefer Sutherland is so hot!" She rolled her eyes and put a hand to her heart and then fanned herself. "Whew!"

Brianna agreed. "I can certainly see the draw. I didn't realize what I was missing! This show is awesome." Famous last words. She was hooked!

By the time **24** was over and they had finished eating, they were all pretty much ready for bed. Brianna put away the leftovers, cleaned up the dishes, and stacked the dishwasher. Angie went to the closet where Terri kept extra pillows, and blankets and bunked on the sofa. It was *so very* comfy, and Louie chose to cuddle with her.

"Traitor!" Brianna told him, as she took her turn in the bathroom.

"Ha! By morning he'll probably be in with you anyway," said Angie, as she snuggled with the furry feline. "You know how fickle these two are. Hey Terri, now that there are three of us, maybe we need another cat!" Angie waited for a reaction and got a withering look from her friend.

"Do you want a place to stay tonight or not?" Terri asked her in all seriousness.

"Night, night!" Angie said then, not pursuing the subject.

They all snuggled in comfy and warm for the night, Brianna kitty-less for now. Tomorrow would be another normal day of work, chilly winter weather, food and friendship, just like any other. Right?

Chapter Five

Angie's phone rang at the disgustingly early hour of 6:00 a.m. It was Rico and of course, he was assuming she was at her own apartment. Angie was half asleep and half-awake when she grabbed the phone, hit the green talk button, and heard her Captain's voice.

"What, *what,*...... *what?*" Angie was so startled by Rico's report that by the third *what,* she was shouting. Louie, who had stayed on the sofa after all, jumped to the floor and feeling Angie's alarm, poofed out to twice his normal size! Terri came running out of her room. Brianna came out of hers with Maria who, upon seeing Louie, also poofed out and started growling! It was a scene of huge eyes and static electricity that would have made anyone howl with laughter. Unfortunately, as it turned out, the situation was anything but funny. Angie was sitting on the edge of the sofa rubbing her eyes with her knuckles like a baby. She looked so stunned that Terri grabbed the phone from her.

"This is Terri. Who is this?" She snapped rather rudely into Angie's cell.

"Terri?" Rico asked, obviously surprised to hear her voice. "What are you doing at Angie's apartment? What's going on?"

Terri almost dropped Angie's cell phone but yelled at Rico instead."What's going on? That's a good question. I might ask you the same thing!" Terri was so startled that Rico was calling at such an early hour, she pretty much gave him hell for it! Then she got a hold of herself and calmed down long enough to explain.

"Angie stayed here with me and Brianna last night because there was no heat in her apartment. Rico, talk to me! Tell me what's wrong, *please!*" Terri begged him to give *her* some answers. She was feeling that weird chill again, even though she was standing in her toasty living room.

"Terri, listen to me," Rico sounded serious and professional. "Just hand the phone back to Angie and she'll tell you. I have to keep moving here!"

"Damn it!" Terri groused in frustration as she thrust the phone back at Angie, who was finally coming out of her stupor. Terri just hated it, *hated it,* when Rico went all cop on her! Obviously, he had to do his job but maybe, just maybe, just this one time, he could cut her a break and not treat her like such a, such a....., a.....*civilian!*"

Angie listened a few more minutes to Rico, saying *yes and no, no and yes,* and then finally hitting end on her phone. She put it down and looked at Terri and Brianna and the two freaked out cats! Amazing the vibes they felt from their humans! Terri and Brianna watched Angie and saw tears running down her cheeks and instinctively waited for her to speak.

"It's Logan. Logan Adams-Buckley, she....she's...." Angie was struggling.

"She's what Angie, what? She's annoying? She's finally gone off the deep end? *What?*" Terri sat down next to Angie and shook her shoulder a little.

"She's dead." Angie said, softly now. "She's dead. She was killed last night. They think...... it was a break-in. She was shot. She's dead."

"My God!" Brianna finally spoke as she picked up Maria, who with her brother, had finally calmed down. "What the hell? Just when you think you can't be shocked anymore! A break-in Angie, you mean like a robbery? What happened? Did she try to confront the guy? Why would she do that?"

"Rico didn't know any of that. Or, at least if he did, he didn't say. We only know just so much anyway at this point. The Buckleys don't live in our jurisdiction so it's not our case. Oh, my God, *Will!*" Angie said then and put her face in her hands. Terri was crying too. Brianna was trying not to. They were all thinking about the kids.

"What's this going to do to Jenni and Benjamin?" Brianna knew there wasn't an answer to that question but she just had to ask it. Obviously, Logan had been a very difficult person to deal with. But Jenni and Benjamin had loved her. No matter how much she had annoyed Terri and Brianna, that didn't mean they wanted to see her dead, much less shot and killed. They had dealt with a similar situation last summer. The man who was murdered was *not nice*, but still, no one had the right to take the life of another person.

Angie finally came to her senses. "I have got to get dressed. I have to get to the station. This is nuts!" Angie had her phone in her hand when it rang again, and they all jumped. "Oh God, it's Will!" She quickly answered. "Will, are you alright? You heard. Oh God, Will. I'm so sorry….. Will, Will!" She covered her phone and talked to Terri and Brianna. "He's crying. This is so horrible. I don't know what to do." She made a quick decision then.

"Will, come over to Terri's apartment, *now!* Are you O.K., to drive? Can someone else bring you? Fine, we'll see you in a few minutes. Will, be careful!" She hit end on her phone and looked at her friends. "Will figures he can drive over. I'll get ready for work." She headed for the shower.

"I'll start coffee," said Brianna. She put her hand on Terri's shoulder and Terri nodded. "Should we make any food? Terri, what do you think we should do?" Then she stopped for a second and sat down next to her boss.

"Terri," she said. Terri looked at her through watery eyes "What in the hell are we going to do with that food Logan ordered? It's all on the way! What are we going to do with it? She paid for all that expensive stuff!"

Terri just shook her head. "We'll figure something out later. Go ahead and make coffee, so it's ready when Will gets here. I think there are some bagels in the fridge, and some jams and cream cheese to go with them. C'mon, I'll help you."

They went to the kitchen, put on the coffee, found the bagels, a variety of cookies and a loaf of banana nut bread. Coffee and sweets, if anyone wanted them, seemed the easiest and not too much.

Angie came out of the bathroom and went into Terri's room to get dressed. There was a soft knock on the door. Brianna opened it *and* her arms, as she let in a sobbing Will.

"Oh, Will," Brianna said, just not able to find the right words to comfort him at the loss of his cousin. Will was in his uniform but this tragedy, allowed Brianna to catch him in a comforting hug. Angie came out of Terri's room, dressed in her own uniform, and engulfed her partner into *her* arms. Terri set up coffee mugs, bagels, and sweets on the peninsula in between the kitchen and living room. They sat Will down on one of the bar stools, set coffee in front of him, and Terri produced a box of tissues. Will took three tissues at once, blew his nose, and sipped the hot drink.

"We don't know what happened yet," Will said, sniffling. "She was shot once through the heart. That's what killed her. It looked like she had struggled with the killer. I just can't imagine why she would have tried......." He couldn't go on, just grabbed more tissues and dabbed his eyes.

"Will, maybe you shouldn't try to work today," Terri said then. "You can hang out here if you want. Brianna and I can take turns staying with you. What about relatives? Do you have people you need to call?"

"I already talked to my mother," Will stammered and sniffed. "She was going to call Logan's mom, my Aunt Rose. They'll contact other relatives. I haven't talked to Alex. I don't know......I really will be better off, Terri, if I just work. Is that O.K. with you, Angie?" Will looked at his partner and she nodded. "Thanks for the offer, Terri. I'm a professional and I have to do my job. Also, I want to stick close to the station, just in case we hear anything from the detectives handling the case."

"Have some more coffee, Will," Brianna said as she filled his cup. "Would you like anything with it? A cookie or bagel, or anything?"

Will took a sugar cookie and munched on it with his coffee. "I need the sugar anyway," he said, justifying the cookie, as if he needed to. Terri set a glass of orange juice in front of him and he drank it down quickly. Along with the cookie, the natural sweetness of the juice would give him energy.

After about 15 minutes, Will seemed to get a hold of himself.

"Angie, if you're ready we may as well get going." Will seemed stronger and now determined to find out what had happened to his cousin. Whatever her personality quirks may have been, family was family. *This was personal!* Angie immediately noticed her partner's sudden change in emotion. He had gone from grief to anger very quickly. She moved to get the rest of her things, grabbed a bagel with cream cheese, and a couple more cookies for Will. They would stop by the shop for more coffee later. Angie and Will scrambled out the door. Brianna watched as they got into the squad car with Angie driving, and quickly took off.

"Whew!" Brianna blew out a huge breath. "This is so freakin' weird, Terri. What time is it anyway? It doesn't seem like we've even been up that long."

Terri looked at her cell phone. It seemed the best way to get the correct time these days. Watches were getting to be almost obsolete and Terri seldom wore one. "It's 7:35," she said, "and all hell has broken loose before we could barely wake up!"

"Do you want me to make anything else, I mean for breakfast?" Brianna asked. "I could scramble some eggs or something."

"Nay, I'll hit the shower and probably just grab some toast with a slice of turkey. That'll be the fastest." Terri moved to her room to get her robe.

By the time they had dressed, grabbed more coffee, juice, and toast with honey-smoked turkey slices for both of them, it was almost 8:30.

They headed down to the shop and saw Amber and Kellie already down in *their* shop. They had a very nice apartment fixed up above their store. Going to work for them just meant walking down the stairs. Terri could see a few lights were on in the back of the store. She knocked on the window and Kellie opened the door to let them in.

"Holy shit, Terri!" Kellie said, as she stood aside and then closed the door against the cold. "What the hell happened with Logan? We heard the news on the radio. It certainly didn't take long for the media to get a hold of this story. Have you seen Will?"

"It's insane," Terri said simply. "Apparently, Logan was shot and killed in some sort of a break-in at their house. Will came over to our apartment and picked up Angie. Angie had stayed over 'cause the heat was on the fritz at her place. Rico called, at like 6:00." Terri said all this and finally took a breath. Amber came from the back and hugged her friends. Terri went on. "Will is pretty broken up, as you guys can imagine. He had some coffee and cookies, and I think he felt a little better. Now he's just plain pissed! You should have seen the look on his face when he and Angie left. I wouldn't want to be the person that killed his cousin, if Will gets a hold of him or her, whatever the case may be. We can't rule out anything at this point."

"I don't imagine there is anything *we* can do," Amber said hopefully, as they all stood there realizing they were pretty helpless.

"I'll tell you what," said Terri, "you two come over for coffee about 10:30 like always, and by then maybe we'll know something. The one thing we all need to do is support Will. Let's admit it right off the top. We did *not like* Logan Adams-Buckley. None of us did. I'm not trying to be mean here, just face the reality of it. Am I right?" Kellie and Amber nodded, looking guilty. They had been through a lot of the same frustrations as Terri and Brianna with Logan. She had been in their shop often. Even though she never complained about their products or the service, Logan had always seemed to find a way to be difficult.

"O.K., just so we're clear." Terri felt like she was giving a lecture. "Once again, no matter what Logan was like to us, no one had the right to take her life. She had people who cared about her, especially Jenni and Benjamin. We might have to come up with something for those kids. We'll have to see if we can help in some way. See you two later, K.?" Kellie and Amber both nodded and Terri and Brianna left their warm shop and went two steps over to their own.

They opened the door, turned on the lights, and Terri locked the door behind them. They shed their outer clothes and checked for messages on the machine. They had kept the land line at the apartment unplugged because of Logan. No problem there anymore, it would seem. There were a half-dozen messages, however, so Terri hit the button. Needless to say, she and Brianna were both pretty freaked-out when the first message was, indeed, the voice of Logan Adams-Buckley.

"Terri," the message began and for once, Logan sounded relaxed and friendly. "This is Logan, obviously." Here she laughed a little. "I hope you haven't taken that check to the bank yet. Turns out, I won't be needing any of that food for the weekend after all. We will be gone instead. I'll get back to you next week. Take care girls." The message was followed by a sharp click as Logan Adams-Buckley hung up the phone.

Chapter Six

Terri and Brianna were gaping at each other when there was a sharp knock on the door of their shop. Brianna screamed and grabbed Terri for support. Terri's heart was beating like a rabbit's as she ran to the answering machine and stopped the rest of the messages. The knocking came again, this time even harder. The shades were still pulled down on the windows, as well as the door, which Terri was thankful she had locked behind them.

Terri put her finger to her lips and went, "Shhhhh," to Brianna. She moved to the left window shade and peeked out.

"Oh, shit," Terri said in a panicked whisper, "it's the suits!"

"The what....the what? The who?" Brianna's eyes were huge and she kept grabbing Terri, in a total panic herself.

"It's those F.B.I. guys. The ones that were sitting across the street yesterday. I recognize the guy who was in the driver's seat. Damn it, damn it, damn it!"

"Who are you, Jack Bauer?" Brianna asked, laughing nervously but shaking, despite trying to make a joke!

"Hardly," Terri quipped back, "but I wish he was here right now. I'm not sure if I can handle this." The knock came again. Terri thought for a second and formed a plan, *of sorts*. She grabbed Brianna by the shoulders and started giving orders.

"O.K., Brianna, the main thing is, we *must stay calm*. Do you have the number on your cell for your family lawyer?" Brianna nodded numbly. "Go into the bathroom. Got your cell with you?" Brianna showed Terri the small phone she had taken from her pocket. "Good, *call him now* and tell him to get here as soon as he can, got it?"

"He's here, in Boston, on business," Brianna said, her teeth chattering. "I talked to my dad yesterday and he had asked me, if we could have him over for coffee or something, since he doesn't know hardly anyone in town. I told my dad, I wasn't sure what we would be doing today!"

"Well we know now!" Terri said without humor. "Call him, *go!*" She gave Brianna a little push towards the small bathroom they had in the shop for their own use. It was on the other side of the freezers and the large walk-in fridge. Brianna scuttled away with her phone in her hand and a finger on the speed dial.

"Terri Springeeee.....," the *Suit* who had been in the driver's seat said now. Terri cringed as always when someone mispronounced her last name. Well, they would straighten that misunderstanding out, *immediately!* Terri slowly raised the curtain on the door. She also took her sweet little time unlocking and opening it. She raised her eyebrows and gave them, what she hoped was a calm, questioning look of surprise. Terri doubted she had fooled them.

"Can I help you gentlemen?" Terri asked, *not* inviting them in.

"Are you Terri Springeee....?" asked Suit No. 1, rather rudely. "We need to ask you some questions. May we come in?"

"First of all," Terri said, trying to sound as tough as they were, "my name is Terri *Springe*, not *Springeee...*, the e is silent. Second, I have absolutely no idea who you gentlemen are. That being the case, I would appreciate it, if you would just leave my shop. So, *unless* you are here to place an order for the Super Bowl or try some of my food, *unlikely*, I would just as soon you go." She moved to shut the door but they pushed their way in. Terri stood her ground, however, as they produced their F.B.I. badges. Suit No. 1 flipped open his badge importantly and pushed it into Terri's face, forcing her to back up!

"I am Detective Davis and this is my partner, Detective Johannsen. We need to ask you some questions, Ms. Springe. First of all, I *humbly* apologize for *not* pronouncing your name correctly. This is a highly irregular situation and if you will just give us a couple of minutes, we will try not to take up too much of your time." Davis made his little speech and seemed polite enough. Terri, however, was not in the position to answer any questions. She figured the smartest thing she could do was stall them and hope Brianna's lawyer could get here *really fast*.

"That's fine," Terri said, trying to sound cooperative. "You gentlemen look pretty chilly, though. I'll just put on the coffee. That's my normal routine as people do start coming into my shop any time after 9:00. Since that will be in about 5 minutes, I trust you do not expect me to keep my door closed while you are here."

Terri had learned over her years of dealing with people, *not* to ask what *they wanted* or if things would be O.K. with them. Just say what you are going to do and do it. Don' t give them time to think about it or make any of the decisions. Always keep the ball, in your own court...... or whatever. Depended upon which game you were playing, *obviously*. Mmmm........ The problem right now was, Terri didn't have the least bit of an idea what kind of a game these two were playing!

Davis and Johannsen looked at each other as Terri made herself busy fixing the coffee. She smiled a little as she heard the toilet flush in the bathroom. Either Brianna was trying for effect, or she had decided to use the facilities as long as she was in there. She came out and looked at Terri but didn't say anything. She nodded her head only slightly and showed Terri five fingers. *Five minutes.* Keep them occupied for *five* minutes.

"Oh, customers already!" Brianna said as she pretended to just realize that someone else was there. She and Terri both tried to *not* think about the answering machine. The repercussions of what Logan had said in that message were beyond belief! Brianna put cookies and more sliced banana nut bread, with butter on a tray and set it on the table for the shivering detectives.

"Coffee will be ready in just a couple of minutes!" Brianna said cheerfully. Maybe, a little *too* cheerfully. Terri put her hand at her side and placing her fingers flat, made a *down* signal. 'Down, take it down a notch,' she was telling her young assistant. Brianna nodded slightly again as the two men took off their gloves and tried to warm up their hands. Terri, suddenly feeling like they were in the middle of a spy flick, was thankful for the cold. It was distracting the detectives and buying the two women the time they needed.

"We really need to just ask you a few questions and get going," said Davis, even though he looked like he could use a cup of coffee. They certainly did not refuse when Brianna placed steaming mugs in front of them. They both drank it black, of course, refusing anything with their drinks, but Johannsen actually took a cookie off of the plate in front of them. Davis looked at his partner and shrugged. *Why not? They had all day, right?* Wrong again!

The door opened then and all looked toward it. A tall man came in, dressed in an *extremely* expensive coat, carrying an equally sharp brief case. He put down the case, peeled off gloves that matched the coat and looked at the group in the shop.

"Wow!" Terri said, half out loud, half under her breath. Standing in the doorway of her shop was the prettiest man she had ever seen in her life.

Brianna looked at her, only a *little* disgusted but not surprised.

"He's married, ya' dope." She said out of the side of her mouth.

"Did I say that out loud?" Terri whispered back. Brianna elbowed her and Terri feigned terrible pain.

"Mm-mm, as usual, yes, you did 'say that out loud.' You want a real education? Watch and learn." Brianna said back in a low voice, referring to her brilliant lawyer.

"Guerrero!" Davis said with obvious surprise, as he put down his coffee. "What the hell are you doing here?"

"I could ask you boys the same question," Nicholas Guerrero said. "My client, Brianna Severson here, called me and asked me over for coffee, just to be friendly. I'm sure you understand."

Terri and Brianna looked at each other again, this time puzzled. These guys knew each other? What a small world it was indeed.

Guerrero pulled up a chair and Terri quickly placed a steaming cup of coffee in front of him before he disappeared in a puff of smoke! Nicholas Guerrero wasn't *just* pretty, he was gorgeous *and* smart *and* genuinely nice. Unlike your garden variety 'bottom-feeder' lawyer type, this one was for real. Brianna had talked about him numerous times but she had never *described* him. He was very tall, about 6'3", had soft brown hair and beautiful blue eyes in one of the sweetest faces Terri had ever seen. It was like the first time she had met Rico. Instant surprise, a guy with good looks *and* a nice personality. What a combination! Rico, though, was the opposite in appearance. Where he was dark, with wavy black hair and brown eyes, Guerrero was fair, blue-eyed and, *at least* two inches taller.

His general physical appearance, however, was merely secondary to his brilliance as a lawyer. He also had a wonderful wife and three little girls, Brianna had told her, which interestingly, added to his charm. Nicholas Guerrero *never, ever* showed undo attention to anyone. He didn't kiss up or make ridiculous statements to butter up prospective clients. Since he *was* honest and genuine, he made all people, men or women, trust him on the spot. He was a 'what you see, is what you get,' kind of person. No hidden agenda with this guy. He laid things right on the line. Davis and Johannsen knew this. They also immediately knew they were beaten.

"Listen Guerrero, you have no business telling us what we can and can not do here," Davis said evenly. "No one is accusing these ladies of anything. We are investigating an important murder case. What the hell are you doing in town, anyway?" Oddly enough, Johannsen made no comment. He was, apparently, Davis' subordinate and rarely spoke. Either that, or he just plain didn't give a damn! One way or another, Guerrero now had complete control of the situation. Davis realized this and he was not happy about it.

"You know, Davis," Guerrero said, nonchalantly sipping his coffee. He picked up a cookie and examined it carefully. His fingers were long and his nails were perfectly manicured. Another nice touch. "I understand you guys have a job to do, so don't get me wrong. I'm not criticizing or anything but sometimes you're just a little too pushy. You sneak around, you scare people, shove your weight around. Ya' got no class." He paused, took a bite of the chewy oatmeal-raisin cookie and nodded his approval. "I know all about *this important* murder case you are investigating. Hell, I'm right smack dab in the middle of it, just like you. Why don't you just give these nice young ladies a little time to get their thoughts together and we'll set up an appointment later. Just a suggestion." It wasn't 'just a suggestion,' however. It was an order!

Davis said a swear word under his breath that Terri would *never say*, grabbed his gloves *and* his partner, and practically ran out the door!

"Oh, my God!" Terri looked at Guerrero with real respect. "That was amazing. What was that all about? You know those guys? Those F.B.I. guys, you know those guys?"

"First things first," Guerrero said, putting out his hand. Terri took his hand for a firm, friendly handshake as he went on. " As you may have already surmised, I'm Nicholas Guerrero but please, call me Nick."

Brianna was still standing by, smirking at Terri's reaction to Guerrero. She had known him and his family for as long as she could remember. She had seen the effect he had on women, *many times*. She also trusted and loved him *and* his

51

family, like her own. He had been their lawyer for at least the last 10 years, and sadly had been called to rescue her alcoholic mother from more than one scrape!

"Hey, Nick!" Brianna said as he gave her a friendly hug after shaking Terri's hand, and wife or no wife, Terri envied her.

"Strangely enough," said Nick then, sobering. "I was in town because I had an appointment with Alex Buckley, *yesterday.* Now this morning, I find out his wife was murdered last night during a break-in. What exactly, is your involvement in this case, young Brianna?" His gorgeous blue eyes missed nothing and suddenly, Terri understood just how important this man was to them. She also realized how much trouble they were all in, and she instantly trusted him. If they couldn't dump *it all on him,* what else could they do?

Brianna started to fill him in. Terri produced all the paper work from Logan's *order* from the day before. They then played the message she had left on the machine yesterday evening. Checking the time, they saw Logan had called Terri's business line at 7:42 p.m., Monday night. By the next morning, she was dead. Guerrero looked over the order forms and Terri's deposit ticket from the check she had immediately taken to the bank. Terri had even made *a copy* of the check, she had been so paranoid. It had been written from Logan's personal checking account. Alex Buckley's name was nowhere on the check. Guerrero listened carefully to the message Logan had left several times, shaking his head.

"I cannot tell you what my business was with Alex Buckley when I saw him yesterday. I am sure you can understand why. It is, of course, a matter of confidentiality." Terri and Brianna nodded. "But I *can* tell you that Alex Buckley had absolutely no knowledge, whatsoever, of his wife spending this kind of money on these items. It would be ridiculous under almost any circumstances. I can also tell you that after what Alex and I talked about, there is no way they would have been planning a large gathering this weekend."

At this point, Brianna spoke up. "I think I know what you were meeting with Alex about, Nick. Now things seem to be making some kind of sense, *or not*. I'm totally confused." She stopped for a second, rubbed her neck, and scratched her head. Terri and Guerrero waited. Brianna sighed heavily and went on.

"A couple of weeks ago we went to a Celtics game and took Jenni and Benjamin with us. Actually, *they took us.* Remember Terri, Benjamin called and invited us?" Terri nodded, *of course.* "Anyway, Alex had gotten these great tickets for us and Benjamin was so proud. Well, I took Jenni to the bathroom and she told *me,* her father had told *her* and Benjamin, that he was going to file for divorce from Logan. Jenni was pretty upset but they had already gone through losing their real mother, so they were pretty much dealing with it." Guerrero just nodded. He didn't comment one way or another. It was obviously what he and Alex would have discussed, though. Brianna, however, was not finished with her story. The rest of it was even more shocking.

"Jenni *also told me,* Logan had told *her,* that she was going to have a baby. Jenni had been pretty excited about it. So, of course, when her father said he wanted to divorce Logan, Jenni was totally confused. It seemed like an awful lot for a 10-year old girl to handle, but she made me promise not to tell anyone." Brianna finished, looking at Terri, whose eyes were almost popping out of her head. This last piece of information finally got a reaction out of Guerrero.

"Alex said *nothing* to me about Logan being pregnant. That is very strange.   Either he didn't know or he wasn't ready to deal with it. This definitely would put a different spin on a divorce. Now that Logan is dead, this will have to be investigated." Nick Guerrero suddenly looked as confused as everyone else. It was indeed puzzling.

"I think I had better get to Alex as soon as possible," he said as he moved to pack up his briefcase. Terri had insisted he hang on to all of the papers she had from Logan's expensive food order. He arranged them in a neat pile and placed them carefully inside, before closing the case.

"Oh, crap!" Terri said suddenly. "I just thought of something and I wish I wouldn't have." Her stupid instincts had kicked in again and it wasn't good. "What if, Alex didn't mention the baby, because if he *did* know about it, the baby wasn't even his? Maybe that was even the reason he was filing for divorce!"

Guerrero looked intrigued but was shaking his head. Brianna, on the other hand, reacted differently.

"Oh, c'mon Terri," Brianna said, laughing nervously, "Logan always crawled all over Alex. She was madly in love with him. What are you talking about?"

"You don't treat someone that way, when you are madly in love with them, Brianna. You show respect by *not* acting like that. The P.D.A. was all a big fat show! When someone is putting on a show, there's a reason. I knew something weird was going on there. I felt it from the beginning. My instincts......"

Brianna rolled her eyes. "Oh sheez, your instincts again!"

"P.D.A?" Guerrero asked, more confused then ever, if possible.

"Public Displays of Affection!" Terri and Brianna said together.

The door opened at that point, with Guerrero staring at Brianna and Terri as if they had both lost their minds! Amber tore in and quickly saw that Terri and Brianna were safe and sound.

"Geez, you guys. What the hell is going on over here? Who *were* those men? Kellie sent *me* over 'cause we have customers......" Nick Guerrero had stood up by this time, and Amber looked waaaaaay up at him with her mouth open.

He put out his hand to her and once again, by matter of introduction said, "Nicholas Guerrero, Brianna's *and now*, Terri's lawyer. Please, just call me Nick."

"Uh......., hi, Nick...." Amber took his hand and stood looking up at Guerrero, completely stupefied. She had such a strong grip on him, however, that he politely looked to Brianna for assistance. Brianna came up to them and carefully took a hold of Amber's arm.

"Let go, Amber, honey," Brianna said, trying to get through to the girl as Amber finally released her grip.

"Uh, yeah, sorry. What was up with those guys anyway? Why is your lawyer here, Brianna? Does this have anything to do with Logan's murder?" Amber finished and finally took a breath of air.

"I'll leave you girls to answer this young lady's many queries. I had better get to my client." Guerrero made a move for the door when his cell phone rang. "If you'll excuse me for a second." He moved off into a corner to answer his phone.

"What the hell, Brianna?" Amber said then, sort of whispering. "No one has a lawyer that looks like that. He is so awesome! Is he....?" The question did not get finished, as Guerrero interrupted.

"Now I need to get down to the police station. If you girls could come with me, please. That was Alex Buckley on the phone. He needs for you, Terri and Brianna, to come and get his children. He has been arrested for the murder of his wife, Logan Adams-Buckley." Nick Guerrero finished calmly and then, strangely enough, Amber, burst into tears!

Chapter Seven

Terri and Brianna had no choice but to close down the shop and accompany Nick Guerrero to the police station where they were holding Alex Buckley. Apparently, not only had they arrested Alex but they had brought the children to the station because Jasmine, Ignacio, and Nadia *had all disappeared!* It was a strange situation but Terri and Brianna were obliged to do whatever they could.

Amber had started crying from just plain nerves. She had agreed to stay at the shop, not only to wonder *why no one ever* answered any of her questions but to accept one of the deliveries due that morning. It was, of course, for some of Logan's expensive items. Terri and Brianna had no idea what they were going to do with all the things Logan had ordered. They had *no idea why* she had placed such an extravagant order in the first place. They only knew the items had been paid for. Terri had taken the check to the bank and had paid for the foods on-line, to guarantee a quick arrival, per Logan's requests. It was so complicated they couldn't even think about it right now. It was all getting weirder and weirder as the day went on.

They got to the police station and walked into the crowded office area. It was much like the station where Angie, Will, and Rico worked. Terri's eyes darted around immediately, looking for Jenni and Benjamin. She and Brianna followed Guerrero's tall frame. He stopped at the desk of one of the officers whom he seemed to know and shook his hand. It was so noisy in the large room, also much like Angie's station, that they couldn't hear anything being said between Guerrero and the policeman he was talking with. They saw the officer point down the hall and gesture to the left.

Guerrero walked, they followed him. It was really spooky for Terri. She could have sworn they were in the same station as the one in their neighborhood. Apparently, they had all been built with a similar design in mind.

Guerrero knocked on an office door that looked exactly like Rico's. He got the same response but a much deeper voice said, "Come!" The officer behind the desk was no Rico, however. More like Fred Gwyne, the goofy big guy who had played Herman Munster on the old T.V. show. He was the first person who came to Terri's mind, anyway. She had seen repeats, on cable. Her mother had grown up with 'The Munsters', of course, and always commented, 'that she had never really liked that show.' It made for a lousy start, in Terri's mind.

"Guerrero," 'Herman Munster' said then, in as deep a voice as the character, "wouldn't have expected to see you today."

"Yeah, Fred," said Guerrero, "good to see you too."

Terri's mind was reeling. *What? Fred?* You gotta be kidding! Well, at least his name wasn't Herman!

"I hope you have a *really good* reason for holding my client," Guerrero was saying. "Otherwise, since you have already ruined my day, I might get a little nasty." The 'munster' guy looked at Terri and Brianna, who shrank behind Guerrero with real fear.

"They've come to get the kids? Good. I had no idea where we were going to go with them. I was getting ready to call social services." Terri winced at this and Guerrero gave her a sympathetic look.

"Please don't let this big, ugly galoot scare you girls! He's really not that bad, at least not all the time." Guerrero was trying to keep things on a friendly level. This guy wasn't in a good mood though, which was typical for the situation. Terri had learned this from hanging out with Rico. Being the police Captain, *was not* a fun job.

"By the way, ladies," the Captain said then, "I am Captain Fred Farrell and I am trying to run this place on a professional basis, despite guys like Guerrero here." Brianna jumped to defend her old friend but Guerrero didn't need help. He put out a restraining hand and got to the business at hand.

"Where are the kids, Fred?" Nick asked then. If Farrell was going to be an old grouch, then so was he. "I brought these young ladies down here to pick up those children. I think they have waited long enough! I also want to see my client, *a.s.a.p!*"

"Fine," said Farrell, as he picked up the phone. "Have a seat, please." Terri was glad to sit down, she was shaking so bad. Brianna sat next to Terri on the only other chair. Guerrero had no choice but to stand.

After what seemed like a terribly long wait, the door opened and a police woman, who was tall and thin but looked kind, came in with the children. Jenni and Benjamin were overjoyed when they saw Terri and Brianna. Jenni ran to Brianna, sobbing uncontrollably. Benjamin, went to Terri's side. Terri could see that he had been crying too, but now he was trying to be brave. She put a protective arm around him and he leaned into her gratefully.

"Are you guys O.K?" Terri asked. Jenni clung to Brianna for dear life and Benjamin nodded.

"We are fine, Terri," he tried to assure them. "They gave us cookies and juice." Benjamin sniffed and rubbed his eyes. They both looked tired and rumpled. Obviously, they had little or no sleep since the death of Logan and the arrest of their father.

"The cookies were stale," Jenni sniffed, switching to practical things as most children do. "The juice was O.K. I'm really hungry now though, Terri. Where is our Daddy? He didn't kill Logan!" Jenni shouted. Benjamin told her to be quiet.

"We need to get these children out of here, *now!*" Guerrero started to show some signs of strain. "I have to see your daddy now Jenni," he bent down by her and put his large, gentle hands on her shoulders. "I'll try to get him back to you as soon as I can, O.K.?" Jenni nodded and sniffed again. Terri could see Nick Guerrero as being a wonderful father to his little girls. She could imagine how he was feeling, thinking what would happen, if he were ever separated from his own children.

He looked at Terri then and addressed her pointedly. "Terri, can you drive my car and take Jenni and Benjamin back to your place? I'll grab a taxi and meet you all back at your apartment. It's up the stairs, down from your shop, right?" Terri nodded and accepted the keys from Guerrero for the Cadillac they had ridden in to the police station. Terri hoped she could stop shaking long enough to drive safely. "Terri," Nick added quietly, "*do not* question the children. If they talk to you, fine, but we have to be very careful not to confuse them. I'll talk to them when I get to your apartment, O.K?"

Terri nodded again and felt a great sense of relief as they left Captain Farrell's office. She and Brianna herded the frightened children through the crowded, noisy office and out into the cold, to the car. They all got into Guerrero's white Cadillac and headed back to the apartment. Both of the kids had hastily packed backpacks, stuffed full of a few clothes and their most precious belongings. As they pulled out of the parking lot, Jenni opened her bag and yanked out a well-used, fuzzy, brown Teddy bear that she called 'Poots.' She snuggled next to Brianna with her precious bear and her thumb in her mouth. Brianna hugged Jenni and smoothed her short, light blond, curly hair.

Jenni's hair, face, and huge blue eyes were still those of an innocent baby. She was an adorable child, and Terri and Brianna had loved her from the start. Benjamin, whose only slightly darker hair, was cut short and standing on end, always tried to look out after his younger sister. It was plain to see that they loved one another unconditionally. Benjamin's eyes were brown and serious. Both children were of slight build but the absolute picture of health. Logan had indeed, if nothing else, taken excellent care of them. Now Benjamin turned around and saw Jenni with her thumb in her mouth and spoke up.

"Geez, Jen," Benjamin chided her, "don't suck your thumb. You're such a baby!" He sounded disgusted but big brotherish. Jenni didn't care. She just simply removed her thumb, stuck out her tongue, and put the thumb back in. Brianna laughed at this exchange and they all relaxed a little.

"C'mon, Benjamin," Terri looked at him, as he was in the front seat with her. "If sucking her thumb makes Jenni feel better, I say why not? My little sister Becca sucked her thumb and carried around a blankie until she was twelve." Benjamin still looked disgusted.

"Yeah well, what about your bunny, Mr. Floppie? You don't go anywhere without him, so there!" Jenni took out the thumb again for the comeback and *again,* put it right back in.

"Ha, busted!" said Brianna, laughing again. "All right. I think you two are about even. Do you have Mr. Floppie with you, Benjamin? We can't get you settled in properly without all your important stuff." Benjamin nodded grudgingly.

"Good. We need to get you guys some food, first and foremost. Terri, what have we got at the apartment for these two?" Brianna wondered.

"Oh, I'm sure we'll find something." Terri wasn't worried. They had just stocked the fridge at the apartment with the basic provisions. It was still only about 10:00 in the morning. They had started this, so far horrible, shocking day, awfully early. Terri already had in mind to feed Jenni and Benjamin a really good breakfast as soon as possible. Juice and stale cookies would hardly suffice for two growing children.

Terri pulled Guerrero's Cadillac in behind her truck and everyone piled out. Suddenly, something occurred to Jenni before they even started climbing up the stairs to the apartment door.

"Oh, Terri," she said excitedly, "we finally get to meet Louie and Maria. Oh, this is so great!" She made it sound like a field trip, instead of the tragedy that had resulted in putting her father in jail. That, along with the loss of their stepmother, all of which had brought them eventually, to Terri's apartment. Terri saw no reason to change the mood. Kids are so resilient, she thought, much like Louie and Maria. They soak up the moods around them and make the best of it. Grown-ups on the other hand, are forced to analyze everything and deal with responsibilities, like taking care of children and cats!

Terri opened the door and, as usual, Louie and Maria came racing up. It was funny to watch their reaction as they saw the kids. It was like they both slammed on the brakes when Jenni greeted them with a delighted squeal! This prompted both cats to quickly retreat and hide behind the sofa. That didn't stop Jenni. She dropped her coat, flipped off her boots, and ran to the sofa. She jumped on it and looked behind down at them, trying to coax them out. Louie and Maria looked up at Jenni with huge blue eyes, just out of her reach, in between the sofa and the wall.

"Give them a little time, Jenni," Terri said, amused. "They're way too nosy to stay behind there for long." She looked at Brianna then. "This might be a good time to mix up some of your famous buttermilk pancakes. If you want to start frying some bacon, I'll go down and see if that shipment arrived so Amber can get back to her own shop. I'll shut our place down for today. Then we'll see what we can do to make these two comfortable. I hope the heat at Angie's apartment has been fixed. We've got a full house here!" Brianna got busy settling the kids, while Terri went down to their shop.

The shipment of most of Logan's order had arrived at about 9:30, Amber reported. She also had lots of questions for Terri, for which they just didn't have any answers yet. Terri told the curious and *frustrated* Amber, to go ahead and go back to her shop and they would keep in touch.

Terri looked over the shipment and checked off all the items on the invoice. Everything was there. Now what in hell were they going to do with it? She looked at a package of truffles and thought for a second. *Well, why not?* These things were paid for. Terri and Brianna had Jenni and Benjamin in their care. They might just as well make the best of it. Scrambled Eggs with Black Truffles, was one of the recipes Terri had found online. She had made copies of all of the pages, she had sent with Ignacio over to Jasmine. After storing away anything that needed to be refrigerated or stay frozen, she grabbed the recipes left next to the computer. Along with the truffles, sealed in an air-tight package for maximum freshness, and a bottle of truffle oil she had on one of her shelves of specialty items, Terri headed back up to the apartment.

The wonderful scent of frying bacon and fresh coffee greeted Terri as she went back through her door. Jenni was sitting on the couch with Maria in a convulsive grip. Maria's tail was twitching at an alarming rate and Terri laughed out loud at the sight. Benjamin was sitting next to Jenni and petting a purring, smiling Louie, who was half-on and half-off of his lap. Brianna came out of the kitchen and Terri handed her the recipes, the truffles, and truffle oil. Brianna raised an eyebrow and Terri shrugged. "Put some eggs with the truffles for tomorrow. I figure, might as well. Got it?"

"Got it! Scrambled eggs with truffles, *yum!*" Brianna took the items and headed back to the kitchen to find the truffle shaver they had purchased last summer on a whim.

Terri went over to the sofa and sat down with the kids. She was glad to see Maria was calming down a little. She was putting up with Jenni merely out of politeness, for the moment. Terri patted her and Maria perked up a bit, raising her previously flattened ears.

"How are you guys doing?" Terri asked, not really looking for any answers but wondering what these two kids really knew.

"We are much better, Terri," Benjamin said politely. "Thank you for having us. We really appreciate it. My dad will be happy to know we are with someone who cares about us."

"You are *definitely* with someone who cares about you." Terri knew Benjamin was trying to be grown-up and she felt sympathy for him. They were way too young to be going through this terrible situation. "What happened to Jasmine,

Ignacio, and Nadia, you guys? Did they run away?" Terri realized Guerrero had cautioned her not to ask the kids questions. This, however, seemed a logical thing to wonder about, since the children were normally in the care of the two women who worked at their home.

"No! They *did not* run away!" Jenni said, finally letting go of Maria. Terri found it mildly interesting that Maria *did not* leave. Jenni went on passionately. "They would never do that! Daddy told them to leave. I heard him. I was up on the stairs listening after someone shot Logan. Daddy *did not* shoot her, Terri. I know he didn't. I heard a noise and Daddy came to my room and told me to wait while he checked to see what it was. I didn't listen to him. I went to the stairs and saw Daddy by Logan. He told Ignacio and Jasmine to, 'pack what they could, take Nadia and go to their family as fast as they could!'" She finished her story and Terri was shocked. Brianna heard the whole thing as she came out of the kitchen. She and Terri looked at each other in disbelief!

"Jenni," said Benjamin then, "Dad told us not to say anything, *to anyone!* You never listen!" He was very upset but Terri chose not to comment on what Jenni had just revealed. It was best to leave it to Guerrero, if he would ever get there, to decide what to do with Jenni's story.

"It's O.K., Benjamin," Terri carefully chose her words. "You are both going to have to tell Mr. Guerrero whatever you know. In the meantime, let's have some breakfast." She looked at Brianna for confirmation that the food was ready.

"That's right." Brianna said. "The special of the day. Bacon, pancakes with warm syrup or jam, and your choice of juice. Whatever you want. Who's hungry?"

"We're starving!" Benjamin spoke for both of them as they moved to the small kitchen. "Can I have some tomato juice please? Jenni will have orange juice!"

"I can ask for myself, Beanie!" Jenni piped up indignantly. *Beanie?*

Terri and Brianna looked at each other and grinned.

"Don't call me that!" Benjamin said. "It's so embarrassing! Can't you call me the right name after all this time? You've called me that since you were two and I was three!"

"It's O.K., Benjamin," Terri said, once again trying to reassure him. "I think it's a neat nickname. Why don't you let it go for now under the circumstances? Besides, time to eat."

Brianna had set the table, the same beautiful way she had set it, the first time she had prepared breakfast for Terri. She had made such an impression back then, that Terri had pretty much hired her as her assistant, right on the spot! Brianna had set the table with nice dishes, perfectly placed silverware and napkins in pretty napkin rings. Benjamin and Jenni both had very good manners but they were obviously ravenous! Brianna had made a pile of scrumptious, crisp bacon and stacked pancakes. Passing around the platters, they all took fluffy cakes, swimming with melted butter, and covered them with warm maple syrup. Brianna poured tomato juice for Benjamin and Terri, and orange juice for herself and Jenni. They all crunched on bacon and enjoyed the perfectly done pancakes.

"This is the best breakfast I have ever had in my life," Benjamin said, his mouth full of pancakes. He took another piece of bacon and pushed a piece of pancake through the warm syrup. "Can I have some milk, please?"

"Me too!" Jenni seconded her brother. "Milk for me too, please!"

"Happy to serve," Terri said, getting up and stopping Brianna. "I'll get the milk, Brianna. You have done more than your share. You guys think this is good, wait until tomorrow!"

"What's for breakfast tomorrow?" Benjamin was intrigued. "It can't be any better than this! I think I'm getting full though. What's for supper, by the way? Terri, you and Brianna are the best cooks in the world!" He couldn't have been any more charming, for an 11-year old. 'Out of the mouths of babes', as they say.

"I'm getting full too, Terri," said Jenni, as she put down her fork and finished her juice, "and I'm really tired. Can I take a nap somewhere? Is Cousin Will coming over sometime? Will we see him today?"

Terri could see that the little girl was exhausted and didn't feel compelled to answer her questions. Right now these kids needed rest and they would probably see Will later. Jenni wiped her mouth with her napkin and yawned. Benjamin looked at his sister and couldn't stifle a yawn himself.

Brianna started to clean up the breakfast dishes and Terri steered Jenni into the bathroom. Terri helped Jenni wash her sticky fingers and face and waited while she used the toilet. Suddenly, poor Jenni could hardly keep her eyes open. Terri asked her if she wanted to put her pajamas on and Jenni nodded. They went into Terri's room. Jenni got her nightgown out of her backpack and changed into it. She gratefully crawled into Terri's comfy bed with her precious 'Poots' and looked at Terri through sleepy, watery eyes.

"Terri," Jenni said, her eyes filling with tears, "am I going to have a Mommy *ever again*? Will they find out what happened to Logan and let my Daddy out of jail?"

Terri's own eyes filled up and she pulled Jenni into her arms. "I don't know, Jenni," she said honestly, as she felt the tears running down her own face. "I wish I had answers for you. I feel so sad for you and Benjamin." Then she had a good thought. "You know what, though?" Jenni looked at Terri and waited. "I think, if you are sure, your Daddy didn't do anything wrong, I mean that he didn't hurt Logan, they will figure it out. Something tells me you know exactly what happened. We just have to find a way to make the police listen. When Mr. Guerrero gets here, after you sleep for awhile that is, we will talk to him and he'll help us, O.K?"

"Yes, Terri, yes," Jenni said, absolutely sure about what she felt. "I know what happened. I do. I'm sure I do. Will they listen to me? Am I too little? Will they listen?" Terri hugged Jenni again and gently laid her down on the puffy pillow with her Teddy.

"Go to sleep now, Jenni," Terri said calmly. "We'll figure it out later. Everything is always more clear after you rest." Jenni nodded and closed her eyes. Maria jumped quietly up onto the bed and laid down next to the little girl. Her soothing purring made Jenni open her eyes for just a second. She saw the cat and smiled, putting her hand on Maria's soft fur.

"Maria," whispered Jenni as she stroked the cat's silky coat. Maria made a soft, calming 'bird noise' in her throat. Terri smiled as she watched cat and child. Maria purred softly as Jenny, thumb in mouth and 'Poots' tucked under her arm, went to sleep. Terri quietly left the room and carefully shut the door.

Chapter Eight

Brianna was in the kitchen putting dishes into the dish washer. The apartment was cozy and quiet.

"Is Benjamin asleep?" Terri asked Brianna in a half whisper.

Brianna nodded. "In my room with Louie, of course. What would we do without those two cats of yours? They have an amazing way of calming even the most upset person."

"I know," Terri smiled. "Maria is in by Jenni. It's like they watch over us as much as we watch over them. Anyone who doesn't like cats has no clue what their potential for healing is. Dogs are the same. No wonder this country is so stuck on their pets."

"Boy, I can sure see it." Brianna said, closing the dishwasher and starting it. "I was never allowed to have a cat or a dog, of course. My mother had these huge aquariums filled with tropical fish and all the fancy crap to go with it. Some guys came every week and cleaned the tanks. Basically, she just kept them to amuse her stupid friends when they sat around drinking and smoking pot, and who knows what else? I was too young at the time to have a clue what they all did to get a buzz. One guy, I think his name was Rupert, would sit on a sofa next to one of the big tanks, higher than a kite and just stare into it for hours. I mean, nothing against fish or anything, but not only can you not pet them or hold them, I would just as soon eat them."

Terri laughed at that and poured herself some more coffee. "Yeah, me too. Nothing beats a nice, perfectly prepared, piece of orange roughy or salmon, *yum*. Speaking of fish, I put away the seafood Logan ordered. It all arrived, along with the truffles, the caviar, the pate, the cheeses. God, I do not know what we are going to do with all that expensive food. Basically, it all belongs to Alex Buckley but I doubt very much, that he is in the mood for a party right now." Brianna nodded and also filled her coffee cup.

They moved to the living room and sat on the comfy sofa with their coffee mugs, finally trying to relax for a bit. "Soooo.....," Terri sipped her coffee and thinking of mundane things said, "whatever happened to Rupert, I wonder."

"Oh yeah, I can tell you that," said Brianna casually. "He was *like totally baked*, my Mother's favorite term for stoned or whatever, one night and thought he was Superman. He must have been on acid or something though, 'cause he jumped off of our roof!"

Terri almost choked on her coffee and nearly split a gut trying not to laugh too loud, lest she wake the kids. "Oh my God," she said, "I probably shouldn't laugh. Did he get killed?"

"Nay," said Brianna, giggling herself, "fell into some bushes and broke his leg. He was even wearing a sheet for a cape. What a moron!"

They were both giggling, probably from being tired themselves and possibly on the verge of hysteria, when they heard a soft knock on the door. *Now what?*

"Geez, I hope *the suits* aren't back." Terri jumped up and ran to look out.

"Whew, it's our lawyer," she said with relief, and opened the door to let in Nick Guerrero.

"Damn, it's cold out!" Nick said, by way of a greeting. "I've lived in this kind of weather all of my life and never seem to get used to extreme cold or miserable heat. Got some more of that coffee, Terri?" He took off his coat and stamped his feet. Brianna took his coat and hung it in the closet, hopefully to dry.

Terri zipped to the kitchen, poured what was left of the coffee, just filling up a mug for Guerrero. She quickly put on a fresh pot. Will and Angie would probably be showing up sometime soon, so it would certainly get drank. Who knew what else might happen on this already bizarre day?

Guerrero had planted his tall frame on the love seat across from the matching sofa. He obligingly accepted the coffee and took a sip, shivering.

"I hope this isn't rude to ask but do you girls have anything to eat? It's nearly noon. I ran out without breakfast and…."

"Say no more," Terri said, immediately interrupting. "You are looking at two chicks who specialize in making sure people get the proper sustenance. Right, partner?" She looked at Brianna, who had immediately moved and was heading to the kitchen.

"As a matter of fact," Brianna said, looking smug, "when you were down at the shop, Terri, along with making breakfast, I surmised the situation, checked our supplies, and prepared a couple of platters for sandwich makings. I figured Angie and Will would be around for lunch, so we might as well start. Nick, want to sit by Terri's counter and fix yourself a sandwich?"

Terri nodded her approval and motioned the way as Nick, nodding appreciatively, got up and moved to sit on one of the bar stools. "Chicks, Terri?" Brianna asked, as they went to the kitchen. Terri shrugged. *Not sure where that came from.* Brianna shook her head, rolled her eyes and opened the fridge.

The girls got out platters of cold meats, cheeses, and tomatoes. They also had pickles, olives, and bright Romaine lettuce leaves. Mayo, mustard, and fresh Kaiser rolls, rounded out the spread for putting together the perfect sandwich.

"This is wonderful," Nick said, as he took a plate and started assembling a turkey sandwich. "I much prefer this to constantly eating in restaurants. Not that there aren't dozens of wonderful places to eat in Boston, mind you." He placed turkey, tomato, lettuce, and Swiss cheese on the bun, and liberally covered all with mayo. Terri placed a bowl of wonderful, decadent *Lays Potato Chips* next to the repast and they were set. She and Brianna, of course, had just finished breakfast with the kids but fixed light lunches to eat with Nick.

After they had each had a couple of bites of sandwich, Nick suddenly had a thought. "Geez," he said then, wiping his mouth with a napkin, "where is my head? Are the kids O.K., asleep I am assuming?"

"You assume correctly," said Terri. "They were exhausted. Brianna made us a wonderful breakfast and they both settled in. Jenni is in my room, with Maria and Benjamin is in Brianna's room, with Louie." Terri waited for his reaction. She could never resist the chance to bait someone. Brianna just rolled her eyes again. Nick took another bite of his sandwich and another sip of coffee.

"Would you like something else to drink, Nick?" Brianna had gotten up to get a bottle of water out of the fridge and he nodded as she offered one to him.

"O.K.," Nick finally gave in, as he twisted the cap off his bottle of water. "I'll bite. Who are Maria and Louie?"

"Well, *actually Nick*, do you like ca.….?" Terri rarely seemed to be able to finish a sentence or a thought these days. This particular day was no exception. The door opened and Angie came through it, dragging her sad, soggy partner behind her. They shut out the cold and started taking off their overcoats and caps. Looking over at the group by Terri's kitchen, Angie got a *what now,?* look on her face and Nick got up.

Now, Terri actually had a chance to watch Angie's reaction to Guerrero, like Brianna had watched hers. She waited for the fireworks but she was to be disappointed.

"Nick!" Angie said enthusiastically as he went to her for a brief hug. Terri threw up hands with a frustrated, "eerrrgghhh!" Brianna just grinned. Who knew?

Unfortunately, the still very depressed Will, looked on *without* amusement. Terri forgot her own disappointment. She could hit Angie up later for whatever her connection to Nicholas Guerrero might be. Apparently, they seemed to be old pals.

Whatever the case, Angie and Will had obviously stopped for lunch and proceeded to fix themselves sandwiches. Will didn't seem to be in the mood to talk much so Terri and Brianna just waited on him and encouraged him to eat. Will did, making himself a generous ham sandwich with all the fixings, along with a handful of chips. He was smart enough to know that in order to keep his strength up and be able to do his job, he had to eat. He picked up his plate, accepted a bottle of water from Brianna and moved to the sofa to eat and try to rest. Terri served him a steaming cup of coffee, and Will liberally laced it with sugar and cream.

Meanwhile, Angie and Nick were talking in general terms about what had happened with Logan. The news had spread pretty fast that Alex Buckley had been arrested and was professing innocence. Alex and Nick had spoken for some time but, of course, Nick couldn't give anyone any information about what he and Alex had discussed. He only assured all of them, including Will, that he felt confident Alex Buckley was indeed innocent. He definitely felt he had a strong case for his defense. Will seemed to accept this but he still appeared to be in shock.

"I really think you need to talk to Jenni, Nick," Terri said, still sipping coffee. She started to feel herself shaking, however. Time to lay off the caffeine, she thought, as she dumped and rinsed her cup.

"Are the kids here?" Will asked, suddenly seeming to perk up. "We heard that you guys picked them up, Terri. Can I see them?"

Terri was about to say they were asleep when her bedroom door opened and Jenni in her nightgown, with Maria behind her and 'Poots' still tucked under her arm, came out.

"Will!" Jenni exclaimed when she saw him. She went running to him and he pulled her in for a tight hug. Jenni began sobbing uncontrollably. The group by Terri's kitchen all watched the emotional scene with watery eyes. Nick took a napkin and blew his nose, trying to keep control. Angie didn't even try. She went to the sofa and sat down next to them, hugging her partner and the little girl at the same time.

Maria, on the other hand, maintaining her dignity even under the present difficult circumstances, proceeded to walk past the group by the counter on the way to her litter box and then her bowl.

"Maria, I presume?" Nick asked, taking his eyes off the unhappy scene on the sofa to watch the cat parade by. Maria briefly stopped to cautiously sniff Nick's shoes. Obviously, finding nothing of interest, she moved on to other business.

"I think I have just been snubbed," Nick said a bit miffed.

Terri would have found the interchange funny, if she hadn't felt so sad watching Will, Jenni, and Angie. Jenni was hanging on to Will with one arm and her Teddy with the other. It was difficult watching them crying and Will was trying so hard to be the grown-up. The rest of them, obviously, had mixed feelings about Logan Adams-Buckley, but Will and Jenni had genuinely loved her. Their grief was painful to see. Will, however, suddenly got a hold of himself and unwrapped Jenni from his neck to look her straight in the eye. Angie sat next to them, blew her nose, and wiped her eyes.

"We are going to find out what happened to Logan, Jenni," Will said firmly. "Do you know what happened? Did you see anything?"

Nick moved to stop Will from questioning the little girl. Jenni, however, was too fast for him!

"I did not see what happened to Logan but I *heard* something," she said, sniffling. Nick went over to the love seat and sat across from Jenni and Will. Angie had moved to one of the bar stools to continue her lunch. She and Will would have to leave, *soon*. Up to this point, Will had shown amazing restraint as they had gone about their morning. They could only hope he would not completely break down!

Nick Guerrero, was having a difficult time controlling the situation. Taking care of his own daughters was one thing. Trying to deal with a very upset 10-year old girl, in a complicated murder case, was something else entirely. He decided then, with her step mother dead and her father in jail, that Will was the closest thing she had to a relative at this point. Alex had given his lawyer complete control of the situation. Maybe trying to question Jenni now, before she forgot or became confused, was his only recourse. Nick looked at Will and he nodded. Will was a police officer, first and foremost, and he realized what was at stake. He hugged Jenni protectively and sighed.

"Jenni," Will said, looking into her sad eyes again, "would it be O.K. with you, if Mr. Guerrero asked you a few questions? You can trust him. He's mine and Angie's friend and he wants to help your daddy, I'm sure of that. What do you think?"

"That will be fine with me," Jenni said, suddenly very mature for her age. "I'm really sure of what I heard. I can tell you, Mr. Guerrero," she said looking at Nick and he smiled at her, reassuringly.

"Just take your time, Jenni," Nick said soothingly, trying to imagine how his girls would react under these circumstances. "All I need for you to do is tell me exactly what you heard. Also, if you saw anything at all, tell me that too."

Jenni then told him what she had told Terri. When she got to the part about her father telling Jasmine, Ignacio, and Nadia, to 'pack some things and get out of the house as fast as they could,' Nick was shocked but regained control quickly.

"Did you hear your daddy say anything else, Jenni? Like maybe, why they should leave fast?" Nick tried to word it, so Jenni could easily understand the question.

Jenni shook her head, *no!* "That's all I heard. I looked over the stairs then. I saw Daddy holding Logan. He was whispering to her. I heard her say, she was sorry and then I don't think she could talk anymore. I think she was dead then. She was dead! I've seen stuff on T.V. like that but this was for real. Logan died. I saw her." Jenni started to cry again and Will held onto her.

"Shit!" Angie said under her breath so only Terri and Brianna could hear. Terri understood Angie's frustration. She was really worried about her partner. If he went off half-cocked, trying to find the Buckley's hired help, or to try to solve this case himself, it would mean nothing but trouble. With the 'Feds' involved and it not being their case, it could be disastrous for Will if he didn't follow police procedure. Rico had already lectured him on leaving it to the *right people.* Will's emotional involvement would only cloud his judgment. Jenni, at this point, broke the spell.

"I have to go to the bathroom, Terri," she said and everyone let out a huge sigh. Terri didn't even realize she was holding her breath, until Jenni spoke up. Once again, mundane, everyday things took off the edge.

"Are you O.K. to go by yourself?" Terri wasn't sure but Jenni just nodded. Taking her Teddy, she headed for the bathroom.

"Are you going to be alright to go back to work, Will?" Angie asked. "Our lunch is pretty much over. We gotta get going."

"I'm fine, Ang," Will said, strong again. "Oh, and I know exactly what you were thinking. *I will not* try to do anything myself. Rico was pretty firm about it. I know, that I am *not* in any position to pursue the few leads we have and lose my job, K.?" Did he know his partner or what?

Angie sighed, again with relief. "Got it, partner. Let's head out!" They grabbed their coats and hats and promised to be back later.

"We'll have supper ready," Brianna promised, and then Will and Angie were gone. Brianna looked out the window again as they pulled away from the curb, with Will driving this time. That too, was a relief. Will seemed to have his emotions, under control for now.

The death of a loved one was difficult, yes, but sometimes it could make those suffering from grief even stronger. This was happening with Will. He also loved Jenni and Benjamin so much that he was striving to be stronger *for them*. There was no blood between them, but their affection for each other was genuine and determined. Determined to keep them going. Determined to keep them close and strong, until they found out the truth about what had happened to Logan Adams-Buckley.

Chapter Nine

Still exhausted after everything that had happened *and* talking to Guerrero, Jenni went back to bed with 'Poots' and Maria to, as she put it, 'sleep a little bit more.' Obviously, a sounder sleeper than his sister, Benjamin had not yet emerged from Brianna's room. Terri and Brianna were relieved to have the place to themselves again for awhile.

Nick Guerrero had left to go back once again, to talk to Alex with the information Jenni had given him. It was obvious they desperately needed to find Jasmine, Ignacio, and Nadia. Nick had put in a call to a private investigator he used in difficult cases named Randy Kucken. *He was good,* Nick had reassured Terri and Brianna. He would figure out if they actually were dealing with illegal immigrants or not, and leave no stone unturned to find them. Terri and Brianna, having had very little personal contact with any of them, had no information for Nick. They had absolutely no idea where the three *runaways* may have gone or why.

"First things first, Terri," said Brianna, turning once again to practical matters. "We are going to have a few people here for supper. Let's see," she counted on her fingers. "Angie, Will, Nick, you, me, Jenni and Benjamin. What do you want to make?"

Terri thought for a second and went to the fridge. Ground beef, ground pork in the freezer, fresh garlic, canned tomatoes, spices....Terri started placing items on the table and counters. She got out mixing bowls and a large pot.

"Ooooo, spaghetti with meatballs!" Brianna exclaimed. "Perfect for a crowd. Does it get any better on a cold winter night?"

"Of course not," Terri confirmed. "Let's get to work!"

Brianna found a large bowl to mix the ingredients for the meatballs. They also got out eggs, breadcrumbs, and milk, along with salt and pepper.

Terri put the ground pork into the microwave to thaw and Brianna began to mince a large onion. All went into the bowl, while Terri started the sauce in the huge soup pot. Brianna mixed the meats and other things, with her hands the way Terri had taught her. Terri added 2 quarts of her canned tomatoes to the pot. Along with one large can of tomato juice, one large can each, of tomato paste and sauce, and various spices, she also cut in fresh, white mushrooms. Terri's cell phone rang and seeing it was Angie, she answered immediately.

"Hey, Ang," Terri said by way of a greeting, "anything happening? How's Will?"

"Not much and pretty good, to answer both your questions. Here's mine, though. What's for supper? Rico wants to join the party." Angie finished her very short report, along with adding another person for dinner.

A few months ago, the idea of Rico coming over to her apartment for dinner would have sent Terri into a tailspin. She cared about him very much but he still seemed too wrapped up in his own world. Terri hadn't wanted to push him, but lately it had become just too frustrating. Right now, having him join them for dinner could only help, though. It was definitely an occasion for, 'the more the merrier.' In times of duress, especially now for Will, it was best to be with friends and family. Logan had been his family but Jenni and Benjamin were the closest he had right now, at least here in Boston. He needed to be with them and as many others as possible. The question now was, how many of them could fit into Terri's apartment? They would manage somehow, so Terri said *no problem* but not to invite anyone else.

"Who else is there? So, what time and do you need me to bring anything?" Angie quickly tried to cover all the bases.

"You shouldn't need to bring anything," Terri said. "I have plenty of garlic bread in one of the freezers down at the shop. I have a couple of bottles of some pretty decent red wine. Oh, I know, what about a salad? Can you run into a market and quick grab a variety mix of greens? Also, I just used up what I had for fresh mushrooms. Then maybe we should have salad tomatoes...." Terri was thinking and Angie stopped her.

"Ah sheez," Angie said, "now I gotta make a list." She wrote down the things Terri needed and promised they would be there by 6:00.

Brianna contacted Nick and found him still at the police station. They were processing Alex and waiting for some information about Logan. The big question now remained. Had she actually been pregnant, like Jenni had said to Brianna? If so, was it Alex's child? Guerrero had not spoken to Jenni about this part of the equation. They would deal with the problem, if it came up. Logan may not have been pregnant after all. She may have been lying to Jenni or Jenni may have misunderstood. They would have to wait for the answers and most importantly, look after the children.

The cozy apartment was full of the wonderful aroma of cooking spaghetti sauce when Benjamin, with Louie meandering behind him, came out of Brianna's room. He was rubbing his eyes and dragging 'Mr. Floppie' by an ear, when he came around the corner of the counter and saw Terri and Brianna busy cooking. Terri was stirring the sauce with a long wooden spoon and Brianna was placing a glass cake pan filled with perfectly formed meatballs, into the oven to brown before they put them into the sauce.

"That smells really good," Benjamin said appreciatively. "Spaghetti, right?" Louie sniffed too but went to his bowl of kitty nibbles, tail straight up in the air, completely ignoring Terri and Brianna.

"With meatballs," Terri said, watching Louie walk by, "one of my specialties. Are you hungry now? Supper won't be for awhile. Everyone else was here for lunch and you slept right through."

While Benjamin used the bathroom, Terri and Brianna proceeded to clean up the mess they had made in the small kitchen. Benjamin came out and asked if they had any cereal. Terri came up with a box of Rice Krispies, as she often made the classic treats for her customers. Benjamin fixed himself a big bowl with lots of milk and sugar. Terri made him some toast and he spread it liberally with Emily Springe's homemade, raspberry jam.

"This is the best jam I have ever tasted," Benjamin said then. "Where did you get this Terri? Do you sell it in your shop?"

"If I ever have enough of it, I will," Terri said then, even though she probably never would. "Actually, my Mom makes this. It's raspberry freezer jam and it takes a lot of picking of those wonderful little berries, just to get one batch! I talked her out of a couple of jars when I was home for the holidays. She's pretty stingy with it though. Just saves it for when us kids are home. I'll let her know how much you like it."

Benjamin finished his cereal and toast and settled on the couch with Louie, who apparently was his new best friend. He turned on the T.V., checking for any kids programs, finally settling on a family cable channel, showing a Disney film. Terri watched them, feeling a calm come over her. The two, boy and cat, had formed an instant bond. She stirred the sauce and checked the meatballs, which were almost ready for the sauce. Brianna was in her room straightening up, after which she was going to do some work on her computer. She and Terri had separate computers set up for homework and business, as there always seemed to be so much to do.

Terri put a load of clothes into the washing machine, stacked with the dryer in the closet next to the bathroom. She looked out the window, watching the never-ending snow falling and thought about Rico.

They had been dating, if you could call it that, since last fall. Terri had first met Rico under some pretty bizarre circumstances, pretty much about the same time she had met Brianna. Not only did she have a mild concussion at the time, but they had been right smack dab in the middle of another weird murder case. That, however, had little to do with their present relationship.

Rico had been living in New York when the World Trade Center had been attacked and the Twin Towers had fallen. He had met a young nurse working in the middle of the disaster. They had fallen in love and had become engaged. She and her sister, had been killed a couple of weeks before the wedding in a terrible car crash. Rico had moved down to Boston after that and had tried to go on with his life. Angie had been the one who had given all this information to Terri about Rico's life, *before* he had moved to Boston.

Terri wished she could be part of his life now but Rico had yet to let her in on his innermost feelings about the tragedies he been through. He also seemed to always be involved in, as he called it, 'family emergencies,' that took him away quite often without any real explanation. Until he could talk to Terri about what had happened, along with what was going on in his life now, there was no way they were going to get anywhere beyond just 'being friends.'

Terri had never taken relationships lightly. In this *day and age,* looking after ones' health, as well as the heart, was important to her. She had dated a little bit in college. However, most of the guys there had been shallow and interested only in *entertainment.* Terri was not going to be anyone's good time or one-night stand. She had needed to fight off more than one so-called *date* who thought she was some kind of an easy mark. Not only had Terri learned to take care of herself, she had developed a reputation of one of the girls, *not to be messed with!* One guy had even ended up with a nice, shiny, black eye, much to Terri's satisfaction and Angie's amusement. He, of course, had been too embarrassed to admit he had 'been beaten up by a girl.' The whole incident had taught *everyone* a good lesson! The guys who *did not* respect Terri stayed the hell out of her way. Angie, already heading towards a career in law enforcement, had dragged Terri to her self-defense classes for women. Along with what she had put into practice thus far, Terri ended up being, *one tough cookie,* which were Harvey Springe's words for his oldest child. Terri's mother Emily, hardily and happily, agreed. Being one of the biggest paranoia freaks around, Angie's words, Emily was confident that pretty much no one could mess with her daughter. So, Terri had hung on to her virtue, as well as her dignity, and gotten out of college unscathed.

Angie, on the other hand, had *not* been so fortunate. Having gotten into what she *thought* was a serious relationship, she and Terri had spent one whole, really long week, anxious and afraid, when Angie was sure she was pregnant. Her boyfriend at the time, 'Jeff the Jerk,' as they had dubbed him thereafter, had run as fast as he could when Angie had approached him with the problem. When it turned out, thankfully, that she was *not* pregnant, Angie had vowed to be a hell of a lot smarter and had not dated seriously ever since.

The most satisfying part of the whole ordeal, however, had been when Jeff had showed up at Angie's apartment with $200.00 in cash. He had offered it to her, in his words, 'to help her get rid of the problem.' Angie was shocked beyond belief that he would even suggest such a thing. Knowing she wasn't pregnant by that time, she had kept her cool in front of Jeff and had humbly accepted the cash.

Terri would never forget the look on 'the jerk's' face when, after graciously accepting the money, Angie had managed to conjure up a tear or two. With Terri standing right behind her, trying to keep the smirk off her face, Angie had looked sadly into her *ex-boyfriend's* eyes and said, "Oh Jeff, thank you so much. You really have solved my problem. Oh, and by-the-way, *I am not pregnant!* But thanks for the cash, dumb ass!" She and Terri had laughed their heads off after *literally* shoving Jeff out of the apartment. They then quickly decided to go on a spending spree for groceries to celebrate.

The girls had purchased thick, juicy Porterhouse steaks and barbecued them on a small grill off of Angie's apartment balcony. Even back then, Terri knew where to get the best beef. Along with the steaks, they had bought fat, succulent shrimp to dip into tangy homemade, seafood sauce. They had also purchased several bottles of reasonably-priced, good, domestic wines, reds and whites, stocking up for future celebrations. Along with salads fixings, some crispy bread, which they dipped in a fabulous, *very expensive* olive oil mixed with some lovely herbs, that normally was not in the food budget, they had quite a meal. And it was all compliments of 'Jeff the Jerk.' They had toasted Angie's victory, as the French say, in vin *ordinaire!* They did not undermine the bad experience, however, and it continued to be an important, *never to be forgotten lesson,* indeed.

Now though, Terri needed to stop trying to analyze her, so far, non-existent relationship with Rico and concentrate on the matter at hand. She took the dish of perfectly browned meatballs out of the oven and carefully spooned them into the simmering sauce. It smelled absolutely wonderful on this cold, winter day, making the apartment feel even more comfortable and safe. Terri stirred the sauce and made sure it was cooking at a temperature that would keep it from burning. She had an excellent pot in which to cook the sauce but it still needed careful watching.

She came around the corner out of her small kitchen, and saw Benjamin on the sofa with Louie still watching T.V. She must have looked tired because Benjamin spoke up with concern.

"Are you O.K., Terri? I know having me and Jen here must be a lot of extra work. I'm sorry." Benjamin looked worried and Terri rushed to comfort him.

"Oh no, Benjamin!" Terri quickly said, moving to join him on the sofa. "Brianna and I are really glad to have you here. I'm just tired for the same reason everyone is else is tired. We got woke up pretty early this morning and……never mind that right now." The last thing Benjamin needed to hear, was that they had all been startled awake with the news of Logan's death!

"I'll tell you what," Terri went on, trying to sound cheerful, "how about if I just get a little shut-eye, right here on the sofa while you and Louie watch T.V.? With all the company we've got coming over for supper, a little nap is all I need."

Benjamin seemed to think that was a fine idea and was reassured, once again, that he and his little sister were welcome. He put his hand on the purring, happy Louie and stroked his soft fur. Terri settled down on the end of the large sectional sofa and the second her head hit a couple of soft cushions, she fell fast asleep.

Chapter Ten

Terri was struggling to wake up! She was having one of those weird dreams where she *thought* she was up, walking around but she was still asleep. She could hear Brianna's voice in the background and little kids talking. Little kids? Here in her bedroom? What was going on? She finally opened her eyes and let out a shriek! Brianna, Benjamin, and Jenni, were all looking at her, at the same time, so they all jumped back in alarm!

"Terri, wake up!" Brianna was shaking her, trying to be gentle. Now she was trying to get her to *sit up*. Benjamin and Jenni were laughing. Terri finally remembered where she was and who they were.

"Oh geez, you guys, sorry." Terri sat up, finally, and ran her hands through her hair making it stand on end. This only sent Benjamin and Jenni into more fits of laughter. "I must have been sleeping like a stone!" Then taking in the reaction of the kids, she could only imagine her appearance and went on. "I guess I probably look like a clown with my hair sticking up and my nose still red from this awful cold!" She reached for a tissue and blew her nose noisily for dramatic effect.

"Yuck," Jenni said then, totally serious, "I hate clowns! They give me the creeps! You look funny Terri, but you are not a clown. Are you awake now?" She looked at her curiously. Brianna just grinned.

"It's a good thing I got done with my work when I did or we would have had a ruined supper!" She stood with her arms folded and tried to look stern, with little success.

"Oh my God, the sauce! Is it O.K.?" Terri tried to jump up and felt a giant head rush, forcing her to fall back onto the sofa. Jenni sat next to Terri and grabbed her in an enthusiastic hug.

"Terri, you are so much fun," she said, "I wish we could stay here forever."

"Jen!" Benjamin chided his sister again. "We can't stay here forever. Besides, Mr. Guerrero is going to get Dad out of jail and then we will be back with him, remember?"

"O.K., everybody," said Brianna, taking complete control and trying to get away from any discussion about the crisis at hand. "Jenni, you and your brother can stay here as long as you need to, right Terri?" Terri nodded as Jenni hopped on to her lap. Louie and Maria were already both on the couch. Jenni grabbed Maria, adding to the weight on Terri's lap. Brianna went on. "Terri, the sauce is fine, perfect as a matter of fact. That pot certainly was a wonderful investment. I turned it down on low and covered it."

"Oh, man," Terri fussed, "what time is it? This apartment is going to be full of people soon. We still have a lot of stuff to do. I'm not quite awake yet after all, Jenni. Could you go to the fridge and get me a bottle of water?" Jenni jumped off of Terri's lap, glad for something to do, and Maria rushed after her. They certainly have formed a fast friendship, Terri thought, amazed as she watched Maria run after the little girl.

Terri couldn't remember the last time she had slept so soundly. Probably when she had that mild concussion last fall. Jenni brought the water and Terri chugged it down. Terri couldn't get enough water. It was fast becoming her beverage of choice and she drank several bottles a day. That having been done, she felt more awake and they all got down to work.

Jenni and Benjamin had changed into jeans and t-shirts but they would need to get them some more clothes tomorrow. Terri dreaded the idea of going to the house where Logan

Adams-Buckley had died but necessity won out. For however long a time they would have the two kids with them, they needed clothes and other necessary belongings. They also had to think about the fact that the children *should* be in school. Benjamin and Jenni attended a private school for *well-to-do-families*, of course. Benjamin assured Terri and Brianna, that they could stop there anytime and pick up homework. Attending school until the murder case was settled would probably not be wise. Everyone at the school knew Logan. She had made herself annoyingly visible there, as well as everywhere else. The two vulnerable children would need to be protected from any scrutiny, for the time being.

Right now, Jenni and Benjamin were enjoying their stay with Terri and Brianna immensely. The four set up a folding table and chairs that Terri had found at, *where else,* a yard sale. Four people could sit at the peninsula, four people at the table. Since Rico had been added to the dinner party, that was eight people. They were set for seating arrangements.

Having so abruptly started their day, Terri, despite a quick shower this morning, still felt rumpled and drowsy. She went into the bathroom and threw some water on her face. She hadn't even bothered to put on make-up this morning. Neither she nor Brianna had been overly concerned with their normal routine. So far, this day had been anything but normal. Now, they both changed into fresh clothes. Terri put on a new pair of dark blue jeans and a short-sleeved soft, red sweater. It was so warm in the apartment, they didn't need to over-dress. They were staying in for the night. Hell, they were having a party! Terri, thinking about Will and his grief, and poor Alex Buckley sitting in jail, tried to cheer up for her company.

She was convinced, though, that Jenni, despite being only 10 years old, knew what had happened. If Jenni said 'her daddy hadn't killed Logan' then it was true. Terri knew she was being over emotional about her feelings in this case. *No one*, on the other hand, could ever underestimate the honest observations of a young child. Children were totally unbiased and innocent, so they usually spoke the truth. Terri suspected however, that something was still missing from the story.

Jenni must have seen or heard something else. She had told Brianna her private secrets and fears. Was she holding back some other information? Had she forgotten something? Only time would tell.

Right now, Terri looked in the mirror of her old-fashioned vanity table and, as usual, did not like what she saw. Her nose was still red but at least she didn't look as tired as she had earlier. The nap had helped after she finally came out of it. She put on some make-up, over doing the mascara. She really had nice brown eyes when she worked on her lashes a little bit. She even applied a touch of shadow and a subtle blush. Satisfied at last, she went out and headed for the kitchen.

Brianna had changed into jeans and a royal blue sweater that went fantastic with her dark, shiny shoulder length hair. Terri looked at her enviously. *Man, to be that pretty one day in her life!* Oh well, Terri loved Brianna so much that her looks were just a bonus. The young guys drooled all over her at school but she just brushed them off with a cold shoulder. Brianna had more important things on her mind these days. She was too young and way too busy to put up with someone who would just be another burden. Whoever ended up getting Brianna's affections would have to be someone really special, Terri always thought. In the meantime, Brianna wasn't interested in some shallow relationship anymore than Terri was. Once again, Terri could not get over how practical and mature Brianna was and she was very proud of her. So far, she seemed to be making all good decisions.

Right now, Brianna was stirring pasta in another huge pot. They would need a lot to serve this crowd. They were making it in batches, carefully rinsing it and keeping it hot in covered bowls.

Angie arrived at 6:00 as promised with her arms full of parcels. The kids and cats ran up to greet her. Benjamin started taking bags out of her arms and Angie gratefully accepted the help.

"Hi Angie!" Jenni said, shouting with happiness. "We are fine! Maria and I are best friends now." She demonstrated by picking up the docile cat and holding her up for Angie to see how happy she was. "Oh, and Terri woke up from her nap before and thought she was a clown!" Jenni screwed up her face at the prospect and Angie laughed with delight.

"Well, sounds like everything is under control," she commented then. "I brought all the fixings for salad, Terri. I'm assuming you have a selection of appropriate dressings?" Terri nodded, *of course.*

"Where is everyone else?" Terri asked then. "It won't be long before we are ready to serve here."

A knock on the door stopped Angie from answering. Benjamin went to answer it and wisely looked through the peep-hole.

"It's Will!" Benjamin gladly opened the door and a grateful, shivering Will came into the cozy apartment and peeled off his gloves and coat. He and Angie had parted ways after work to change, and he was wearing jeans and a Red-Sox sweatshirt. He pulled both of the kids into his arms but there was no more crying. They were happy to be spending the evening together, that was all.

The door was still half open and Nick Guerrero made his entrance, seeming to fill up the room as usual. Suddenly, Terri and Brianna's little apartment felt like it was full of people. Rico, however, had yet to make an appearance. Terri was just starting to wonder where he was when there was another knock on her door. Benjamin ran to it again and opened the door to let Rico in. He was carrying a bottle of wine which he handed to Terri with panache. She accepted it gratefully with a smile and a thank you. She had missed him so much lately and was genuinely glad to see him. That good feeling was short-lived however, because *unfortunately,* as Terri quickly found out, he *was not alone.*

"I brought someone with me," Rico announced then, as he stood aside and another person came through the door. "I hope you girls made enough food." As it turned out, enough food was hardly the problem since the *mystery guest* was none other than, Tabitha Hughes!

Part 2

Chapter Eleven

Everyone stood in stunned silence as Tabitha and Rico removed their coats. Benjamin politely took them into Terri's room to add to the pile on her bed. Angie looked at Terri, waiting for an explosion she hoped would not come. It had been a difficult and emotional day. Terri was still fighting a bad cold along with the stress, from all that had occurred in the last couple of days. First Logan and her demands, then her shocking death. Angie wasn't sure just how much more her friend would be able to handle. Tabitha suddenly crashing the party could be the proverbial, *straw that broke the camel's back!*

Tabitha, of course, looked fantastic. Her gorgeous, blond hair, loose from her police cap, fell onto her shoulders in soft waves. She was wearing slim-fitting, black slacks and a bright, white sweater. She smiled at the room, obviously thinking nothing of her last minute intrusion.

Suddenly Terri spoke up and *seemed* to recover nicely. "Well, Tabitha," she said smoothly, "what a nice....... *unexpected surprise.*" Just the use of the word *nice* was painful but she forced herself to be sincere.

Angie and Brianna looked at each other, barely able to contain themselves at the obvious redundancy. It was also a signal from Terri to her friends, as to exactly what she was feeling.

Terri hated surprises with a passion, even the *good* ones. She had never dealt with them well but was forced to make an exception, under the present circumstances. If need be, she could freak out later. At the moment, she had guests. Of course, Guerrero had no idea what was going on. Rico appeared to be as innocent and clueless as ever. Benjamin and Jenni just looked puzzled. Even Will forgot his own feelings for a second and looked at Terri with concern. Louie and Maria had disappeared. Terri assumed they were under her bed. This was a little too much company, *even for them!*

"Well," Terri said, finally moving on as all in the room seemed to relax, "everything is ready. We need to find another chair though. Brianna, could you get out a couple of small folding tables? They are in the closet in your room, I think. If everyone would like to start fixing a salad, we have some wonderful garlic bread to go with it. There is wine, for anyone who would care for a glass, as well as soda and beer." Terri strained to be the perfect hostess.

They had set up salad fixings on the counter and everyone moved to pick up plates, napkins, and utensils to start. Brianna, relieved that Terri seemed to be alright for the moment, brought out a couple of old-fashioned T.V. tables and put them by the sofa. Benjamin and Jenni *volunteered* to sit at the small tables to eat and watch T.V. Benjamin had fished through Terri's vast selection of DVDs and the resounding theme for 'Pirates of the Caribbean: Curse of the Black Pearl,' blasted out of the surround sound speakers, making everybody jump.

'Yo, Ho, Yo, Ho, a pirate's life for me.....'

"I think we had better turn that down a little," said Will wisely, as he picked up the remote. Everyone relaxed a bit more and the movie played in the background at a much more reasonable level of sound.

Terri felt her head throbbing. Fearing she would lose control, she quickly slipped into her small bathroom for sanctuary. Normally, she enjoyed entertaining but this was ridiculous. What in the hell was Rico thinking bringing Tabitha? Terri just could not understand what was wrong with him. Surely he could have figured out, it would not be something Terri would be O.K. with. Maybe Tabitha had invited herself. Maybe she had left him no choice, without being rude. Whatever the case may be, Terri couldn't stay in the bathroom all night. Then again, maybe they wouldn't even miss her. This was not to be, however, as Angie started tapping on the bathroom door.

"Terri, we need you out here," Angie said then, in a *please just come out and handle it* tone. Terri could usually figure out every inflection in Angie's voice so she went out with a smile on her face.

Everyone was in the living room area, however, so she immediately dropped it. Angie looked at her and in a low voice asked. "Uh, are you O.K.?" Terri nodded a little. "Everybody has their salads. Let me help you and we'll move this party along as fast as we can." Angie gave her a reassuring hug and Terri smiled at her best pal gratefully.

She moved through the rest of the evening numbly. Everyone seemed to be perfectly comfortable, despite the close quarters. They were all, of course, extremely complimentary of Terri's spaghetti with meatballs. 'Perfect meal for a cold winter night,' everyone said. 'Fantastic drinks, terrific bread and salads, etc., etc., etc.' Terri accepted the compliments and smiled away. She suddenly felt like Princess Diana, on a very small scale, of course. Stuck in the middle of a situation where she had to smile and smile, even though she was absolutely miserable. Terri's mother, Emily, had always been enamored of Diana and had passed it down to her daughters. So Terri thought of her often.

Had she not felt so lousy at the moment, Terri might have found it more than mildly entertaining, to watch how differently everyone ate their spaghetti. The men piled their plates high with pasta, sauce, and meatballs. They tucked napkins into their collars, twirled large forkfuls of the perfectly cooked pasta with the tangy sauce and enjoyed their meal with gusto! They all clinked bottles of beer and laughed for some reason, known only to them. Even Will was taking it easy and having a good time.

Sounds of *mmmm*....and *yummy*, *did* make Terri smile, though. It really was nice to be appreciated. The kids took medium-sized plates of spaghetti, along with crispy wedges of garlic bread. They ate happily at their own little tables and watched the movie. Angie and Brianna filled their plates, carefully cutting pasta and meatballs, in an effort *not* to splash sauce on their sweaters. Terri ate very little, even though it was one of her better efforts. As a rule with the sauce, especially with such a large batch, most of the cooking and adding of spices was done by taste. It seemed to turn out different every time but was always delicious. Everyone seemed to be enjoying themselves and Terri's cooking immensely.

Tabitha, on the other hand, took only a bit of salad and ate a small plate of pasta with no sauce. Heaven forbid, a little sauce might splash on that blinding white sweater!, Terri thought cattily. She didn't just feel a little grumpy now. She felt down right ugly. She felt fat, ugly, and mean enough to spit tacks! What was happening to her anyway? *Obviously*, between the worst cold in memory and the weird, untimely demise of Logan Adams-Buckley, she just couldn't think straight right now. Terri also knew, somehow, that she wasn't being fair to Tabitha. She just wasn't sure why.

Mercifully, as fast as it had started, the dinner party was over. Everyone got back into their winter clothes. Guerrero went back to his hotel. Obviously, he needed to stay in town for at least a couple more days. He told Terri he would call her tomorrow to discuss arrangements for the children. Terri told him, they needed to go to the Buckley home to pick up some things for Jenni and Benjamin. Angie volunteered to be the police escort, along with Will, of course. Terri felt more than a little upset when Rico left with Tabitha, as he had brought her along in his car.

What was going on here? Was there anything going on and did she even have the right to care? Not only was Tabitha way too young for Rico, she didn't seem to be really interested in him as anything more than a work colleague, nor he in her.

Also, she couldn't have been any nicer. So she didn't have a big appetite, so what?

Terri was thinking about all of these things and trying to calm down as she and Brianna finished cleaning up. Angie had helped with the worst of it and had headed back to her apartment to which, fortunately, the heat had been restored. She was totally wiped out after a long day in the cold and snow, along with trying to look after her grieving partner. Will had headed out after hugging Jenni and Benjamin good night, promising he would see them tomorrow. The children were both exhausted, so Brianna and Terri quickly made preparations to settle them in for the night. After a quick bath, Jenni settled down in Brianna's bed, with Maria. Brianna would join them later. Benjamin bunked down on the comfortable sectional sofa. Terri had plenty of blankets and pillows and the apartment was cozy and warm. The T.V. was shut off, 'Pirates' put away for another time. Louie snuggled on the sofa with Benjamin and they were soon both snoring away. Brianna and Terri finally had a moment alone in the kitchen to talk about the latest happenings.

"Well," Brianna started, as she watched Terri fixing more tea for her sore, dry throat, "that was quite the interesting evening. Are you doing O.K.?"

"Not really," Terri said, as she set out cups, spoons, lemon, honey, milk and sugar once more, to go with the tea. "I am sure that I will get over it, however. I always do. Unfortunately, we have more important things to worry about, then what *Captain* Rico Mathews is up to this time. I am pretty sure though, that he is not the least bit interested in Tabitha other than as a work colleague and friend. He treated her just like he treats everyone else. Pathetically this evening, he didn't act a whole lot differently towards me. As usual, I haven't the foggiest idea where I stand with this guy. So, this begs the question, do I even have the right to care? Weird, as always." Brianna didn't respond to Terri's wondering because she knew there really wasn't an answer. At least not yet.

The girls both fixed their tea the way they liked it. Terri, as usual, with honey and lemon, Brianna with milk and sugar.

"Yeah, weird," said Terri's as usual, 'all wise for her age' young business partner. "I agree. Rico just brought her along to be polite. I heard Tabitha say, that her roommate was out for the evening. She had mentioned it to Rico. He had brought her along. That's pretty much it."

"Sheez," said Terri, rubbing her eyes and yawning. "As usual, nothing goes like you plan. We got this all arranged and it seemed like a great idea. Suddenly, someone crashes the party and the mood changes. I'm still not feeling all that great either, so that didn't help. I think I need to just get some sleep. I feel like the walking dead." No argument came from Brianna on that observation.

They finished their tea and Brianna took the bathroom first. Terri cleared up their dishes, looked out the window and saw that it was snowing again. Terrific! Tomorrow was Wednesday. She needed to get together a final list of meats and cheeses for Super Bowl sandwiches and trays, and call in an order to Jack. They had to go over to the Buckley home to get clothes for Jenni and Benjamin.

Where will the children go, if they can't stay here with me and Brianna? Terri pondered this question and she could feel herself starting to panic. She didn't want to think about it. They were *way too* attached to Jenni and Benjamin, to say the least. Besides, there was no where else for them to go. With their stepmother tragically murdered and their father in jail, these children needed someone they could rely on. Alex Buckley seemed to be completely stunned by his arrest and unable to make any decisions at this time. If the courts sent the kids to a foster home, it would be a disaster and Terri just couldn't bear to deal with that possibility. Until, hopefully, Alex was cleared of the charge of murder, Terri hoped she and Brianna could keep them. She knew Brianna and Will felt the same way. Hopefully, so would the authorities.

Brianna came out of the bathroom, said goodnight, and headed for the cozy bed she would be sharing with the vulnerable Jenni and her new best friend, Maria.

Terri finished her nightly routine and went to bed all by herself. She lay in the dark thinking about everything, when her room door slowly opened and a small stream of light showed itself. Louie jumped up onto the bed and plopped down next to his mistress.

"Louie, you old softy," Terri said as she stroked his smooth, silky fur. "You knew I needed you, eh?" Louie made a soothing noise in his throat and purred softly as he settled in for the night. Terri smiled in the dark. She was never alone. Right now, she was being comforted by her loyal pet. She had wonderful friends and a terrific family. What did Alex Buckley and his two young children have? Only each other and they couldn't even have that right now.

There has to be a way to fix this mess, thought Terri, as she drifted off to sleep. I'll think about it tomorrow. *Tomorrow is another day.* O.K. Scarlett, go to sleep, Terri told herself as she drifted off. Louie purred and it continued to snow. All was peaceful in Terri's little apartment, in January, in Boston, for tonight.

"I've had it Rico," Terri said, finally at the end of her rope. "If you can't let me into your life, into your heart, there is no way this is going to work. I can't believe you brought Tabitha over to my apartment." She grabbed him by the shoulders, despite the stupid policeman's uniform and shook him, trying to make him talk to her. Rico looked deeply into Terri's eyes, his face filled with sadness. Sadness and shock......*and horror!* In those deep, dark brown eyes, suddenly Terri could see *the 'Towers.'* She saw smoke and fire, pouring out of the buildings. She saw people running, falling from the buildings. She could hear them screaming. The air was filled with what looked like snow, from the dust and debris. She also saw the shadowy outline of a beautiful woman, a nurse. Her face and hair, covered with dust, tears streaming down, as the buildings crumbled and fell, first the south tower, then the north.

"Rico, talk to me. Tell me what the hell is going on with you. Tell me!" Terri was shaking him again as hard as she could, pleading with him.

"I can't, Terri," Rico said, grabbing her and shaking her back. "I want to tell you but I just can't yet. Terri….. Terri, can you hear me? Are you O.K.? Terri! Please, wake up!"

Terri sat up and turned on the light. Jenni was on the bed with Maria in her arms. Apparently, 'Poots' had been abandoned for the moment in favor of the real thing.

"Jenni!" Terri's brain was racing, the nightmare still fresh in her mind. The same nightmare she had already had, more than once. The nightmare Rico probably had on a regular basis, maybe every night. Maybe, that was why he worked so much. Maybe he, along with thousands of others like him, kept seeing those same horrible images and hardly *ever* slept. "Jenni, what's wrong? Why are you up?" Terri was groggy and her heart was pounding.

"Terri, are you awake now? You were talking to someone. Were you talking to Louie? Were you talking in your sleep?" Jenni looked puzzled and was shaking her gently. Terri looked at Louie but he just appeared sleepy and cranky at having been so suddenly disturbed from slumber. He yawned and hopped down onto the floor, presumably heading to his litter box. Maria, spotting her brother, squirmed out of Jenni's arms and followed him. Even disturbing human nightmares, would not stand in the way of the ever important routine of the cat.

"I'm sorry, Jenni," Terri said then, pulling her in for a hug. "I was having a bad dream. I was probably talking in my sleep because I've been sick and overtired. Did I say anything that you could understand?" Please don't let me be saying Rico's name in my sleep now, on top of everything else, she thought.

Jenni however, had something else on her mind. "You were just calling out something. I don't know what it was. But Terri," she said then, with a sense of urgency, "I remembered something else, something else that I heard *before* Logan died! I heard sirens. The police or someone, were already on the way. I heard the sirens and Logan was still talking to my daddy. How could they be on the way so fast, Terri? How? Who called them?" Jenni's young brain was putting the events together and it did not make sense. Something was *definitely* out of joint.

Chapter Twelve

The next morning, more snow had piled up but Terri, Brianna, and the kids, had places to go and things to do. Terri had told Jenni to wait, to tell Mr. Guerrero what she had remembered. Brianna had called Nick as soon as she could, to inform him there was a new development in the case. He had promised to come over that afternoon to talk with Jenni again. They needed to find out who had called the police and what exactly were the chain of events in this weird case. For now though, they had more immediate things to take care of.

First things first, was a fantastic breakfast prepared by Terri, from one of the recipes she had gotten on the internet. Scrambled eggs with truffles, were the order of the day. Terri had not tasted truffles for some time. Brianna had eaten them years ago but had not even realized, at the time, what she had been eating. From the look on her face as she ate, however, the sensation was coming back! Jenni and Benjamin had rarely had anyone serve them much for breakfast besides cereal or frozen toaster meals. Both had hesitated at first but after being coaxed to try just one bite, they had dug in enthusiastically. Along with toast, liberally covered with more of Emily Springe's fabulous, raspberry jam and smoky, perfectly cooked sausage links, they were all starting out this busy day right. The most important meal of the day took on a whole new meaning, for all of them. They all savored the fluffy scrambled eggs with the savory dark dots, of the best truffles money could buy, thanks to Logan's mysterious order.

It was a taste that was difficult to describe. Woodsy and earthy, yet sweet and fresh. Like an *extremely* expensive mushroom, appealing to all the senses, making them all feel like they were right there. Right there in Provence, somewhere in the deep woods, where eager hands had dug at the bottom of a huge oak tree. Terri tried to explain it to them.

The determined hunter had to know where to look, know where to dig. The old-fashioned idea of using pigs to search for the precious, black gold nuggets of unimaginable worth, was of another day and time. No pig, in its right mind with an appetite, and *what pig does not have an appetite,* would surrender over the precious, delicious treat. They wanted the truffles for themselves, dirt and leaves and all. Many truffle hunters now used dogs, carefully trained to go for the smell of the truffle, rubbed onto a piece of meat. Still, the precious tubers were difficult to come by.

Terri had been to Provence years ago, back when she was in college. Back before they had all been afraid to fly but, of course, Terri had been petrified anyway at the time. The trip had been a memorable experience, just the same. She and several other students, had taken the excursion for a once in a lifetime chance to meet and learn from a great chef. At that time, they had gone on a search for truffles, feeling foolish as they poked with sticks and looked for likely spots under huge oak trees. But one, *only one* of the twenty-five students, had actually dug up a small piece of the precious treasure. It had been a wonderful trip and Terri hoped to go back again some day.

For now, though, here she was, still in Boston and savoring the delicious treat was taking her back to France. Oh well. In her cozy, little kitchen with Brianna and the kids, it was delightful to still be able to enjoy such an amazing treat. How it had all come about unfortunately, was obviously disastrous by comparison. For now, they could only make the best of things.

You didn't have to be a genius, however, to figure out that when Logan had placed her order with Terri for all those expensive items, it had somehow ended up being tied to her untimely demise. There had been a plan there. Terri was thinking, when she should have been enjoying her truffles and eggs, about the way Logan had acted, the way she had talked when she had called. Logan had been distracted. She had been way too off-hand. She hadn't cared how much she was spending. She really hadn't been very specific either, with what she was buying. Logan had been completely reckless, beyond even what she normally was. *If* you could have called the way Logan *ever* acted, normal. Terri's instincts, and as Brianna would say, 'Oh, geez, here we go again, with Terri's instincts!' were definitely working overtime. The whole thing had been one, big, fat set-up! Logan knew she wasn't going to need or use all of that expensive food. She had not expected Terri to go right to the bank with the check, that was for sure. It also may have been, that *someone* was supposed to die but contradictory to Logan's plans, it had turned out to be her. Why place the order though and then cancel it the same day?

"Terri!" It was Jenni again, trying to get her attention. "Are you day-dreaming this time? That is what our teacher always asks us, when we aren't paying attention. 'You look like you are in outer space' she always says. These eggs are really good. Aren't you going to finish yours?"

Jenni and Benjamin were both finished with breakfast. Brianna took one last bite and started cleaning up the dishes. Terri looked down at her plate, saw that she had eaten only half of her share and quickly finished. Jenni was right. The eggs really were fantastic and she wasn't going to waste them.

"Sorry, Jenni," said Terri, trying to clear her head. "You're right, I was day-dreaming. First you wake me up from a nightmare, then you catch me *in outer space*, like your teacher says. I better start paying more attention. There's so much to think about and we have a lot to do. So let's get going."

They all helped finish clearing and Brianna stacked the dishwasher. Terri threw a load of laundry into the washer and everyone helped make beds. Benjamin put his blankets and pillows back into the closet for the day. It was assumed, the children would still be with them for the rest of the week. At least that was what they all hoped.

Benjamin and Jenni watched T.V. while Terri and Brianna quickly showered and got dressed. Terri made the all important phone call to Jack, with what she hoped would be her final order for Super Bowl supplies. They would also need to assess how many loaves of bread that would be needed and place the order, with their favorite bakery.

Everything would have to be coordinated so the bread could be picked up the morning of the game. The meats, cheeses, and vegetables would, of course, all be on hand. All they would need to do, is put everything together. They would *not* be delivering the sandwiches, however. All customers in this case, had agreed to pick up their own orders at prearranged times, thus keeping everything as fresh as possible. Terri had also gotten an excellent price, on liters of several different kinds of sodas. They would be included with the sandwiches. Any other extras, such as chips, alcoholic beverages, etc., would be the responsibility of their customers. Terri also hoped they would be able to enjoy the day themselves, not just work. Being in the business of making food for other people hardly ever took a holiday. People wanted to eat during special occasions, but they did not want to have to work for it.

They were just getting ready to go out the door. Jenni was hugging Maria good-bye for the day, as the cat tried to wriggle from her grasp. Benjamin was putting on his boots. He and Jenni would leave their backpacks at the apartment, along with their favorite stuffed animals. Terri had already put their laundry into the wash. They would pack suitcases at the Buckley home. The plan was also to stop at their school and pick up homework. The best laid plans, however......Terri's cell phone suddenly let out a sharp, briiiittttttt!

"What the....?" Terri groused, seeing a number that she *did not* recognize.

"Yes, this is Terri," she answered rather crankily. She just wasn't in the mood to talk to anyone, who might make this day anymore complicated than it was already.

"Terri, this is Nick Guerrero. I'm sorry. Am I disturbing you?" Guerrero sounded startled and apologetic.

"Oh, Nick," said Terri, feeling immediately guilty. "No, it's O.K. I am so sorry. I didn't mean to sound so crabby as I answered. I didn't recognize the number, but anyway, I have to calm down. I'm a nervous wreck, I guess." She laughed, sounding a little hysterical. "What's going on? Some good news, I hope."

"It's alright, Terri," Nick said. "I don't blame you for being edgy. We all are, I'm afraid. I'm also sorry to call and tell you, I will have to change whatever plans you have at the moment. First let me ask, are the kids doing O.K.?"

Terri's heart sank as she realized Nick was *not* calling, to tell her something she wanted to hear. "Uh, they're fine, as a matter of fact. We were just leaving to go to the house to pick up some more of their clothes, and whatever else they think they might need." Terri was sure Nick was contacting them to say someone was coming to take the kids away. So she was totally shocked when he finally said why he had called.

"If you can get away from the kids for awhile, I mean if they don't need to have both you and Brianna with them, I need to pick you up. Alex Buckley would like to speak with you, as soon as possible."

Chapter Thirteen

Terri found herself an hour and a half later, in a large room with several long tables. She wasn't even sure where they were as she had fallen asleep in the car. As soon as Nick had noticed Terri's obvious fatigue, he had pulled a comfy afghan out of the backseat. She had snuggled under it, leaned against the door, and snoozed. By the time Terri woke up, they were being allowed through a heavily guarded gate. She asked no questions about their location. Whoever Nick spoke to, seemed to be only interested in him. No one gave Terri even so much as a second glance. Apparently, being with Nick Guerrero gave anyone with him, all the credibility they needed. Pretty impressive, thought Terri. She could, however, have come up with about a hundred other places she would rather be at that moment. The way things were, she was committed. They got out of the car, faced the cold, entered the facility, and went through more security.

Now Terri was waiting for Alex Buckley to make his appearance and enlighten her as to why she was even here in the first place. Thus, as Terri waited, she carefully scrutinized her surroundings, not wanting to miss any details, to relay to Brianna and Angie later. Scattered around the room, far enough apart to prevent anyone else from hearing their conversations, were several sets of people. In most cases, it was a man and a woman. One was a woman with a young child, apparently talking to *daddy*. There were several sets of two men. One couple appeared to be a father and a son. *Why* you were there, depended on which side of the table you were on and what you were wearing. Prison issue clothing, plain shirts and pants, north side of the table. Outside clothing, colorful sweaters and jeans or suits, if it was a lawyer speaking with a client, south side of the table. Coats, hats and gloves, were left in the outer room. The room was clean and comfortably lit and much to Terri's relief, several **NO SMOKING** signs were very much in evidence. That was the last thing she could handle right now. This cold was really taking its toll on her, sapping precious energy. Also, not getting the proper rest was making the cold, all the more difficult to shake. It was a good thing she had been able to sleep in the car!

A very polite police woman had respectfully searched Terri for any weapons or other unauthorized materials, *not* allowed in the room where the meeting with the prisoner was to take place. Terri had started to sneeze ferociously, and *damned this cold!* The lady was holding her purse as Terri looked around for a tissue. A nice officer behind the desk handed her a purse pack of tissues, then seeing Terri's dilemma, handed her an extra one.

"Take two, they're small," he grinned a little. They had also provided her with a fresh bottle of water. Her throat was horribly dry and still felt scratchy, so Terri had accepted it gratefully. The mornings, of course, were the worst. She would have loved a cup of tea right now but was thankful for the water and their kindness.

Terri, now gratefully clutching the precious tissues, took a swallow of cool water and tried to look relaxed and casual, which was pretty much near impossible. There were several prison guards in the room, even though there *appeared* to be only one door. Terri assumed, the number of guards were there to keep order, as opposed to stopping anyone from leaving. Terri *wanted* to leave, right here, *right now!* She realized that she was free to go, if she chose to do so but her curiosity, of course, was killing her.

She had no idea why Alex Buckley wanted to see her. She hardly even knew him. No more than five words had ever passed between them. Logan had always been there to embarrass both of them, without ever really involving them in any conversation or interaction. He appeared to be an O.K. guy, however. Also, judging from how much Terri and Brianna found themselves caring for Jenni and Benjamin, he was obviously a good and loving father. The children had been raised well, despite the loss of their mother *and* despite the bizarre personality of Logan. Terri tried to keep in her mind how much Jenni and Benjamin had adored Logan. It was very hard. She had always treated everyone else, as if *she* were the superior human being. Apparently, she had been a totally different person with the children. It was, once again, a conundrum of gigantic proportions!

Logan's situation really was a classic scenario. Babysitter moves in on father, gets pregnant, breaks up family, marries husband. However, in this case, the situation had been just a little bit different. The mother of the children had actually died, of natural causes no less, leaving it wide open for Logan to move in and marry Alex. Unfortunately, most people in these cases, almost always forgot their humble beginnings and took on a high and mighty attitude. It was very strange but only too typical.

Terri was finally getting to the point, where she was wondering what was taking so long, when Alex Buckley came into the room. So there was more than one door, Terri realized, as a second door opened off in a corner. If you hadn't been looking for it, you would not have seen it. The door blended in with the wall. There was no door knob, only a small place to insert a key, thus opening or closing it.

Alex Buckley certainly appeared different from the last time Terri had seen him. He had always, of course, been immaculately attired, no doubt more of Logan's influence. No casual wear for her man. He really was unusually handsome and looked fantastic for a man in his early 60's. Terri's own father was only 57 and a nice comfortable looking fellow.

Alex Buckley, on the other hand, was much more striking. He had very thick, black hair with just a few gray streaks in it, a straight nose and a firm mouth. Normally, his hair had been slicked back, giving him a bit of a gangster appearance, despite his friendly smile. He just seemed to Terri, like the type who could be charming when it suited his purpose. He had a great smile, however, with perfect teeth, which he now flashed at the guard bringing him into the room.

As Alex Buckley sat down across from Terri though, he seemed much more vulnerable. His hair was soft but still combed back making him look less threatening. After the guard moved away, Alex looked at Terri directly, with very dark, intense brown eyes, startling her immediately. Rico's eyes were brown too, but always appeared calm, if not thoughtful. Often times, he appeared just sad, in his own world, like he didn't even *see* the people around him. Alex's eyes, on the other hand, pierced through Terri now, like he knew her thoughts and feelings. She suddenly felt completely panicky and vulnerable herself, feeling as if she had to leave. He noticed her reaction and stopped her.

"Don't be afraid, Terri." Alex spoke then and suddenly, *it was as if she had never heard his voice in her life! Gone* was the quiet, meek gentleman who had followed Logan around like a puppy, obediently doing her bidding. *Gone* was the man, who had always barely muttered a greeting to Terri and Brianna. Suddenly, here was a firm and determined man. Definitely *not* what Terri was used to, or had expected from him at all. He was taking complete charge of the situation, something he apparently should have done a long time ago.

"What!" Terri exclaimed then, spooked *beyond belief.* "How…how did you know…" she stammered and then felt defensive. "What makes you think that I'm afraid? Why would you say that to me? You are giving me the creeps, Mr. Buckley!" Terri blurted out. "I do not appreciate someone I hardly know, getting one step ahead of me. I'm not so sure this meeting is a good idea…..I…." Alex interrupted her protests, this time sounding anxious and a bit frightened himself.

"I'm sorry, Terri. Please, forgive me. Obviously, my trying to calm you down has had the opposite affect. I don't know how I can tell what people are feeling. It's always been my way." He put his head in his hands and ran his fingers through his hair. Terri was glad to see that at least his wrists weren't shackled. Either this facility kept a really tight ship, or they didn't feel Alex Buckley was an immediate threat to anyone.

Terri could also see, that Alex Buckley was a very sad and tortured man. She felt genuine sympathy for him, being separated from his beloved children, losing his wife suddenly. Was he sad about losing Logan, though? She needed to find out!

"First of all, could you please just call me Alex?" He was begging Terri, now, for understanding and friendship. "You are young enough to be my daughter, for heaven's sake. Of course, so was Logan, but anyway, I really do need all the support and friends, I can get right now. You also must realize, how much I trust you and your friend Brianna. Otherwise, I would have certainly made other arrangements for my children. They are the most important thing in the world to me and I truly believe they are safe with you. Am I correct in assuming that?" He stopped and waited for reassurance from Terri.

"Yes, Alex," Terri said, trying out his first name and feeling much calmer. The mention of the children, also made her feel better and she immediately warmed to the subject.

"Oh, Jenni and Benjamin are just wonderful! They are smart and funny and sweet and polite. You have raised them well." She hesitated but felt she needed to say it. "They really did love Logan, too. I…I'm so sorry for your loss." Now Terri looked intently at Alex, trying to gage what he was feeling. She was making an effort to put aside her feelings and see if she could figure this man out. Terri needed to figure out, what *his* feelings were. As it turned out, she didn't need to. He came straight to the point.

"Thank you, for saying all those things about my kids. You are right about everything, when it comes to Jenni and Benjamin. *On the other hand,* you may have already guessed this Terri, so I am going to be completely honest with you. I married Logan for only one reason. You are correct. Jenni and Benjamin did love her, very much. She was wonderful with them. She wanted them for her own. *That was the problem.* She wanted my children, she wanted my money. I thought, *fine!* After Julia died, it seemed just as well that I marry Logan, no matter how many of my friends and colleagues told me what a bad idea it was. I just didn't want people talking about her living in our house with just me and the children. If I was married to her, it would put the situation above reproach and be better for Jenni and Benjamin. I have to admit and I'm ashamed to say it, but the first couple of months with Logan were pretty great. She was exciting and loving. Suddenly, though, she changed her tune and shut me out. In the last year or so, we have had a completely separate relationship. She went her way and I went mine." He put his head in his hands again and stopped for breath.

Terri, on the other hand, strained to hide her shock. Not to mention the embarrassment of finding out the intimate details of Logan and Alex Buckley's weird marriage. This also certainly put what Jenni had told Brianna, in a completely different light. If Logan had been pregnant, who was the father of the child? Terri knew that she *could not* bring this up to Alex. It may not have even been true. Jenni might have misunderstood or Logan may have been lying to her for some strange reason. Obviously, the question of whether or not there was a baby, would be answered by someone other than *Jenni or Terri*. Terri was sure that Nick would be checking into it. If Logan had been pregnant and it was proved that Alex was not the father, it could spell disaster for Alex! If it had been the child of another man, it would give Alex a very strong motive to want to kill his wife. Crime of passion and all that, never an easy thing to prove but not unheard of. Also, what about the way Logan had always acted with Alex? *The P.D.A., what about the P.D.A?* What kind of game had this woman been playing? Terri's mind was reeling and she was more confused than ever. She just could not bring herself to ask Alex about it, though. What he had already told her, fell under the category of *way too much information!* Alex finally went on and Terri was forced to snap out of her reverie.

"I obviously, have my company to run and couldn't be with my children as much as I would have liked to. When Logan came into the picture, it had seemed the perfect fit. At first, she was supposed to be temporary, of course, just until Julia recovered. My children and I, as you can imagine, were devastated when Julia was diagnosed and then died so quickly. The doctors tried everything our money could buy to save her, but nothing could stop the cancer. It was already too far gone. It certainly puts things in perspective though, doesn't it? No amount of money can buy a life!" Alex finished and looked down.

Tears were streaming down the eyes of Alex Buckley now, and Terri did see his feelings. She saw what was in his heart. His one and only real love was Julia, the mother of his children. Marriage to Logan had been convenient and logical, *at the time.*

Silly as it seemed, Terri took two tissues out of one of the little packages and handed them across the table. Alex accepted her offer. The guard closest to them, saw the interchange and didn't move. Alex wiped his eyes and blew his nose, waiting for Terri to respond.

"Now I am going to make a few statements myself, Alex," Terri said finally, trying to sound firm and confident. "Also, I am going to ask a couple of questions. Is that O.K. with you?" Alex nodded, accepted a couple more tissues and wiped his eyes again. Terri went on.

"First of all, being your friend is about all I can offer you right now. That being the case, Brianna and I hope that Jenni and Benjamin will be able to stay with us as long as necessary." Alex nodded gratefully and looked relieved. "Also, I certainly do not expect you to tell me everything. You've already told me too much the way it is. I am *not* the police and I am *not* your lawyer. According to Brianna, however, they don't get any better than Guerrero! Do you agree?" Alex nodded again.

Terri could tell, that saying as much as he had up to this point, had sapped a great deal of his energy.

"O.K. then, first question," Terri suddenly wished she had a notebook and pen. Maybe she could pretend to be a hotshot reporter for the Boston Globe, getting an exciting scoop for a story. 'Did you kill your wife, Mr. Buckley?' she would ask, expecting him to confess *only to her.* Mmmm....probably a bad idea, for starts. As usual, Terri was letting her 'Nancy Drew' imagination run wild. There were other things to worry about, at the moment. Get a grip girl, she told herself and went on.

"Do you have any close relatives at all?" Terri inquired then, still trying to keep Jenni and Benjamin's best interests to the forefront. She was worried that suddenly someone would show up out of the blue and demand the children be handed over. But Alex calmed her fears.

"No," he said firmly, and then smiling a little he figured out where Terri's thoughts were going, *again!* "At least not anyone who would turn up and try to take my kids away. My only sister lives in Europe and plays the social scene. She could care less about her niece and nephew. Both of my parents are deceased. That's what you were worried about, right?"

"O.K., you can stop that now!" Terri smiled a little at Alex. "Fine, stay one step ahead of me if you want to. It will save time. Speaking of which, how much time do we have anyway?" They had only been talking for about fifteen minutes. Was there a limit?

"As much time as we want," Alex said confidently. "You are right again. Guerrero is the best. One thing is for sure, I think he has more info. on some of the high-up people around here, than anyone can imagine. He's also trying to get the judge to post bail and get me the hell out of here. You can't believe how well I have been treated in the meantime. I don't think anyone believes that I shot Logan either. What do you think Terri? I will save you some time on that one. Here it is. Jenni told you she saw me bending over Logan. She heard Logan talking. Is that correct?" Terri nodded numbly, amazed, once again, at this man's insight. "I feel terrible that my daughter had to see that. But it *could* help my case. What she saw is what it was. I had heard a noise, gone to the rooms of both of my children and told them to stay where they were. As you know, Jenni let her curiosity get the better of her but it may save the day. When I got to Logan, she had been shot, *once.* The gun, unfortunately *my gun,* was lying on the floor next to her. Jenni also heard sirens, meaning that someone had already called the police and we still do not know who. Jenni *also* heard me tell Ignacio, Jasmine and Nadia, to leave and get away as fast as they could. *I did do that,* for a very good reason."

He suddenly ran out of breath again and had to stop for a minute. He looked up then, and said, "Hey, Jasper," addressing the nearest guard, who looked back respectfully. "Do you think you could grab me one of what Ms. Springe here is having?" *Jasper* immediately went through the door that Terri had come through and returned with a bottle of ice cold water for Alex. "Many thanks," Alex said, "you're a good man!" Jasper merely nodded as Alex went on.

"Logan had hired Ignacio, Jasmine, and Nadia. They are from Guatemala, but I don't think she even knew that much. All she did, was make some kind of a connection with one of her so-called friends and she had her hired help to push around. *My lovely wife* completely forgot what she herself had been, and always treated them like shit!"

Shades of Brianna's mother, Elizabeth Severson, thought Terri, as she waited for Alex to keep talking.

He didn't apologize for the cuss word, just unscrewed the cap from the bottle of water and took a long swig. It seemed to refresh him as he went on. At this point, Terri saw no reason to question him about anything else. He seemed to be answering her queries before they even came to her.

"Here then, is the problem. I don't think they are in this country legally. Somehow, one of them may be tied to Logan's death. I am not saying that I am willing to *take the rap*, as they say, for someone who may have murdered my wife. I was shocked as hell when they arrested me. All they have for evidence is *my* gun. No solid motive, no gun powder on my hands. They needed to make an arrest fast and I was the prime candidate." Alex paused for another drink of water and went on. "But the truth is, whoever shot her had a good reason. *She was bad news*. I know that sounds terrible. There is never an excuse for taking someone's life." Where had Terri heard that before? "Look at all the war casualties. Is it being excused? No, but someone is reasoning in their heads that it is necessary. What are all these killings about anyway? All the suicide bombings? It's all about *someone* thinking they have a good reason to kill, not only themselves but other innocent people along with them. Sorry to go on and on. I have a cousin in Iraq. Obviously a much *younger* cousin but he has been in the military for twenty-five years and it's never enough. Since I have very little family, he and I have always been close. Now, he's over there." Alex stopped and took another drink of water so that Terri could get a word in.

"I sort of know how you feel," she said. "Brianna's brother, Brad, is over there and she worries about him constantly. Terri sighed heavily and then looked intently at Alex. "So you are saying, directly *to me*, that you *did not* kill Logan. You think you may know who did but you can't do anything about it? How are you going to find out what happened if you can't contact Ignacio or Jasmine or Nadia? If they are illegal aliens, they have probably disappeared by now. This is impossible!" Terri threw up her hands. Not only was she exasperated, but once again, she was surprised that she and Alex Buckley were exactly on the same wave length.

Terri had been so sure that she was just being paranoid about Ignacio. Turned out, she had more than likely been right. This still didn't quite explain the F.B.I. being on *her* doorstep, however. She beat Alex to the punch then, by making that her next concern before she even let him comment.

"O.K., fine, so what about the F.B.I. showing up at *my* shop? Why would they be interested in three people, out of possibly thousands, that may be in this country, illegally? It doesn't make any sense to me. They were not very friendly either. Nick had to come to our rescue. He…..." Alex jumped in then.

"Ah, yes! Davis and his side-kick Johannsen. Nick told me about your unfortunate experience with those two. Sorry about that." Alex sat back in his chair and looked rather pleased with himself. Despite his present predicament, he didn't appear overly concerned with the outcome. Terri as much as told him so, thinking he may be feeling a little over-confident.

"Why should I be worried?" Alex said, seeming more together and relaxed. "I did not kill my wife and, as we both agreed, Nick Guerrero is the best. I'm convinced he'll get me out of here and soon. My main concern, at the moment, is Jenni and Benjamin. You have assured me they are being well looked after. That is all I needed to know. Oh, and don't worry about Davis and Johannsen. They have been trying to get something on me for years. A past old grudge. You know nothing so they can't bother you. If they do again, however, just call Nick. If they're actually dumb enough to wait for him, he'll take care of it." Then Alex sobered again.

"You can't even imagine some of the people I have to work with, Terri. Big business isn't just mean and nasty. It can threaten your whole life. I'd give every penny that I have right now to have Julia back. I really screwed up by not just sending Logan off from the beginning. I should have looked for someone, good and kind to be with me and the children. Oh, and about that order Logan placed with you, for all that expensive stuff, I haven't a clue what that was about. She was playing some kind of a weird game, I guess. But if we can make some kind of a connection, it may have something to do with why she was murdered. It may not. If you can come up with any ideas, let Nick know."

Terri nodded in agreement to all Alex had said as he went on. "So, after all of that Terri, here is the bottom line. Here is the *most important reason,* that I needed to see you today." He took another drink of water and Terri waited patiently, dreading what he might expect of her. She was right to be afraid after all as it turned out, when Alex Buckley finally clued her in on why she was really there.

"I have been informed," Alex said then, lowering his voice a bit, "that there is a large population of Guatemalans living in the city of Boston. I know this is a lot to ask but I also know, that Ignacio and Jasmine, *trusted you.* I believe, they may still be in the city and they would talk to you. Besides, *I'm helpless* stuck in here. I can give you an idea of where they might be. Then I need for you, to go out there and find them."

Chapter Fourteen

erri realized, unfortunately sometime *after* they had left the prison where Alex was being held, that she had forgotten to ask him what to do with all of the food Logan had ordered. Her obvious plan to cancel the order and not even pay for it, had apparently backfired on Logan Adams-Buckley. Now, Terri and Brianna were stuck with it. Even though it was indeed paid for, she had no idea what to do with it. She mentioned as much to Nick Guerrero as they drove back to Boston. The weather had calmed down, for the moment, and the roads were passable. Nick drove his luxurious new car, expertly and safely, traversing the ice and snow. Terri was, again covered up with the soft, warm afghan. She was shivering, despite the warm interior of the vehicle. Nick put her concerns about the food stuffs to rest, however.

"Don't worry about it, Terri," he said then. "When I showed Alex all the receipts from the purchases and the copy you had made of the check, he was as confused as you were. I'm rather surprised you two didn't talk about it. Anyway, he said, to tell you, to just do what you want with the food. You are looking after Jenni and Benjamin, after all. Taking care of children is expensive. It takes time and it costs money. I should know. My wife and I decided, after daughter number two, that it made more sense for her to be home with the kids. Alex is in no position at the moment, to pay you and Brianna for what you are doing to help him out. His assets have all been frozen. He wants you to keep the food and use it at your discretion. Perhaps some of it can be used directly to look after Jenni and Benjamin," Nick wondered. Terri just shrugged her shoulders. Most of what Logan had ordered, was hardly appropriate for feeding growing children!

"Well, we did talk about the food a little but not what to do with it. I didn't have the heart to ask, I guess. We certainly talked about plenty of other things, that's for sure. So we barely touched on Logan's mysterious order. Basically, he knows about as much as we do. Pretty much nothing. I doubt, however, that Jenni and Benjamin, would be interested in incredibly expensive caviar and pate. But I gotta tell ya,' Brianna and Angie and I would love it!" Just thinking about the caviar and pate, made Terri's mouth water. "Sorry, but I do not intend to let it all go to waste, you can bet on that. I hope we can get this all figured out before the Super Bowl. 'Cause if we do, we are going to have one hell of a party and we would love for you and Alex to be there!" Nick laughed at that and Terri went on. "We did have some great scrambled eggs with truffles for breakfast this morning. Jenni and Benjamin really seemed to enjoy them. Brianna and I certainly did." Terri rubbed her eyes and yawned. "I had almost forgotten all about it. That seems like days ago. Those kids miss their dad so much, though. Oh, don't get me wrong. I love having them but they need to be with their father. Also, my apartment is pretty small. They just plain need more space!" Terri let out a huge sigh and Nick Guerrero agreed.

"I want to get Alex Buckley and his children back together again as soon as possible too, but as you know, the wheels of justice seldom turn quickly. What we really need to do is find out who did do this, as in, *not* Alex!" Nick looked sideways at Terri then, and she felt uncomfortable under his scrutiny.

She had not told Nick what Alex had asked her to do. Terri did not want to even *imagine* Angie's reaction! It would not be pretty and was bound to be explosive. She tried to think over her conversation with Alex and continued to at least tell

Nick about some of it, *for now*. She wasn't sure what she was going to do about Alex's request. She needed to think it over for awhile. In the meantime, she did have some feelings about Logan's weird actions the day before her bizarre death. She told Nick about the way Logan had acted, the way she had sounded. There was definitely some weird plan in the offing there, but what?

"Mmmmm….," Nick wondered, thinking over what Terri had told him.

"Your instincts again?" He grinned at her as he skillfully navigated the slippery roads.

"They haven't let me down yet," she said with confidence. "Logan was always pretty out there but this…..this was bizarre, even by her standards. I tried everything I could to talk her out of it, too. Ask Brianna, if you feel like it. She was there when I was on the phone with Logan. She watched me place the order and we were both dumbfounded! Then Ignacio came to the shop with this *huge* check and a ridiculous tip! We sat him down, for hot soup and coffee and then he left. Then *I* left to go right to the bank, something Logan apparently did not count on. You heard what she said on the answering machine. 'Hope you didn't take that check to the bank yet.'" Terri mocked Logan's little whiney voice and then went on. "It was just way too much money and it had technically been already spent. I did not feel comfortable keeping that check in my possession, not even overnight."

Nick nodded and Terri went on. "Of course, when I walked out the door to go to the bank, I looked across the road and there were those two F.B.I. goofballs! Since then, nothing has been the same." She sighed again and pulled the afghan up over her head, feeling like a little kid who wanted to hide and pout.

Nick laughed and pulled at the afghan. "C'mon Terri," he said teasing her a bit, "hiding won't help. We'll get this all figured out, I promise. One step at a time, O.K.?"

Terri peeked out of her hiding place and looked at him hopefully. She had already forgotten how gorgeous he was, 'cause he was just so damn nice! Yikes! "You promise, huh?" She asked then. "That's a pretty tall order. Are you telling me you have worked on cases, even more weird than this one?"

"Well," Nick said then, hesitating, "not lately but…..I'll tell you what. I'll give you some homework to do." Terri rolled her eyes at that one. *Oh, great!*

"When we get you back to your apartment, I want you to sit down at your computer and open up a file. Call it, oh, I don't know……"

"Alex Buckley vs. The people of the state of Massachusetts?" Terri suggested then, trying to sound smart.

"Whatever you want," Nick grinned at her. "Anyway, put down everything that has happened since this all began. Keep a diary, beginning with when Logan first started calling your apartment on Saturday. Try to remember *exactly* how she sounded, *exactly* what she said. Put down as much of your conversation as you can remember, if you like. Try to recall if Ignacio said or did anything, that seemed unusual. Was he acting the same as he always did?" Terri shrugged again, not sure. She would have to ask Brianna and see what she thought.

Nick went on. "Also, put down all the dates, and even the times if you can recall them, of each thing that happened. I know it may take you awhile but get down as much as you can, including your experience today, talking with Alex. Try to remember as much of your conversation as possible. Once you get caught up with everything, continue as the case goes on, not leaving anything out. Do you think you can do that?" Terri nodded. "Also, as you remember more things, just go back and get it down. Keep a notebook with you so that if you are away from your computer, you can scribble down thoughts to put in your file later. That's what makes computers so great. You don't have to erase or scratch off. You can have a record for each day. Then just add to it as we go along. O.K.?"

"O.K," Terri said then. "I think that is an excellent idea. It would help me to not be so confused, too, if that's even possible. Mmmm……..if I put everything in order, maybe it'll give me a chance to sort it all out and......" The screeching of her cell phone broke up Terri's train of thought. It was Angie.

"Where in the hell are you, woman?" Nice way to greet a friend.

"Out with a gorgeous lawyer," Terri quipped, and now Nick rolled *his* eyes. "Where in the hell are *you*?"

"At work where I'm supposed to be. Will you get serious? What happened? Did you talk to Alex Buckley? What did he want? When will you be home? Brianna called me. Jenni and Benjamin are wondering what's happening. Will is driving me crazy and....."Angie drew a breath.

"Angie!" Terri took her voice up a notch. "It's O.K. Yes, I talked to Alex. Mostly we discussed the children. I'll be home in a little bit. I'll call Brianna. See you tonight for supper. Later, bye!"

Terri quickly ended the conversation, probably pissing Angie off. She just didn't know what to tell her friend right now. Terri then placed a call to Brianna. Nick said they would be back to the apartment in about a half hour. Brianna assured Terri that Jenni and Benjamin were fine. They had picked up plenty of fresh clothes, school books, along with homework, and a few more favorite toys. They were presently in the middle of trying to *organize* their stuff. Terri hung up, assured they would be busy until she got home.

"Hey, c'mon," Nick said then, "what's with all this *gorgeous lawyer* stuff, anyway?"

"Hey, have *you* looked at *you* lately?" Terri asked with a laugh. He raised an eyebrow but made no comment. It was starting to snow again so he kept his eyes on the road.

"O.K., yeah Nick," Terri felt like it was confession time, "you're one of those guys, that the first time a single girl sees you, probably married ones too, it's like....*whoa!* But I gotta tell ya' it's not *just* the fact that you are married with three kids, that makes women like me back off fast. It's the fact that you are just so..... oh I don't know, so damn appropriate! You treat *everyone* the way you are supposed to. You don't flirt or put on a show to get what you want or need. You do things the way you are supposed to and accomplish what you have to, by just plain doing the right thing. You possess real integrity. That's rare these days and refreshing."

"Great," said Nick, having absorbed Terri's summation of his personality. "So, basically what you are saying, is that I am boring. I'm not so sure, I'm happy about that." Now he laughed but he also appeared a little disappointed.

"No, you are definitely *not* boring!" Terri assured him. "C'mon Nick, there is nothing wrong with being a nice person. I'm a nice person too. People like you and I, we *try* to do what we're suppose to do. Has it always been easy? Hell no! We have choices to make everyday. No one is perfect, that's for sure. We all make mistakes, sometimes big ones. Show me anyone, who says, 'they have never told a lie and I'll show you a liar!'" Nick laughed again and nodded in agreement.

"You know, Terri," Nick said, totally serious now, "I have been very fortunate. I love my wife and girls more than anything in this world. But do not think, it has always been easy for me. O.K., fine, I'm not ugly." He looked at Terri sideways and now *she* raised an eyebrow.

"Yeah, that's one way to put it," Terri confirmed. No argument from *any woman* on that one. "Well, whatever it is, that keeps you on the straight and narrow, if it works for you, don't question it." Terri sighed then and finally didn't feel cold anymore. She folded the soft afghan and put it into the backseat of the car. "I sure wish that *someone else*, would be just a little more, oh well, I don't know, *friendly*. Someone single, also *not ugly*, as you put it. Also, nice guy, just like you. Treats everyone the same. Blah, blah, blah....geez, I'm sorry. But men, in general, seem to confuse me more than ever these days. Especially this man. I'm just about ready to give up!" She threw up her hands in exasperation and looked out the window at the falling snow. For a few minutes neither one of them said anything.

"Soooo....., *what is* going on between you and Rico then?" Nick asked finally, breaking the silence. Obviously, it wasn't difficult for him to figure out who Terri was referring to.

"In a word," Terri said then, with a frustrated sigh, "nothing! Not a damn thing! Huh, what do you know? That's five words." Terri pinched the bridge of her nose and stifled another yawn. She was so tired. She continued her grousing however. "What's the difference anyway? With this stupid murder getting everyone so screwed up and this damn head cold, I don't even have the energy to think about it right now. It's just so complicated." Nick waited for Terri to go on, realizing she needed to talk about it, whether she had the energy or not.

"How did you guys meet anyway?" He asked then, attempting to draw Terri out without seeming too nosy.

They were coming into the city now and Terri would be back at her apartment in a few minutes. She tried to put the story of how she and Rico met, in a nut shell. Finally, she finished with Angie's heartbreaking revelations about Rico's past life. So far, any effort Terri had made, to break through the wall Rico had built around himself, had been for nothing. Sometimes, Terri felt like maybe...... *maybe,* they were finally getting close. Then something would come over Rico. Perhaps a memory or a flashback, of the nightmare he had lived. Then the wall would just go up again and leave Terri heartsick and disappointed.

Nick listened and nodded occasionally. He didn't really have an answer for Terri and she didn't expect one. She would just have to wait and be patient. In the meantime, they had some serious facts to sort out. They had the kids to look after and Alex to get out of prison. That was *one hell of a tall order!*

Nick had just maneuvered the car onto Terri's block, when her cell phone chirped again. It was Angie. Terri was almost afraid to answer it.

"Hey Ang," she started cheerfully, hoping her friend wasn't *too upset* with her. "Anything new?"

"Oh, yeah," Angie sounded like the cat that had swallowed the canary. "I've got something new all right." Terri was nearly blown away by what Angie told her. She quickly signed off and looked at Nick.

"What is it?" Nick asked, as he stopped the car below Terri's snow covered staircase. "What's the matter? What did Angie say, Terri?"

Terri was stunned for a few seconds and then she got the words out. "She somehow found out something. I've no idea how, mind you." She took a deep breath and came out with it. "Angie found out, that Logan *was* pregnant. She was about two months along. Oh shit, Nick!" Terri was now on verge of tears. She knew what this could mean for Alex and it would *not* be good. He had told her, that his marriage with Logan, had been all but over for nearly a year. If that was the case, *he was not the father.*

"Well," said Nick, trying to absorb the information. "I guess we need to find out if Alex knew. If he didn't, then that would explain why he never mentioned it to me. If he did, well……" Terri had to interrupt Nick then and tell him what she knew he would not want to hear. He would find out anyway, sooner or later. She might as well let him know, as soon as possible. How she wished now that Alex Buckley had kept this intimate detail, *to himself!* He had passed the responsibility onto Terri and now she had to deal with it.

"Nick," she said finally, grabbing his arm for emphasis. "This is bad, *really bad*. If what Alex told me, back at the prison about his relationship with Logan, is the truth, *he was not the father of that baby!"*

Chapter Fiteen

For the first time in several days, Brianna and Terri had the apartment to themselves. Will had taken Jenni and Benjamin to see an early movie and then out for dinner afterwards. Terri had insisted they be home by 7:00 or 7:30, at the latest. Even though they did not have to get up for school, Terri felt it wise to keep them on some kind of a schedule. She and Brianna were both so tired from all of the activity and stress, that the earlier bedtimes were doing them good as well.

At the moment, they were having leftovers for supper and waiting for Angie. Terri had barely touched on her conversation with Alex Buckley to Brianna. She figured she may as well wait until Angie arrived and tell them both together.

"That must have been weird being at that big prison, huh?" Brianna asked as she took a bite of the Chicken Divan she had warmed up in the microwave, along with a generous scoop of creamy macaroni and cheese.

"Weird is hardly the word," Terri said, shivering. She had decided on leftover spaghetti with meatballs. Terri had been so miserable during the dinner party, with her cold and the confusion she had felt when Rico showed up with Tabitha, that she had not been able to enjoy one of her own favorite dishes. They had also made some fresh garlic bread to go with their supper, along with an aromatic pot of soothing hot tea.

"Hey, hey…"said Angie then, as she came through the door with her key and made a big fuss of stomping snow off her boots. "Where are the munchkins? This place looks empty!" She took off her coat and gloves and tossed them in a chair.

"The kids are at a movie with Will, which is nice. So we can talk. Leftovers for supper, so take your pick. Spaghetti, chic. divan, mac' and cheese, or make a sandwich if you like. Oh, and there's also chicken and dumpling soup. Never a lack of food around this place, as always." Terri twirled another generous forkful of the delicious pasta and sauce and took a bite. "Mmmmm….."she said pondering, "why are spaghetti sauce and chili, always so much better the next day?"

"You know the answer to that question as well as I do, so quit stalling. Obviously, I have a few questions of my own," said Angie, as she put a generous portion of pasta on a plate and added sauce, with the tender meatballs. Terri had reheated and drained the pasta and warmed up enough sauce for two or three people on the stove top. Angie went on then, trying to sound tough. "What did you and Alex Buckley talk about? Oh, and don't you dare leave anything out!" She looked at Terri suspiciously, like she knew her friend might try to hold something back.

Terri made a big performance out of thinking this question over as Angie finished preparing her supper. When she had gotten home earlier, Terri had done just exactly what Nick had told her to do. She had sat down at her computer, with a mystified Brianna standing by. By the time she was done, Terri had filled several pages full of whatever she could think of from the last five days. When Brianna saw what she was doing, she sat down next to Terri and helped fill in where she thought of something her boss didn't.

Terri had begun her *report* naming it, something a little shorter then she had suggested to Nick, however. She aptly titled the file……

The Murder of Logan-Adams Buckley

Saturday, the 21ˢᵗ of January, 2006. Wake up with terrible cold. Telephone rings, let machine take it. Logan Adams-Buckley leaves *urgent* message. Brianna finally speaks with Logan, who responds with anger and disrespect at not being able to speak with me. She seems desperate and even a bit threatening but not out of the ordinary for her. Consequently, Brianna and I did not find Logan's attitude to be all that unusual. She already had a history of being rude and demanding. Brianna handles Logan, pretty much hangs up on her and unplugs phone in the apartment. We basically ignore it and have a laugh over the incident.

Sunday, the 22ⁿᵈ of January, 2006. Uneventful, watched some football. Rested most of day, sick in bed with horrible cold.

Monday, the 23ʳᵈ of January, 2006. Find answering machine in shop blinking with a dozen messages, most of them from Logan. At exactly 9:00, phone rings. It is Logan. I finally speak with her. Brianna and I are completely shocked at the extravagance of Logan's order. She claims to be *put out* at my *not* speaking with her on Saturday. Logan indicates that she is having husband's relatives for the coming weekend and wants to impress them. (I find out later that Alex basically has no relatives, with which he keeps contact.) She goes beyond her usual ridiculous spending, to completely outrageous (list of order, copy of check, and invoices attached). Nothing I say to her, convinces Logan to back off. She proceeds to order as many expensive items as she can come up with. She convinces me to go ahead with it, promising to send Ignacio over with a check as soon as possible. I add up the costs. Logan seems to flinch only slightly at the amount of money involved, and agrees to send Ignacio over with a check immediately.

Ignacio arrives shortly thereafter with check, eats lunch and leaves. He seems to be his normal self, as far as Brianna and I can tell. Brianna and I are then shocked as we open the check, to find *not only* payment for the order but a large tip also attached. I quickly prepare to get to the bank, go out the door, and notice a car sitting across from my shop. I mentally take down the license plate and write it down when I get to my truck. I find out later from police officers, *Captain* Rico Mathews, Tabitha Hughes, and Angie Perry, who are all in agreement, that the license plate is F.B.I. issue.

Angie spends the night, as she has no heat in her apartment. We have supper and settle in for the night.

Tuesday, the 24th of January, 2006. Angie's cell phone rings at 6:00 a.m. The caller is Captain Rico Mathews reporting the *death* and/or homicide of Logan Adams-Buckley in an apparent break-in. We are all shocked and saddened (sort of) but mostly concerned about Alex, Jenni and Benjamin, and, of course, Officer Will Collins, Angie's partner, who just happens to be Logan's cousin.

Terri went on from there, from stopping to talk to Amber and Kelli, to covering their experience with Davis and Johannsen. Then she went on to Guerrero coming to their rescue, to picking up Jenni and Benjamin at the police station, and getting them settled in at the apartment. Also, dealing with Will's grief, he, Angie, and Guerrero coming over for lunch that day, etc. etc. She described the dinner party, which actually had nothing whatsoever to do with Logan's murder but Terri included it anyway, trying to cover as much of the time as possible. Both Tuesday and Wednesday had been *very* full days. Terri's conversation with Alex Buckley went on for a couple of pages, even though she tried to just hit the high spots. Brianna left her to it, as she had not been at the jail with her. By the time Terri got to the present time, the evening of **Wednesday, the 25th** of January, 2006, she had filled several pages, with as many details as she could remember, for now.

Terri had been pretty drained by the time she had gotten through her report, trying to document as much as possible. Obviously, documenting actual dialogue with Logan and Alex, would have taken forever. Terri couldn't imagine writing, '*he* said and then I said and then she said…..blah, blah, blah….,' it would just be too much. She was almost afraid to put down some of the shocking details from her conversation with Alex. Since no one would be checking her file, however, at least not for the time being, she left nothing out. That being the case, she found no reason to inform Angie of the existence of her personal report, *for now*. Whatever information Terri chose to disclose, or to whom, she would do so in her own good time, *even to her best friend*. Her best friend, who now seemed to be drilling her for answers, in the fashion of the police officer that she was.

"Angie, give me a break, will you?" Terri begged, as she took another forkful of the delicious spaghetti. "It has been a totally crappy day. Going to a prison, to talk to a guy, who has been accused of cold-blooded murder. Yeah, not exactly something that one does every day of the week! I am completely wiped. Let's just finish dinner, please!" She sipped her tea and gave Brianna a careful look. *Do not tell Angie about my file, in my computer!* Miraculously, Brianna understood completely and remained mute. Angie looked at them both suspiciously. Terri tried to appear innocent. Brianna's face revealed nothing.

"You two are up to something, but fine," Angie, said suspiciously. "I'm a little bushed myself. Another day of fender benders and the usual minor mishaps. No murders, thankfully, at least not on my beat." Angie, temporarily distracted, finished the wrap-up of *her*, mostly uneventful day and sat down with her plate.

They finished eating and cleaned up the dishes. Brianna prepared a fresh pot of tea. Just the aroma itself, was intoxicating. Terri seemed to prefer tea, to an alcoholic drink these days. It was winter, after all, and aside from what one would call a hot toddy or maybe apple cider with a kick, tea or hot chocolate seemed to better fill the bill. It also had a more calming effect on Terri, who never had been able *to hold her liquor* well. Where most people reacted to alcohol as a depressant, with Terri it almost always had the opposite effect.

She would get home, try to sleep, and toss and turn. No, she had learned a long time ago to drink in moderation. It had been a good lesson.

For the time being, it seemed as if Brianna had been to Amber and Kelli's shop once again. Thus, a new flavor of tea was on the tray, along with more biscuits and, of course, the usual honey, lemon, sugar and cream.

"Wonderful, Brianna!" Terri gushed, exaggerating for Angie's benefit. "What a jewel you are, my darling girl. What fabulous potion did you pick out this time?" Also, as usual, Brianna handed her the elaborate box of tea bags. Terri sniffed appreciatively and Brianna poured. This one was called, Babie Black-Berrie Brue.

"Mmmmm......, catchy name. Who knew that blackberries even have babies? Obviously, someone wasn't using a spell check when they named this one! I love it, though." Terri sighed with contentment, chose a biscuit from the tray, and leaned back into the comfortable sofa.

"I know of your fondness for blackberries, Terri, which was another good reason to try this. Tea, Angie?" Brianna asked then pointedly, trying to sound calm and casual, as she addressed their disgruntled friend.

"Martini, Brianna?" Angie shot back with a little snip in her voice. Terri ignored her, as always. Brianna raised her eyebrows pretending to be shocked.

"Fine, I'll have some damn tea. Anything to get you guys to tell me what the hell is going on here. This is ridiculous! I've never seen two people stall so much and I'm a cop!" Angie finally finished ranting and accepted the steaming cup, taking a careful sip. "O.K., yeah, I guess this weather calls for tea. This is nice." She also selected a biscuit from the tray and leaned back on the comfy sofa cushions. As if on cue, Maria jumped up next to her. "Tea, Maria?" Angie asked the clueless cat, who merely proceeded to groom herself. "Seems like that's all they have to drink around here. Where have you been, anyway? Where's your brother?" Maria politely sniffed Angie's cup of tea and backed away with snooty disinterest.

At that point, Louie came sauntering out of Terri's room and headed for the kitchen to his bowl. Maria spotted him and hopped down to follow. Terri moved to get up, presumably to check their food and water. Brianna stopped her.

"I took care of their bowls, Terri, so just relax. Everybody, please just relax. We cannot do anything right now, to move the process of this investigation along, Angie. Besides, Terri hasn't even told *me* what she and Alex talked about yet. Isn't that right, Terri?" Brianna was comfortably ensconced on the love seat. She pulled an afghan over her knees as she balanced her hot cup of the fragrant tea.

"She's right, Angie," Terri affirmed what Brianna had said. "I *have not* told her what Alex and I talked about. I figured I may as well wait until you got here and tell you both at the same time. But please, Ang, do not expect a word-by-word, blow-by-blow, account of our conversation. We didn't even talk that long." She suddenly didn't feel like talking about any of this, *to anyone, anymore.* Not tonight, anyway.

Why, she wondered, was it her responsibility to solve this stupid crime? Had it even been a crime? Had it even been a murder? Logan was dead. That was one thing for sure.

It suddenly occurred to Terri, with no doubt in her mind, that whatever *had* happened, Logan had truly brought it on herself. Terri's musings, however, would have to wait, as Angie's curiosity would not. So, she went ahead with a condensed version of what she felt comfortable telling them. The high spot for Terri was, of course, that *no one* was going to come and take Jenni and Benjamin away from them. Brianna and Angie were also relieved at this news. Terri told them why Alex had married Logan in the first place. No, she had not asked Alex why Logan had treated him the way she had in front of other people. Terri just felt that was too personal a question and Alex did not bring it up. It had, obviously, always made him uncomfortable. Logan may have just been acting foolish to put on a show. That part probably had nothing whatsoever to do with her death. Her outrageous order for all the expensive food and it's sudden cancellation however, definitely had some weird connection to all of it.

On this fact, they totally agreed. Brianna and Angie were also both enthusiastic about the fact that they were allowed to do whatever they pleased with all of the food. This revelation brought an interesting comment from Angie. She seemed to be satisfied with what Terri had told them, moving on to other things, including a musing of her own.

"So, speaking of truffles.....," Angie started, choosing a biscuit and taking another sip of tea.

"Ah....who was speaking of truffles?" Terri grinned as she carefully placed her delicate tea cup down on it's matching saucer. Brianna motioned to Terri, for more tea. "Thanks, Bri, but no more. I'm floating as it is. It was wonderful, by the way." She leaned back on the sofa again and could not stifle a huge yawn. "O.K., that's it!" Terri said then. "I *have got* to get to bed. What time is it anyway? Will and the kids should be back pretty soon, I would think."

Just then, they heard Will and his charges clattering up the stairs. Angie jumped up and opened the door to let them in, leaving her truffle comment hanging, for the time being. Jenni and Benjamin looked happy but also tired. Jenni dropped her coat and flicked off her boots. She ran immediately to Terri for an enthusiastic hug.

"Terri, we really missed you today. Did you see my daddy? When is he coming home?" Jenni was so sure, she had gone off to fix everything, that tears came to Terri's eyes once again. What was she going to tell this little girl who had so much faith in her? How could Terri let her down, more than she already was? Maybe she did have the responsibility to do what she could, to find out how this had all happened. But how could she do that, without putting herself in a possibly dangerous situation?

Terri looked at Benjamin standing behind Jenni. The look on his face, was asking the same questions. Terri realized then, at that moment, she had absolutely no other recourse. She would *have* to find Jasmine, Ignacio and Nadia, and try to find out what happened. She simply had no other choice.

Chapter Sixteen

erri had typed, **Thursday, the 26th of January, 2006,** into her file. Now she was just sitting in front of her computer, trying to figure out what to put down. Well, it was still early morning, after all, and not much had happened yet. She quickly typed in two words. *Got up!* She had actually been checking the file over, adding to what she had already put down, trying as hard as she could *not* to leave anything out. She *did*, however, omit her conversation with Guerrero. Talking about his looks and personality, along with her pretty much *going nowhere,* relationship with Rico, had absolutely nothing to do with the death of Logan Adams-Buckley. Terri wanted to stay completely on subject with this report. Anything personal, need not be included.

Terri could have not even imagined, the terrible disappointment that came over Jenni and Benjamin, when she had to break it to them that there had been no change with their father. It was terribly heart-breaking. They couldn't understand the reason why anyone would think, that their daddy could have done such a terrible thing. Terri couldn't understand it either. From what she had surmised of the charges against Alex, they were based on very little evidence. The gun had been fired, obviously. The bullet from Alex's gun, had resulted in Logan's death. Now, unfortunately, they find out that Logan *was* pregnant. Aside from what Alex had told Terri, the possibility that the child was or *was not his*, had yet to be addressed.

Terri closed the file and would come back to it later. Benjamin was watching T.V. Brianna had gone to an early class and Jenni was still asleep.

The little girl had been completely exhausted, to say the least. They had seen 'The Lion, the Witch and the Wardrobe' and then gone out for supper. Coming back to the apartment and finding out her father wasn't going to be released from jail anytime soon, had been too much for her. Jenni had cried and cried, as Benjamin stood by, still trying to be brave. Finally, completely wiped out, she had fallen asleep on the couch, with 'Poots' gripped in her arms and her thumb in her mouth. Brianna had picked Jenni up, taken her into her room, changed her into her pajamas, and tucked her in. Jenni had hardly even responded, she had been so zonked! She could sleep as long as she needed to. Terri was glad of that. School would have been impossible, under the circumstances.

Now Terri rubbed her eyes and sighed heavily. She picked up her empty coffee cup and headed to the kitchen for a refill. She opened the fridge and took out bacon and eggs. French toast, with bacon and fruit, would be a good way to start the day. She found a loaf of thick slices, of sour dough bread to make the French toast. Jenni would be up soon, so Terri started breakfast. She heard the door open and looked around the corner. It was Angie, coming in quietly this time, thinking there might still be sleepers.

"Hey!" Angie raised a hand in greeting and took off her coat. "What's for breakfast?" She said hi to Benjamin, who currently engrossed in his cartoons, just raised a hand in greeting. Coming into the kitchen, Angie grabbed her favorite coffee mug from the cupboard. After filling the mug and emptying the decanter, she started a fresh pot.

Terri sighed again. Her whole world seemed to gravitate around food. Oh well, that was O.K. She enjoyed feeding people. Angie was definitely one of those people, since she rarely cooked for herself. Angie fought the bad guys. Terri cooked the food. It was the perfect arrangement.

"Oh, let's see," Terri said then, "I was thinking French toast, bacon, a little fresh fruit, such as it is this time of year. Not sure if there's enough for you though." Angie gave her a puppy-dog look and made whining noises.

"Uh, would you like a little cheese with that whine?" Angie completely ignored that silly 'Wisconsin' question and Terri went on. "Fine then. If you would please clean and cut up the fruit, that would be great." Terri motioned towards the fridge.

"It's done!" Angie reached in and took out a cantaloupe, grapes, oranges, and strawberries. "Where did you get all of this? Looks pretty good for dead of winter." Angie carefully dumped the strawberries into a colander and rinsed them under the faucet. She then proceeded to cut the cantaloupe in half, covered one piece with cellophane, and placed it back in the refrigerator. She drained the berries on paper towels, cut the cantaloupe into bite size pieces, added a few grapes, and cut two oranges into quarters. "Looks beautiful!" She admired her own work arranged on a platter and placed it in the center of the table.

"Gorgeous," agreed Terri, "and oh, I do have my *produce* connections. It's still not as nice as the Farmer's Market but we can make do. It's not winter all over the world you know, even if it feels like it right now." Terri was draining bacon on more paper towels. Angie was setting the table when Jenni walked through on her way to the bathroom. She had 'Poots' under one arm and a very crabby-looking Maria, under the other. Maria struggled and Jenni let her slip to the floor. The rumpled cat shook herself thoroughly, making disgruntled, squeaky noises in her throat. She then headed in the direction of her own breakfast.

"You O.K. Jenni?" Terri asked the sleepy little girl. "Did you get enough sleep?"

"Yeah, Terri. I'm O.K. Hi, Angie," Jenni said, straining to be cheerful. "I will try to be more patient, I promise. That's what my teacher always says. 'We must be patient. Good things are worth waiting for' she says. When daddy comes home, it will be great so I will wait patiently for that." Angie and Terri looked at each other. That must be some teacher! Jenni certainly seemed to have her mind made up that it would all work out. Terri wished she felt as confident as the little girl.

Angie tried to reassure Jenni then, as she pulled her in for a tight hug. "Mr. Guerrero is working really hard right now, to get your daddy home as soon as possible Jenni. So we will *all* try to be as patient as you, O.K?" Angie waited for Jenni to respond and was startled by the look on the child's face. Had she said something wrong?

"O.K.," Jenni said then, "but Angie? I have to go potty *really* bad right now, so could you let me go?"

Terri started to laugh as Angie immediately released Jenni, who shot into the bathroom. Just as quickly, Maria followed her in and Jenni slammed the door.

"Oh God, Angie," Terri was still laughing, "you're quite the maternal figure, you know that?" She wiped away the tears running down her face, she had been laughing so hard, as she refilled her cup, with the freshly brewed French Roast.

"Yeah, thanks a lot," Angie said, just a tad embarrassed. "Didn't see that one coming. I'm feeling extra glad right now, though, that there aren't any diapers to change!" She started laughing too and Terri raised her mug in total agreement.

"Amen to that," Terri said. Then she remembered Angie's reference to truffles from the night before and asked her about it.

"Oh, yeah," Angie took a sip of coffee and went on. "I just happened to mention our *truffle dilemma* to Judith. I think you can guess what she suggested."

Judith was Angie's *sort-of,* step mom, but in truth, they were mostly just very good friends. Angie's mother had died nearly nine years ago after a courageous battle with breast cancer. Eventually her father had remarried. Judith was a wonderful wife and companion to Angie's father, George Perry. She was also a fantastic gourmet cook and fabulous hostess. From preparing and serving several beautiful courses with carefully selected wines, along with setting a gorgeous table of crystal, china, and heirloom silverware, her dinners were always memorable events. Terri and Angie, and now occasionally Brianna, enjoyed the dinner parties immensely. Thus, Terri responded enthusiastically to this news.

"Oh, Angie," Terri was relieved, "that would be fantastic! I know I could try some recipes with them myself but as precious as truffles have become, I doubt that I could ever do them justice. What did she say about the pate' and caviar?" Terri had been wondering what would be an appropriate way, to use these extremely expensive items. She had thought about selling some of them back somehow but that didn't seem right either.

Angie's response to this question was quick. "Bring it on! She wants to do it Saturday night, and get this. She wants you to invite Rico and she wants me to invite Will. Do you think Brianna would mind babysitting? I got the idea Judith wants to do couples. Although, I hope she doesn't have the silly idea of getting Will and I together, on her mind."

Before Terri had a chance to comment on this weird thought, they heard the toilet flush and the water running. They dropped the subject, for the time being, as Jenni came out of the bathroom with cat and teddy. She sniffed the air around her and was obviously hungry. So was her brother, who finally made an appearance in the kitchen looking for breakfast.

Angie proceeded to set the table with help from the kids. Terri stacked up crisp pieces of French toast on a warm plate. The syrup had been taken out of the fridge and was warming in the sink. By the time they sat down, they were all famished. The crisp bacon, French toast with warm syrup, and luscious pieces of fruit, served as the perfect meal to start the day.

"Terri, when our daddy comes home, could you make us breakfast everyday?" Benjamin asked, as he bit into a crispy piece of bacon and popped a piece of cantaloupe into his mouth.

"Yeah, could you, Terri?" Jenni seconded as she chose a pretty strawberry off the tray. "You are the best cook in the whole world!"

"Well, thanks guys," Terri appreciated the praise, "but I can hardly get my work done the way it is." Jenni sighed with disappointment, so Terri went on in an effort to distract her. "Besides, by the time your daddy gets home, you'll be so glad to see him, you won't miss my cooking. Now, what does everyone have to do today?"

Jenni and Benjamin had homework and Terri had her regular chores. Angie was heading to work by 10:00, so after helping Terri clear up the kitchen, she took off. Will picked her up but didn't stop to see the kids. They had been through enough emotional upheavals, for the time being.

Benjamin settled with his school books at the kitchen counter. Jenni sat by the sofa with her homework spread out on the coffee table. Louie and Maria perched on the window seat and watched the birds, before their usual morning nap. Terri sat down at the computer again to plan menus for next week. The Super Bowl was a week from Sunday. The idea of the case being solved by then and Alex Buckley back together with his children, seemed almost impossible. *Almost* impossible, *unless* Terri put aside her fears and found a way to contact Ignacio. Fears that were completely justified, from what Terri had heard about the Guatemalan community in Boston. Many of the people in these areas were desperate. Desperate, *not to be found*, thus dangerous to disturb, to disrupt, like the proverbial sleeping bear. Terri had been in danger before. She *did not* want to experience that feeling again. Also, what if she did find Ignacio, what then? She had no idea if Ignacio knew anything about Logan's death. What made Alex Buckley think that he did? They must have been witnesses for Alex to ask her to do this.

Suddenly, Terri's cell phone chirped, jarring her out of her dark thoughts. It was Rico and Terri answered immediately. She really had missed him lately.

"Rico," she said warmly, into the tiny instrument. "How are you?"

She heard him laugh a little on the other end. "Whatever happened to people answering their phones and saying hello? There are no surprises left in this world since the invention of caller I.D., I swear!" Rico sounded like he was in a good mood. Terri could picture him, sitting back in his comfortable chair trying to relax. She imagined his beautiful, brown eyes and thick dark hair and *please, the uniform!* Terri and Rico had gone on plenty of dates and, of course, he was dressed in street clothes, like everyone else. But there was still something about that uniform.

Snap out of it, she told herself. This guy is actually your boyfriend! Stop trying to analyze everything and enjoy it! Hearing his voice made her feel so much better, she couldn't believe her good fortune. She tried to sound casual though, wondering why he had called but just very glad that he did.

"Well, sorry, can't help you there. All I do is cook! Besides, you know I *do not* like surprises. So caller I.D., has been nothing but a miracle for me." Terri got up and walked into her bedroom, to have some privacy. She described the fantastic breakfast she and Angie had just had with the kids.

"Sounds wonderful," Rico said longingly. "All I've eaten so far is a bagel and cream cheese. Not a very good bagel at that. My problem, I guess. Anyway, I didn't call to talk about food. Well, not directly anyway. I was wondering if you would like to take in a movie tomorrow night. I'm sorry about the dinner party Tuesday evening, speaking of surprises. I know you were not expecting Tabitha. Are you still mad at me?" He sounded like a petulant child and Terri laughed.

"No, I'm not still mad. I wasn't really mad to start with, but I was sick and still in shock from the news of Logan's death. The combination was not a good one. Tabitha is O.K. I mean, she is your partner. That's important when you're a police officer. Oh, and you guys are just good friends, right? Besides, she is *much too* young for you!" Terri waited for his reaction and got the one she wanted.

"Oh, thanks a lot!" Rico sounded dreadfully offended. "I'm not exactly a senior citizen you know. Besides, lot's of men get together with younger women. How about Michael Douglas and Katherine Zeta-Jones? Now there's a hot couple. Whew!" He whistled, obviously thinking more of the gorgeous Ms. Jones, than her fortunate husband, Mr. Douglas.

"Ah, fine," Terri was starting to get perturbed now. "Did you call to ask me for a date, or did you not?"

"I did! Sorry to get off the track. What time? Say, maybe 7:00?" Rico was leaving it up to Terri and she made up his mind for him.

"Make it 5:00, but could we catch a movie another time? I would really love to go out for a nice dinner. I've had enough of cooking and serving everyone else this week. As much as I love what I do, sometimes I need a break. Oh, and *you* pick the restaurant, someplace really fantastic, and *you* make the reservations!" Suddenly, she felt like giving orders and being a little selfish. Rico took the hint.

"Yes ma'am," he said smartly. "I like a woman who knows what she wants! Oh, and before you worry about the kids, Will has agreed to baby sit. Or, had you forgotten about them already?"

"As a matter of fact, I had forgotten," Terri admitted then, feeling a little guilty. She also knew better, then to assume that Brianna could stay with them. On Friday nights, she normally had plans. Terri also suspected, that Brianna might be seriously dating someone and wasn't quite ready to talk about it yet. Needless to say, she was relieved that Rico had immediately solved the problem.

"Five it is then and dress up! I'll pick some place really special for dinner, Terri. How about French food? I know a really fantastic place! You deserve it. You've been working way too hard lately." Rico sounded concerned and sincere. Terri suddenly felt appreciated and cared about.

"Thank you, Rico," she said gratefully, "that means a lot to me. See you tomorrow then, at 5:00." Terri shut her phone and sat on the edge of her bed for a few minutes. It suddenly occurred to her, that since she rarely dressed up, she may have just caused herself a bit of a problem.

"Great," she said out loud to the empty room. "What in the hell am I going to wear?"

Chapter Seventeen

"Terri?" Jenni poked her head around the door and looked in with a confused look on her face. "Are you still talking on the phone?" Terri looked at the little girl and her dilemma must have shown on her face.

"What's the matter, Terri? Are you not feeling well? You look like you're not feeling well. Do you have a fever?" Jenni was very concerned.

Terri laughed as Jenni and Maria hopped up onto the bed, and she grabbed the little girl in a convulsive hug. "No, Jenni, I'm fine. Actually, I'm feeling better than I've felt in days. I just suddenly have a bit of a *grown-up* problem. Are you all done with your homework?"

"Yes I am, and it's ready for you to look over. What is your problem then, Terri? Maybe I can help." Jenni looked so hopeful that Terri decided to run it by her. Why not? Girls are girls, no matter what age you are. As soon as you're old enough to look in the mirror, you start to analyze the reflection looking back.

Terri told Jenni that Rico had called and asked her out on a date. *A fancy date at that,* she told Jenni, thinking the old-fashioned term might be easier for the young girl to understand. "I have nothing to wear! What will I do Jenni?" They proceeded to ponder the problem and then heard the door open. Brianna was back and Maria hopped off of Terri's bed to greet her.

"What are you two up to, sitting in here looking so goofy?" Brianna asked, joining them as she sat on the edge of Terri's bed.

"Terri has a fancy date and she has nothing to wear Brianna!" Jenni spit out the problem before Terri had a chance to respond.

"Mmmmm......a fancy date, huh? Would this *fancy date* happen to be with a certain Police Captain of our acquaintance?" Terri and Jenni both nodded and Brianna smiled. "It seems to me, that the answer to your problem is very simple, Terri. We need to go shopping and we need to go now!"

"Shopping!" Jenni started bouncing on the bed and Maria beat a hasty retreat. "Yes! I wanna go shopping, Terri. Please let me go with you! Are we going now?"

She was so excited that obviously Terri could not say no. Benjamin, however was another matter. He would not want to go shopping with a bunch of girls, which was made apparent when he stated that fact right out.

"I can stay here by myself, Terri. I'm 11 years old, almost 12. You guys go ahead. I'll be fine." Benjamin was determined but Terri wasn't so sure.

"I really believe that you can stay by yourself Benjamin. But I would feel better, if you did not stay alone at this time." Benjamin looked disappointed at this. What to do though? Brianna had to go along. Terri had no idea where to start or even what to look for.

"Amber!" Brianna said then, as if by inspiration. "She can come up and stay with Benjamin while we girls go on our shopping spree."

"Well, I don't know if it's going to be a spree exactly....." Terri could feel herself getting more edgy by the minute.

"I'll call her right away," Brianna volunteered. She quickly got on the phone, before Terri could think about it any further. Amber agreed to come right up, as it had been a fairly quiet day.

Benjamin seemed a little hesitant when he first saw who would be staying with him for the afternoon. They had tried to stay away from the word, *babysitter*. However, when Amber spotted the X-Box 360, along with the video games Benjamin had brought along and started playing quite expertly, his face brightened and he joined her. Terri watched them, amazed. Video games were definitely not her bag. Amber's expertise in this area though, quickly solved their problem of a suitable companion for Benjamin.

Terri still felt uncomfortable about the whole situation. She was ready to call Rico back and say, 'forget the dinner, let's just go for a movie after all.' She could put on her jeans and boots, along with a comfy Patriots hooded sweatshirt, and enjoy their evening in comfort. What could be better after all, than leaning on your boyfriend's shoulder and digging into a big bucket of buttery popcorn? She could make her own French food at home, in her pajamas if she wanted to. Getting all dressed up, suddenly seemed like just *way too* much trouble.

"This is going to be so much fun!" Brianna, her enthusiasm building, was not to be stopped. Jenni, on the other hand, had picked up a controller and joined Benjamin and Amber on the sofa. She also played expertly and both Maria and Louie watched the bouncing characters on the screen, in complete fascination. Looked like she was staying home too.

Terri and Brianna prepared to leave, thinking that everything was totally under control, *for once.* They should have known better. The front door of Terri's apartment door opened suddenly before they could even get into their coats. There stood a very grim Angie. There was a bandage on her head and she was in plain clothes, as opposed to her uniform. Will was standing behind her, also out of uniform, with his arm in a sling.

All in the room looked at Will and Angie in shock and disbelief. Terri finally came to her senses and quickly went to her friends.

"Angie," Terri looked at her and then at Will as they stood by the door, seemingly mute, "what the hell happened? Are you guys alright?" She put her arm around her injured friend and Angie suddenly began to sob. Terri carefully held onto her distraught friend and looked to Will for answers. Brianna, Amber, and the two children waited for them to speak. "We were in an accident this morning," Will finally started to explain. "It was a hit and run. They totaled our squad and took off. We just came from the hospital."

It had definitely been a traumatic experience, for Angie to be losing control the way she was. Both Benjamin and Jenni ran to Will. He quickly reassured them that he and Angie would be fine. They had both been released from the hospital and a fellow officer had dropped them off.

Terri immediately snapped herself into a *take charge* mode. The shopping trip would have to wait as they took care of their friends. "Brianna," she said, "could you please start to fix lunch? Get out the chicken and dumpling soup and warm up enough for a crowd. Also, find whatever you can for sandwiches, along with the fruit and some cheeses. Jenni, could you please help her?" Brianna and Jenni both nodded and quickly headed for the kitchen.

Poor Amber watched helplessly from the sofa and looked to Terri for something to do. Terri saw this and thus gave her an important task. "Amber, could you please take Will and Angie's jackets and then help Angie into my room?"

"Absolutely, Terri." Amber, anxious to be of help, quickly moved. She took Will's coat, which had merely been draped over his shoulders because of the sling on his injured arm. Terri handed the still, softly crying Angie over into Amber's capable hands and turned to Benjamin.

"Benjamin, could you make Will comfortable on the sofa and then get some bottles of water from the kitchen?" Benjamin swiftly moved to his appointed tasks.

Both Maria and Louie, immediately feeling the alarm in the room, had run to hide behind the sofa. Maria now peeked out from their hiding place and followed Amber and Angie into Terri's room. Louie jumped up on the sofa, as Benjamin moved Will towards it. Apparently, the cats too, wanted to help.

Will gratefully allowed himself to be guided to the sofa and sank down with a heavy sigh. He held onto his injured arm as Benjamin went to the kitchen for bottles of water. He came out carrying four and gave one to Will. Terri took two bottles and headed to her room. She twisted the cap off of one of them and handed it to Angie, who was resting on several pillows that Amber had propped up behind her.

"There are bottles of pain pills in our coat pockets," Angie said then, starting to slowly recover her emotions. "They gave us both prescriptions. *I do not want* to take them damn things!" She suddenly was turning into her old self and Terri smiled a little. Nothing, short of death, would stop Angie from being her usual stubborn self! Fortunately, she and Will were still very much alive. They could only hope, that fact would help them find out who had done this foolish thing. For right now, Terri sighed with relief and put an arm around her friend.

"Gee Ang, you scared me there for a minute," Terri teased her a little. "I thought you had gone all soft on me crying like that!" She tried to keep the mood light as she gave her injured friend a quick hug, and then plumped up the pillows and straightened the blankets.

Amber retrieved the pills from Will and Angie's coats and handed them to Terri. "I'll go help Brianna and Jenni with lunch," she said then, wisely leaving the room and closing the door behind her. She could see that Terri and Angie needed to spend some time alone. Maria had plopped down next to the patient, purring soothingly as Angie stroked her silky fur. Terri sat down on the edge of the bed.

"Terri," Angie said then, completely sobering. "I have to tell you what happened! Please!" The tears started running down her face again, taking away Terri's temporary sense of relief. She struggled to calm her friend down, by saying soothing words.

"Angie, why don't you wait until you've gotten some rest? I don't have to know exactly what happened. The most important thing is that you and Will are both O.K." Terri placed a reassuring hand on Angie's arm and was shocked when her friend grasped it desperately.

"You'd like to think that!" Angie said suddenly. "It *was not* an accident, Terri! Someone did this on purpose. I saw them. I saw the car coming straight at us! There were two men in it." She stopped for a second and Terri looked at her friend in complete disbelief.

"What do you mean, someone did this on purpose? Why would anyone wreck a police car deliberately? Angie, you *are not* making any sense. Do you have a concussion? Maybe I should call the hospital and….." Angie gripped her hand harder and interrupted Terri.

"No, Terri, listen to me!" Angie's tone finally got Terri's attention and she went on. "They came out of an alley like they knew we were going to be there. I saw them, out of the corner of my eye. I think someone may have even been following us but I thought at first, I was just being paranoid. They must have been communicating with one another by cell. They came right at us and slammed into the car. We were spinning, totally out of control. Then we stopped and they rammed us again! One of them jumped out of their car, which of course, was *a total piece of shit!* The guy came up and leaned in my window. There was broken glass, all over the place! He was wearing a ski mask over his head. It looked so creepy, I thought I was having a nightmare! He leaned in the car and spoke to me." Angie started crying again and Terri waited for her to go on.

"What, Angie?" Terri suddenly started to feel the genuine fear from her friend. "What did he say to you? What?" She took Angie's hand in both of hers and was alarmed by how much her friend was shaking.

"He got really close to my ear, Terri. I could feel the blood on my face. I had my seatbelt on but the broken glass, had been flying all over us. I could hear Will groaning and this guy whispering in my ear. He had some kind of an accent, Hispanic, I guess. He said, 'Angie Perry, you a tough cop, huh? You tell your friend Terri Springe, this is only a warning. You tell her not to look for Ignacio or *someone else* might die!'"

Chapter Eighteen

Once again, Terri's small apartment was full of people and they had all been or were going to be, *eating*. What else was new? Terri would have been perfectly content with this arrangement had it not been for the *reason*, they were all there. Here they were, dealing with another crisis and everyone had to have food.

Terri, obviously for her part, had no choice at this point but to let the police know exactly what was going on. *The police*, in this particular situation of course, being Captain Rico Mathews. The weirdest part of all was, Terri had put absolutely no effort into looking for Ignacio, at least not yet. How did they even know she had been *asked* to do such a thing? How desperate could these people be, to deliberately destroy a squad car and injure two police officers? Someone must have been reporting back from the same correctional facility, currently housing Alex Buckley. Alex had told Terri, he had talked to someone in the jail about Ignacio, Jasmine and Nadia, *possibly* still being in the city. Up to this point, Terri had proved to be of no threat to any of them. So why were they suddenly threatening her and her friends? Who in the hell were *they*, anyway?

Terri had also called Nick Guerrero after Angie's revelation and he had come over to the apartment, as quickly as he could. He had listened to the details of the accident and Terri's possible involvement in it. They provided him with a quick soup and sandwich, and a cup of coffee. He also quickly contacted Randy Kucken, the P.I., *he* had hired to get information on Ignacio, Jasmine, and Nadia. Since the possibility existed, that his part in the investigation may have caused the attack on Angie and Will, Nick told Randy to immediately back off on any further inquiries. He then headed off to see Alex Buckley to get whatever information he could from him.

Rico had left *his little partner*, Tabitha Hughes, back at the station with a pile of paperwork. Terri was at least grateful for that. She still did not feel threatened by Tabitha in any way but under the circumstances, they did not need another bystander around. Besides, someone had to get some work done. It seemed as if the rest of them, found their lives at a complete standstill once again, following this latest strange occurrence. When would things get back to normal, Terri wondered, if ever?

Rico, of course, wanted some answers, *now!* Terri suddenly felt like they were playing *cops and robbers* again, as Rico questioned her on the conversation she had engaged in with Alex. He was *not* happy with her. She was feeling extremely defensive, to say the least.

As far as she was concerned, at this moment, he could take his fancy date and *shove it where the sun don't shine!* Angie was still resting in Terri's room, with Jenni and Maria, by her side. She had managed a bowl of the chicken and dumpling soup, with saltine crackers and a couple of scoops of strawberry ice cream. Jenni opted for cereal, also followed by a bowl of ice cream. You never knew with kids, and Terri saw no reason, to make a big deal out of it. She was satisfied that Jenni had something reasonable to eat, along with the treat.

Will and Benjamin had made ham sandwiches and eaten them with big bowls of the hot, savory chicken soup. Now they were playing a video game, and considering that Will had a sprained wrist, he was giving Benjamin a pretty good battle. The poor, hapless Amber, had gone back down to the shop to try to tell Kellie what was going on. Terri had sent along enough soup and ham sandwiches for the both of them, for their lunch. Needless to say, the shopping trip had been cancelled until further notice. Brianna had retired to her room for a nap after lunch. She had been up since 6:00 a.m., to get to her early class and was exhausted. That left Terri to deal with Rico on her own and *she wasn't happy either, so there!*

"This is a terrible situation, Terri. What in the hell were you thinking? You weren't, were you?" Rico was giving her major crap about all of this and she was very close to the breaking point herself! They were sitting in Terri's small kitchen trying to keep their voices down, so as not to upset the kids or their injured friends. This with much effort, considering the explosive nature of their discussion. "What if Will or Angie had been killed? What if something had happened to you? You should have told us what was going on, as soon as Alex Buckley asked you to do this fool hardy thing. He had no right to expect you to do this! If Guerrero doesn't kick his ass, I will!"

"Are you through?" Terri asked him, when he finally stopped to catch a breath. She could be tough too and had *definitely* taken about all she could for one day and it was barely noon! She had also taken pretty much all she could stand from Rico and proceeded to tell him so.

"What are you anyway, my mother?" Terri shot back at him with both barrels! "My conversation with Alex Buckley was *yesterday,* for crying out loud. I haven't even had time to consider any of the things we talked about. There was *also* a private investigator looking into these people, you know. *Anything* could have set them off. Of course, the fact that they actually mentioned *my name* is pretty obvious, I guess."

Terri paused to make sure she had Rico's attention. When he made no comment, she went on. "Besides which, I've been looking after his kids remember, and trying to do my regular work on top of that. I certainly *did nothing at all* to provoke anyone and I would *not* have done anything fool hardy, as you put it. So, if you will *pardon me, Captain* Mathews, since I am *not* afraid of you anymore, I have no problem telling you,

S. Kay Weber

*right here, right now, that you are being a total ass! You are pissing
me off and I have had just about enough!"*

Rico leaned back in his chair in surprise and Terri couldn't
believe his silly response. "You were afraid of me? When were
you afraid of me? I've never done anything to make you feel
that way. I can't believe this....." He kept going on and on until
Terri literally banged her head on the table.

That was all he had gotten out of everything she had just
said to him? *That she had been afraid of him? That was it? Men!
Arrrrggghhh!* Terri sighed heavily, ran her hands through her
hair, and decided to put an end to it. What was the difference
anyway? They were both so upset right now, that neither
one of them could even think straight. She was hungry and
exhausted and she knew Rico was too.

"Just stop!" Terri said finally, in a loud stage whisper. Rico
stopped talking and watched, mystified, as she got up and
started fixing some of the blackberry tea Brianna had bought
yesterday. "I am going to make some tea. You are welcome
to join me." She looked at Rico and he nodded wordlessly.

"Good! Now, fix yourself a sandwich, *please!* I'll get you
a bowl of soup. Then you will sit here and eat a decent lunch.
You never eat right, for Pete's sake. Have you had anything
else to eat today since that stale bagel you mentioned to me
this morning? I thought not! Now, get busy making that
sandwich."

Rico, finally calming down, proceeded to do as he was
told. Terri ladled out a generous serving of soup into a large
bowl. She placed it on the table. Rico sat down with a ham
sandwich, composed of fresh dark rye, with Swiss cheese and
brown mustard and ate heartily. Terri placed steaming cups
of tea on the table for the two of them, along with fresh bottles
of water. Then she sat down with her own bowl of soup,
with crispy fresh saltines. For several minutes they just ate
and rested. No more questioning, no more ranting. Will
and Angie were going to be just fine. Terri had done nothing
wrong. Rico, however, *had* revealed his deep feelings for Terri,
having allowed himself to be as upset as he was. They both

realized it and now they were trying to understand it. Finally, Rico put down his spoon and reached across the table for Terri's hand. He twined his fingers through hers, making her feel warmer all the way down to her toes!

"I am so sorry, Terri," he said then, sincerely apologetic, "that was terrible of me to speak to you like that. You deserve better. You're not some common criminal who I can just strong-arm into a confession or something. O.K., that sounded dumb too. Man, I don't know what I'm doing right now. I'm not eating right, just like you said. You have every right to be concerned. This is the best meal I've had, well.....since your spaghetti two nights ago. What would I do without you to take care of me and at least fix me a decent meal once in awhile?" He smiled weakly then and squeezed her hand.

"Strong-arm, huh? Do that often, do you? You know, that doesn't really sound all that bad." Terri had regained some of her sense of humor and smiled weakly. "You are right about one thing, though. I'm not satisfied unless the people around me are well-fed, warm and rested, especially in *this* weather. My mom is like that. She gets all nuts, if someone isn't eating right or taking care of themselves. Oh, and speaking of rested, when was the last time you had a decent night's sleep?"

Terri suddenly realized, she might be pushing it with this question. That would be getting into a part of Rico's life she still hadn't been allowed. He still wouldn't talk about the past. He worked until he was so tired he nearly passed out, more times than not on the sofa in his office. It was a wonder why he even bothered to keep his apartment. He hardly ever went there, from what Angie and Will had told her. Good thing he didn't keep plants or a pet! They wouldn't survive for long.

"Well...." Rico hesitated at the question. Terri felt uncomfortable immediately.

"It's O.K., let's not go there right now." Terri withdrew her hand and took another spoonful of the delicious, soothing soup. Then she strained to change the subject. "Oh, and about our date tomorrow night? We probably should just postpone it for another time. I think I'd better look after Angie for the next day or so. She did it for me when I had my concussion last fall. I want to make sure she's alright. Do you mind?"

At this point, Rico looked really dejected. "O.K., fine. This whole thing really sucks but I have to agree with you. The circumstances have completely changed with this accident, or whatever the hell it was. We will thoroughly investigate exactly what Angie told you, Terri. This is pretty serious business, someone deliberately trying to injure two of my police officers. Not to mention, totaling a City of Boston squad car in the process." He stopped to take a long swig of cool water and tried to make further amends. "We'll have that date though, Terri, I promise. You work so hard to take care of everyone else. Now Angie needs you and here you are again, willing to put yourself out for her. That's one of the reasons I care about you so much. You are one of the most unselfish people I have ever known."

Terri glowed under the praise but didn't pursue it. "Well, Angie is my best friend, has been since grade school." She got up then, to clear the table and began stacking dishes into the dishwasher. Rico went into the living room and picked up the dishes left behind by Will and Benjamin. They were still in a hot video game, with Louie blobbing and grooming at Benjamin's side.

"Hey, Will." Rico addressed his friend and fellow police officer. "How ya' doing? Need anything?"

"I'm O.K., Rico, thanks," Will said and then looked at Benjamin. "Hey buddy, what do you say we quit for awhile? My arm is killing me and you're beating me hands down."

Benjamin agreed, yawned, and put down his controller. "I need to take a bathroom break anyway," he said, heading off in that general direction.

"Will," Rico said then, sitting next to him on the sofa, "what can you tell me about what happened this morning? Did you see the car? Did you hear the guy talking to Angie? Anything that you could remember might help us catch these jerks. No one is going to assault two of my best officers and get away with it." Rico was getting himself worked up again.

Terri came out of the kitchen and sat down in the love seat across from them. "Mind if I listen in?" Maybe Rico would stay calm, with her sitting there listening.

"It's O.K. with me, Terri," Will said and Rico nodded. "Rico, I wish I could give you more information than I already put in my report. Nothing else comes to mind. It all happened so damn fast. I saw the guy talking to Angie but what he was saying to her, was merely a whisper. He gave her his threatening message, the bastard, got back in their wreck of a car and disappeared! I couldn't believe that thing still ran so they could take off, it was such a piece of junk! I saw no license plate. The whole back bumper was covered with snow. It appeared to be put together with several different pieces, doors weren't the same color, one of the fenders was missing. The whole grill in the front was busted out. I wouldn't drive my worst enemy around in it. They definitely had *that* vehicle, knowing they were going to do damage to something, *or someone*, and then probably ditch it!"

"Agreed," said Rico solemnly. "My bet is we will find it in an alley somewhere and the I.D. numbers, if they're even still in the car, will turn up as stolen or abandoned. I'm sure we won't come up with an owner. The car itself will probably just be a dead end." Will nodded and they all looked toward Terri's room as the door opened and Angie came out. She sat down next to Will and he put his good arm around her shoulders. They leaned into each other and Will kissed the top of Angie's head in brotherly fashion.

"So, how ya' feelin,' Sweetie?" Will asked his partner and Angie sighed. She reached up and touched the bandage on her head and then laid her other hand on Will's injured arm. Tears starting running down her cheeks again and she reached for a tissue to impatiently wipe them away.

"O.K., I guess. My throbbing head tells me, though, that I'll probably need one of those damn pills after all. Shit! I hate taking pain pills. They always lay me out and make me feel like 'Alice in Wonderland' falling down the rabbit hole. Every character in that damn story is stoned!" They all laughed at this comment, breaking the tension in the room. Terri got up to get the bottles of offending pills from her room.

"Where do you think the book and the song came from?" Terri asked. "Go Ask Alice!" She had read the book for high school English. Definitely not a happy story. No wonder the author preferred to remain *Anonymous*.

Terri wasn't surprised to find Jenni sound asleep, with Maria snoozing next to her. Everyone was so wiped out. The cold, the snow, and now this accident, or whatever it was. She quietly took both bottles of pain pills from the bed-side table and grabbed Angie's water bottle.

Back in the living room, Benjamin had joined the group, so all talk of the mornings events had come to a halt for now. Angie and Will both willingly took their pain pills knowing that waiting would just make things worse. They would both need to get a good night's rest, although neither one would be reporting to work for a day or two, doctor's *and* Captain Mathew's orders. It was agreed then, that Angie would stay with Terri, although that had already been a given. Rico actually asked Will to come stay with him for a couple of days, much to everyone's surprise. Will happily agreed and they prepared to go to his apartment to pick up some fresh clothes and toiletries.

As Benjamin helped Will with his jacket, Rico motioned for Terri to come with him to the kitchen. *Now what?*, she thought. One last chance to give her crap about something? Rico said nothing however, as he put his hands on Terri's shoulders. He held her from him at arm's length for a moment and looked deeply into her eyes. *Uh-oh*, thought Terri, when she realized what was happening. *I'm not sure if I'm ready for this.* Rico pulled her toward him and Terri, trying to avoid the inevitable, mostly out of nervousness, moved her head to the side for a hug instead. Rico, however, was not to be deterred. Terri felt his soft lips on her neck. She closed her eyes as he slowly moved up and lightly kissed her chin. She felt herself tense up as Rico's mouth, touched the corner of hers. His hands were in her hair now and he moved his soft lips full

154

onto hers, for a kiss like Terri had never before experienced. It was sweet yet demanding, gentle yet possessive. She felt the blood rushing to her face and then forced herself to relax as Rico put his arms around her. She finally let herself respond and started kissing him back. Terri realized then, for the first time in her life, she felt safe and cared for. It was a feeling she had never known with anyone else she had ever dated. She wanted the kiss to go on forever. It was the single most romantic moment, she could have ever imagined or dreamed about, *ever! But this was not a dream. This was for real!* When the kiss ended, however, she could only respond with the first dopey question that came to her mind.

"What was that for?" Terri asked, in sheer wonderment, as Rico pulled back and looked at her. Before answering, he put his hands on her hot cheeks and planted another quick kiss, on her trembling mouth.

"You needed to feel better," Rico simply said. Then he was gone.

Chapter Nineteen

Of course, Terri tormented herself for the next day or so, analyzing, reanalyzing, and remembering the kiss over and over again. Their relationship had been so casual up to that point, it had taken her completely by surprise. Since Terri absolutely hated surprises in any way, shape or form, she was having a very difficult time dealing with this one.

Oh, it wasn't like she had never been kissed before. She was 31 years old, for crying out loud. She had dated in high school and college, obviously sometimes with disastrous results. She had never let anyone get very close, though. Maybe it was because all the boys or men, as they may have imagined themselves, that she had dated before Rico had all been so immature, or stupid, *or drunk.* They didn't have the foggiest idea how to handle a girl like her. Terri had to admit, if only to herself, that she was absolutely petrified of a so-called 'serious' relationship! She had not wanted to go through what Angie had gone through, *not ever.* Even before Angie *thought* she was pregnant, even before they had gone from high school to college, Terri had been accused by more than one person of being overly paranoid. She, however, preferred to think of herself as cautious. Any guy tried to go too far and she dropped him like the proverbial *hot potato,* as it were. She had seen too many couples stay in relationships or even get married and *oh, hey!*, there was baby too. *Forget it!* She was way too practical.

Terri wanted to believe too, that it was about doing the right thing. Or as in the case of sex, *not doing* the wrong thing. Since *not doing* the wrong thing ended up in her best interests, allowed her a clean conscience *and* kept her out of trouble, then it was a bonus. Terri Lyn Springe knew how to take care of herself. She knew what she wanted and perhaps more importantly, she knew what she *did not* want. That was not going to change.

Oh, and what about Rico's attitude? She needed to feel better? Did he have a high opinion of himself or what? Terri had to admit though, she *did* ask a silly question and the kiss *did* make her feel better. She had almost given up hope, that anything other than friendship, would ever be possible between them. Perhaps she had been mistaken, after all. That kiss had not been between two people who were just friends.

Right now, though, Terri was pretty sure that she *did* want Rico. She wanted to be his wife. She really felt like he was the person she wanted to spend the rest of her life with. How long she would have to wait for him to figure out if he felt the same way, however, was another matter. He had obviously been very much in love with his fianceé. It was extremely difficult to compete with someone who had died, especially under such tragic circumstances. Terri definitely *did not* believe in ghosts. She had never felt that dead people could come back and haunt the living. It did not make sense! The memories were there, though, and they could be just as difficult to combat.

Terri had been thinking about all of these things, as she added additional information to her file, on **The Death of Logan Adams-Buckley.** Once again, a lot had happened in the last couple of days. She tried to document it all the best that she could. She finally closed the file and moved on to other business. It was Friday and there was, as always, much to do.

As it was, Terri and Rico, *would* have their 'fancy date' after all, in a manner of speaking. It had been decided last night.

They would all go over to Judith and George's lovely home the next evening, that being Saturday, for, as Terri and Angie had dubbed it, 'The Truffle Gourmet Feast'! Brianna had indeed, gladly acquiesced to stay home with Jenni and Benjamin. She had a date tonight with some friends for supper and a movie and had no problem spending the next evening with the kids. She also needed time to study and rest, as the next week would be another busy one for her at school.

For today, Terri and Angie were going over to see Judith and George, to take over the supplies for the dinner *and* tell them about the accident. Angie had already gone from self-pity and fear, to being really, really pissed off!

The night before, Terri had all she could do to keep her friend from going out on her own *'to find these bastards!'* These were Angie's words, of course, on the subject. She was being held down now, *only* by the fact that her head just plain hurt. It wasn't physically possible for her to drive or take any kind of action against anyone. So after taking another pain pill, with much fuss and complaining, Angie had settled down and stopped going on and on about revenge.

"Let the police handle it," Terri had said with a little smile, throwing Angie's own words back at her, as she tucked the blankets around her friend.

"But I *am* the police," Angie was saying weakly, as she had drifted off to sleep. Terri smiled again, shut off the light and closed the bedroom door.

After getting Angie settled down, Terri had bunked on the comfortable sofa. Benjamin, with his sleeping bag piled on several blankets, had slept on the floor next to the sofa, with Louie. Brianna and Jenni, of course, were cozy in Brianna's room with Maria.

Benjamin would have liked to have gone to Rico's apartment with Will but Terri hadn't felt it would be wise to separate the children. They were still her responsibility and she couldn't take any chances. Besides, she figured Rico would have his hands full just trying to look after Will. The children were settled with Terri and it was best, if that didn't change for the time being.

Now it was still pretty early on Friday morning. Along with adding to her report, Terri had been trying to plan meals for next week, as well as double checking Super Bowl sandwich orders. She also paid several bills online and checked her e-mail. Both of her sisters usually messaged every day and several other family members sent news of mundane things. Angie was still asleep. Brianna had gone to another early class so Jenni was also still slumbering. Benjamin was sitting on the sofa reading a book for school with Louie on his lap.

Terri needed to go shopping. Not for food so much anymore. Most of their food supplies were usually delivered to the shop. She needed to pick up more personal items, such as shampoo and toothpaste, maybe some bubble bath for Jenni, make-up and paper products. Terri had also decided, that she really would love something new to wear tomorrow night. Maybe she and Brianna could leave Angie with the kids tomorrow morning for awhile and quick go look for something. Today was already pretty full. By the time she and Angie went over to Judith and George's, stopped by Benjamin and Jenni's school for their homework, and then the doctor to have them check Angie's head injury, the day would be pretty much shot.

Terri's bedroom door opened then and Angie came out, looking like she had the worst hangover of her life. She shaded her eyes as if the light was way too bright, and groaned. Terri jumped up to help her and got her to the sofa before she fell down.

"Oh, my, God!" Angie leaned into the sofa cushions and held her head in her hands. "I am going to die, I swear. That, or I'm going to kill the jerks who did this. Arrggghhh!"

"Angie, don't start," Terri warned. "You are not going to die, not from this anyway. I also doubt that killing anyone would make you feel better. Now take it easy, or I'll shove another pill down you."

"Fine, I'll try to relax but I'm just so pissed-off! I.....," Angie started to rant some more and then just looked at Terri helplessly.

"I know and I don't blame you. But it saps your energy, when you get so upset." Terri tried to say calming words, as she covered Angie with a blanket from the bed clothes still on the sofa. Benjamin had gone to the bathroom and came back to sit next to Angie.

"Can I get you anything, Angie?" Benjamin looked anxiously at her, hoping he could help. Before Angie could answer though, Terri spoke up.

"You can stay right here, Benjamin, and keep an eye on her. Make sure she doesn't try to get out the door or anything." Terri was *pretending* to be serious.

"Oh, very funny," Angie said then and looked at Benjamin gratefully. "Thanks, Ben," she said. "I won't move, I promise. I can't move, I promise that, too. Uh, any coffee around here, by the way?" This was directed at Terri.

"Of course," Terri jumped up. "What kind of an establishment do you think we're running here?" She went to the kitchen and fixed a tray with mugs of freshly brewed coffee, cream, sugar, spoons, and napkins. She also added two glasses of orange juice for Angie and Benjamin. Jenni would be up anytime and hungry, so Terri would start breakfast soon. Right now, she just wanted to sit and calmly drink a cup of coffee with her best friend. Hopefully, they would have an uneventful day, get their errands done, *safely,* and then spend a quiet evening in the cozy apartment.

It had been a terrible week. Terri and Brianna hadn't even been down to the shop since Tuesday morning when, as they were dealing with the news of Logan's death, the F.B.I. had shown up at their door. From Logan's ridiculous order, to her murder, to Alex's arrest, and having the children with them, Brianna and Terri's world had been literally turned upside down. Rico and Guerrero had both cautioned the girls *not* to be at the shop alone, especially after the attack on Will and

Angie. The threat had been leveled at all of them, so no one was to take any chances until this mess had been cleared up.

Terri and Angie would spend most of the afternoon together. Brianna would be home by lunchtime to stay with Benjamin and Jenni. Terri's cell phone rang as they were finishing their coffee. It was Brianna saying *she* would pick up Jenni and Benjamin's homework and help them with it this afternoon. Terri relayed this information to Benjamin and he made an exaggerated face at the thought. So much for enjoying the time off from school, *even a little bit.* They still had to have some kind of a structured schedule, at least as much as Terri could manage to control, anyway.

Terri took a last drink of coffee, saw to it that Angie was calm and comfortable, and went to the kitchen to start bacon and scrambled eggs. Jenni got up, came through the kitchen with 'Poots' in her arms and Maria at her heels. She sniffed appreciatively, and said good morning, rubbing her eyes. Maria followed Jenni into the bathroom. Apparently, the cat was now the child's constant shadow and companion. They did everything together, except sit at the table. Maria had her own food and facilities, of course.

Benjamin came into the kitchen with Angie and they both claimed to be ravenous. Terri relaxed with relief. It was good to see Angie feeling better and if she had an appetite, that was a good sign. She sank down in a chair with a big sigh and Benjamin proceeded to help set the table. Jenni came out of the bathroom, sat 'Poots' on the counter, and planted herself next to Angie.

"Are you going to be O.K., Angie?" Jenni suddenly looked concerned and Angie put a comforting arm around the little girl.

"I am going to be fine, Jenni. Absolutely, positively, *fine.*" Angie sounded determined and perfectly calm. "There is no way, I am going to let a little thing like this get me down. I'll be back to normal in no time." She hugged her tight and Jenni sighed with relief.

"Yeah," said Terri, not to let any opportunity slip by, "whatever normal is for you Ang."

"Are you going to feed us or talk smart? I'm injured here!" Angie was starting to enjoy the attention. "Or have you *no sympathy* for a mortally wounded, helpless officer?" She put the back of her hand to her head, for dramatic affect.

"Oh, I have loads of sympathy for a mortally wounded, helpless officer," Terri said, as she set a plate of crisp bacon on the table. "But you are neither one of those things. *Especially not* helpless, as far as I'm concerned. Now eat up!"

Terri added a steaming bowl, of fluffy scrambled eggs to the table and sat down. No truffles this time. Just large fresh eggs, mixed with a little salt, pepper, milk and dried chives. Benjamin grabbed hot slices of toast and stacked them onto a small plate. They all ate heartily, needing a good breakfast to get them through another cold day. Jenni and Benjamin wanted to go out and play in the snow. Terri wasn't so sure. She was feeling just as concerned about the safety of the children, as the rest of them.

"I'll sit by the window seat and watch them Terri, while you do your chores," Angie volunteered prompting whoops of joy from Jenni and Benjamin. Terri decided that would be fine.

"Do not talk to anyone, though," Terri reminded them, "and if you see anyone driving by or *anything* that looks suspicious, come right back up, O.K.?"

"We will, Terri, we promise," Benjamin said solemnly. "We won't stay out too long, will we Jen?"

Jenni nodded and quickly finished her juice. "I want to build a snowman! Could you help us, Terri? You know," she looked at Terri then and sounded just like a grown-up, "you could use a little bit of fresh air yourself."

Terri laughed and agreed to go out as soon as she got a couple of things done. Maybe the little girl was right. *She could* use some fresh air, clear her head, get one with nature, all that.

The kids put on their boots and snow pants and went out, clattering down the stairs and immediately flopping into the snow. Angie laughed as she, with the cats of course, watched the youngsters play. They went through the preliminary throwing of snowballs at one another and the making of *snow angels*. Then they started rolling up a huge ball of snow for the bottom of their snowman.

Terri quickly stacked the dishwasher and threw in a load of laundry. Angie watched them enviously, wishing she could go out too. But like the sick little child with the fever, she could only watch from the window. By the time Terri got dressed and joined them, Jenni and Benjamin, almost had a huge snowball ready for the bottom. Terri had been out there for no more than 10 minutes, when another little boy, who said his name was Jason, along with his little sisters Jessica and Jade, twins as it turned out, joined them. In no time, they had built, not only a pretty impressive snowman but a snow fort as well. They were having such a good time, that Terri couldn't believe it when Brianna drove up.

"What in the world? What is the meaning of this?" Brianna tromped over in her fancy dress boots and wool coat, trying to look fierce and not exactly dressed to play in the snow. Nevertheless, she suddenly took a splooshy snowball, *right in the face!* Everyone stopped and waited for her reaction.

"Well," she said, wiping wet snow, out of her eyes, and *straining* to look even more stern. "All right, who threw that?" Terri started laughing uproariously!

"Guilty! Ah!" Terri yelled, as she and Brianna started chasing one another. Pretty soon everyone was screaming and laughing and chasing each other and falling in the fluffy, white snow. Terri couldn't remember the last time she had so much fun.

By the time they got back up to the apartment, Angie had abandoned the window seat and was making hot chocolate with marshmallows. Jason and his little, twin sisters headed home. Jenni and Benjamin said a sad, good-bye and could they come back tomorrow? They were missing out on a lot, not being in school, and Terri was glad the other children had shown up.

Everyone peeled off their wet clothes and made a hug mess. Terri didn't care about the mess at all. She had to admit, she did feel much better. Everything had been perfectly normal, no one driving by, no strange looking vehicles or people hanging about. She sipped her hot chocolate and tried to relax and not worry so much. Angie had set out sugar cookies and scones, with butter and honey.

Everyone was warming up, sipping their hot drinks, laughing, and enjoying themselves, when there was a knock on the door. Benjamin ran to it and stunned the whole room when he yelled, "Daddy!" Terri nearly spit out her hot chocolate. Angie stood up suddenly, bumping her head on the cupboard above the counter, with an indignant, 'Ooowww!' Brianna gasped and Jenni screamed. There stood Nick Guerrero. With him, was a smiling Alex Buckley!

Chapter Twenty

Terri was sitting in front of her old fashioned dresser mirror, taking extra care with her make-up and hair. She sighed and plucked her eyebrows before applying a light pencil line. She wasn't happy with her hair. She was *never happy* with her hair. It seemed to change from day to day. It was a little longer than she usually wore it but with it being so cold, she had put off getting it cut. She finally got it to look presentable and lightly sprayed it before applying mascara and lipstick.

"Hey," said Brianna from her bedroom door. Terri turned around and Brianna came in and sat on her bed. Maria sat down on the floor next to Terri and looked at her with sad eyes. "You miss the kids, don't you?" Brianna asked Terri and didn't wait for an answer. "So does Maria, it would seem." She picked her up and the fluffy feline started purring loudly, as she stroked her creamy, silky fur.

"We knew they wouldn't be here forever," Terri said then. If she thought about it too much, she felt herself getting choked up. The apartment seemed so empty without them. "Can you imagine how happy they are to be back with their father? Jenni was beside herself with happiness when she saw her beloved *daddy*." Terri smiled weakly and resolved herself to be happy for them. "I'm not surprised he got out on bail, though. Guerrero is awesome and we know Alex

165

did not kill Logan. They had nothing for evidence to speak of and, obviously, he is not a danger to anyone. Otherwise, they wouldn't allow him access to his children either, you would think." Terri sighed again and put down her mascara wand.

"Terri," Brianna tried to comfort her. "Go to this dinner tonight and have a wonderful time. You deserve it. You have been working your butt off for everyone else, and *worrying,* about everyone else. Give yourself a break and enjoy this evening."

"You know, that's funny," Terri said as she got up from her chair to put on her new, *very* expensive, red cashmere sweater and comfy charcoal gray, wool slacks. "That is exactly what Rico said. Almost the exact same words, so I guess you must both be right."

"So did Alex, remember?" Brianna reminded her before she left the room.

She had already fixed herself some leftovers for a light supper and was drinking tea as she did her school work. Judith had wanted Brianna to come to the dinner also, once the children were gone. Brianna was exhausted, however, and decided to pass. It had been a tough week, *for all of them.*

Terri definitely agreed with Brianna but was still dumbfounded by the way Alex continued to react, to Logan's extravagant spending.

"Please, girls," he had begged them. "You have taken such wonderful care of my children. I haven't seen them this happy and well looked-after, well, since their mother was with us," he said sadly and went on. "Just take the food and enjoy it. You deserve it and I don't want to see any of it, *ever!*"

Alex had even made the decision, *not* to take the children back to the mansion Logan had insisted on living in. He called it a monstrous waste and intended to sell it, as soon as possible. He had also dispatched several trusted assistants to pick up *only* what they needed, from the house and move it to a luxurious but serviceable hotel. He had booked a suite with nice accommodations for each of them, and room service to take care of meals. Alex hoped to find a more modest home for himself and his children soon.

"Something with a backyard," Alex had said determinedly. "Then I will find a respectable housekeeper who can look after us and keep it simple. Also, Terri, I would like to have some of your wonderful meals delivered again, to our new home when we get settled. I want good, old-fashioned food, casseroles, and stews, that kind of thing. Oh, and can you make a good meatloaf? I'm dying for some."

Terri had laughed at that. "I knew it," she had said to Brianna later. They had known it all along. It had been all about Logan, all of the time. She had been a piece of work, that one, from the start.

The last thing Terri needed to think about tonight, however, was Logan Adams-Buckley's untimely demise. She also couldn't let it ruin this evening. Rico and Will, after picking up Angie, would be arriving soon, so she needed to get moving. She would be plenty warm as they wouldn't be out playing in the snow this time. From one warm building to a warm car, to George and Judith's toasty, cheery home, the cold would not be a factor. She had also gone all out and bought herself a new leather jacket, on sale, naturally. It had a warm, cozy hood, lined with fur, *faux, also* naturally. Terri was not a big fan of fur but leather was another matter. She loved the smell. She loved the feel. She already had the perfect, short winter boots, an over-sized leather bag, and gloves to go with the coat.

She was also looking *very forward* to seeing Rico again. They had spoken only briefly yesterday to make the arrangements for this evening. Angie had gone back to her own apartment, to get a good night's sleep last night, and had promised to rest most of the day. Even Angie had a difficult time seeing the kids leave. It had been a very emotional moment, for all of them.

When Guerrero and Alex had shown up at the apartment yesterday afternoon, Terri had felt a dozen different emotions. *Of course*, Jenni and Benjamin needed to be with their father. *Of course*, he should not be incarcerated if he had not committed a crime. Thus, the murder of Logan Adams-Buckley remained a mystery, pending further investigation.

Alex had apologized profusely to Terri, for putting her and her friends in any kind of danger. He also found it difficult to imagine, that Ignacio would try to harm anyone. Terri felt the same way. Obviously, Ignacio, Jasmine, and Nadia, had very good reasons to stay hidden. But why try to harm Will and Angie? Why threaten Terri?

Taking all of this into account, a large part of the investigation, had now turned to *the attack* on Will and Angie, as it could only be called. They had indeed been deliberately injured and the vehicle totaled. It appeared as if the culprits were admitting their guilt by these actions. They seemed to be saying, 'Stay away and leave it be. We don't want to hurt anyone else.' But a murder was a murder. A life had been taken. Thus, *someone* needed to find out who else was involved to *completely* exonerate Alex. Terri certainly had no desire for it to be her. She had no need to play detective anymore.

Oh, and then, there was the phone call to the police! Definitely, to no one's surprise, it turned out that Logan herself, had called the police. The 911 emergency recording had revealed her voice calling, 'to report an intruder.' Guerrero had listened to the tape and heard Logan's *frantic call!* He was not fooled anymore than Terri was, however, and she mentioned she would also like to hear the tape. Terri knew how Logan was. She could put on a pretty good show, if the situation called for it.

"I think I know what you're getting at, Terri," Nick had said. "This woman was up to something. She was laying it on pretty thick when she made that call, and there was no evidence of any kind of break-in. If she was setting the whole thing up, that was one detail she forgot to attend to."

By the time Alex had gotten to Logan, as he had told Terri, the police were at the front door. He knew, that telling Ignacio, Jasmine, and Nadia, to leave quickly, was his only recourse for their protection. He had never imagined the police would arrest him so quickly. They had no time to find out anymore details before Alex found himself in jail.

Now, *Terri* was wondering *what* to think about Ignacio, Jasmine, and Nadia. It wasn't like she had really known them at all. If Ignacio had anything to do with the attack on Will and Angie, what then? Angie had met Ignacio on more than one occasion and had no reason to think it was he who had directly threatened her. Someone had used his name, on the other hand, so obviously Ignacio was involved. It seemed to be getting more complicated. For now, Terri needed to stop thinking about it for a couple of hours. As Brianna *and* Rico *and* Alex had advised, she needed to just, *relax and enjoy the evening*.

Chapter Twenty-One

erri and Rico, with Angie and Will, in Rico's sleek, black Pontiac Grand Prix, arrived at the Perry home at exactly 5:00. Promptness was very important to Judith, and this dinner called for everything going exactly right and *on time*. The day before, Terri and Angie had delivered everything needed for the recipes Judith had chosen. Because of the importance of the meal, the incredibly expensive truffles, caviar, pate, etc., Judith had hired two of her close friends, who were in the catering business, to assist her with the meal. Cynthia Grossman and her daughter Lauren had helped Judith prepare the courses, six in all, and would serve the meal. Cynthia also prided herself, on her expertise at selecting the proper wines, to go with each course of the meal. The entire dinner, from appetizers to dessert, would take *at least* 3 hours to consume and, *hopefully*, completely enjoy.

Angie and Will, recovering nicely from their minor injuries, had both been looking forward to the meal. Will was more than a bit puzzled about how it had all come about, as far as the truffles and other food items were concerned anyway. Angie and Terri had wisely decided not to enlighten him about the situation. Will would find out, in time, exactly what kind of person his cousin had been. Either way, it would be difficult for him to deal with and now was not the time. He had also been deprived of going to Logan's funeral. His

Aunt Rose had come to Boston and taken her body back to Cleveland. He definitely needed cheering up and this evening would hopefully be a start.

Terri, on the other hand, would have preferred to be alone with Rico for the evening, particularly to talk things out. *Oh well, another time perhaps.* They were with good friends and there were few things in life as enjoyable, *or as memorable,* as one of Judith's dinners. So, enjoy they would. Terri had made up her mind, to truly relax *and not think* about Jenni and Benjamin for awhile. She would miss them but it was time to move on.

They were greeted warmly *and* enthusiastically by George and Judith, who both excessively fussed over Angie and Will. George had been very distressed when they had told him what had occurred. Angie had considered *not* telling her father the whole story but decided against the idea. George knew his daughter's job as a police officer could at times be dangerous. She and Will were fine and they would eventually discover who had done this foolish thing. For tonight, they would not dwell on it.

Also joining them, as it turned out, were George and Judith's neighbors and close friends, Carrie and Don Spencer. So, 'they would be eight for dinner.' Ten, when you counted the fact, that as they served, Cynthia and Lauren, would also eat. Terri was glad to see the extra couple as they did introductions all around. The more the merrier, along with plenty of conversation, would keep her mind off worrisome matters. For tonight they would not think about anything negative, just indulge themselves. Terri would have felt a little guilty but *indulging* herself was something she so seldom did. She rarely found a need to. That was why, occasions such as this were such a treat.

For now, the guests were admiring their impressive surroundings. Judith's antique dining room table was gorgeous, sparkling with crystal, fine china, and shining silver pieces, against flickering red and white candles in shining crystal holders. The center of the table held a beautiful, silk flower arrangement of red and white roses, baby's breath, and expertly arranged greens, another one of Judith's many talents and hobbies. As they entered the warm, welcoming home, the scent of truffles filled the air with an intoxicating aroma. Nothing else smelled *or tasted*, like this rare substance. This dinner would be a well-deserved reward, after the miserable week they had all experienced.

To get their meal off to the proper start, an expertly presented, delicious selection of hors d'oeuvres, was arranged on the sideboard in the Perry dining room. George stood behind a small bar next to it and served drinks. Cocktails and champagne, in tall sparkling flutes, were served with the appetizers. The very costly, Beluga caviar, was being kept properly cool in a small bowl, placed in a larger crystal bowl of crushed ice. Nothing could be a better match with caviar than a really good champagne. *Blanc de Blancs champagne*, George said, as he handed Terri a bubbling glass. After tasting it, she knew it was more than likely very expensive. *Nothing but the best for their guests!* George and Judith both glowed with satisfaction, as everyone admired the table and fussed over the appetizers.

Small gold-rimmed china plates on which to place caviar, pate, and smoked salmon, served with assorted crackers, breads, and several fine cheeses, were placed next to the bar, along with pretty cocktail napkins, knives and forks. There were also savory deviled eggs, with truffles, of course, and for variety, one hot appetizer was served. Asparagus Parmesan Pastry Rolls were presented, hot out of the oven, by Lauren. She skillfully scooped them off of a beautiful crystal serving platter with a small silver spatula and a flourish. The delicious cheesy bites, with tender cuts of asparagus covered with flaky pastry, had each been drizzled with a drop or two of Black Truffle Oil and were addictive, to say the least. They all enjoyed them immensely, as they sipped cocktails or delicious sparkling champagne and munched on a little bit of everything.

Lauren was friendly, pretty and personable, as she moved easily amidst the guests, making sure everyone was served. She and her mother had a very successful catering business and the easy temperaments, to smoothly handle mishaps and keep their clients happy. Lauren quickly removed used plates and napkins. She also helped George see to it that everyone had drinks and a taste of all the hors d'oeuvres offered.

"I have never been quite sure what to think about caviar," said Angie, as she tasted a morsel on a cracker and wrinkled her nose. "I just don't think I'm a fish egg person. It is very unique though. The deviled eggs are fantastic! Terri, did you try these asparagus things?" Angie popped one into her mouth and took a generous drink of her champagne.

"Angie, for crying out loud," Terri said, shaking her head. "This is Beluga Caviar! Do have any idea how expensive this stuff is? At least *try* to appreciate it. Oh, and take it easy on the champagne. The night has just begun." Angie wrinkled her nose again, this time at her over-protective friend, as she spread some pate on a crisp, toasted cracker.

"*You* are supposed to be relaxing, Terri," she shot back. "I know *I'm* going to. Oh, yummy! This pate is fantastic! I am going to be full before the main course." Angie groaned and everyone agreed enthusiastically.

Lauren assured them, however, that there would be plenty of time between courses, so they should all be sure to try everything. She and her mother, wanted opinions from everyone, on how everything tasted and was presented. This dinner was serving more than one purpose, apparently. Cynthia and Lauren were reveling in the experience of preparing the food, and getting opinions from all of the guests, along with their own taste buds to savor and critique the meal themselves.

Terri loved caviar and *it did not* get any better than this. It had been another one of the wonderful delicacies she had first tasted in France. The banquet she and the other students had helped prepare *and eaten*, on their last night before going home, had also been memorable. That seemed so long ago but she had never forgotten it.

Rico, Will, and Don Spencer, were involved in what appeared to be, a serious discussion on current world affairs, along with, of course, the Super Bowl. How they managed to talk, eat, and drink so smoothly, not to mention all the exaggerated gestures, all at the same time, never ceased to amaze Terri. She also couldn't get over how handsome Rico was tonight. *How did I ever get such a cute boyfriend?* Terri pondered this silly thought, feeling like she was back in high school, for like *the millionth time,* since she had met him. *Is he even my boyfriend? How in the world will I know?*

Terri watched him, as she sipped her champagne and munched on a crispy cracker, spread with the delicious pate. Rico's soft dark hair was cut the perfect length. She imagined herself, running her fingers through it and sighed. He was wearing a pair of perfectly fitted, black slacks and a dark maroon, long-sleeved dress shirt, open at the neck. From the side, Terri could see how long his eye lashes were, and his soft mouth beckoned. She sighed again and looked away, *unfortunately,* right into Angie's face, who had been *watching* Terri, *watch* Rico. Terri jumped back a little, rather startled but she quickly strained to compose her expression. She could feel her cheeks getting red and hot. *Damn it!*

"Oh, brother," Angie said, in her most disgusted tone.

"What?" Terri asked innocently, as her friend just rolled her eyes. Terri laughed at Angie though, in spite of herself, knowing exactly what she was thinking.

"Sigh," Angie said, exaggerating terribly, as she placed her hand over heart. "Would you two just get on with it already?" She said this in a low voice only Terri could hear.

Terri simply ignored her, like always, *pretending* not to know what Angie was talking about. She suddenly became very interested in a painting on the wall to her left, opposite her pesky pal. In truth, it was the most atrocious thing she had ever seen! Terri wasn't going to voice her opinion of this particular art object, in the conversation anytime soon, however, but it certainly was distracting! Well, I guess there's no accounting for taste, she thought, emptying her glass and wondering if she should have another. Probably not. More alcoholic beverages were yet to come. She wanted to be able to *actually taste* her food or there would be no point in this whole event.

The cocktail hour was soon over. At this time, they were all encouraged by Lauren, to move to the beautiful dining room table. Judith had gone all out with the place settings and told everyone where to sit. She placed George at one end and Rico at the other. Terri was pleased to be sitting at Rico's right hand with Carrie Spencer on her other side. Angie was across from Terri, with Will next to her. Don Spencer sat next to his wife and Judith was next to Will, with George on the other end.

Once they were seated, Cynthia and Lauren served the next course. Truffle-infused French Onion soup, in gold-rimmed soup cups, was placed before them. To compliment the soup, Lauren poured a gorgeous, raspberry-rich 2003 Marcel Lapierre Morgon, into shimmering wine glasses in front of their plates. They savored the rich broth, the combination of caramelized onions and black truffles, giving the delicious soup, an earthy, sweet taste. Along with the soup, they sipped the pretty wine out of *the first,* of Judith's beautiful crystal wine glasses, placed in front of their plates.

"Just exactly how many sets of wine glasses do you have Judith?" Angie asked, grinning at her father.

Now it was George's turn to roll *his* eyes. "Just exactly as many she needs, no doubt," he commented, looking fondly at his wife.

"Quite a few I suppose, but I am not frivolous as I buy," Judith defended herself. "Obviously, we love to entertain and I always watch for sales to keep my collection fresh."

"Only to sell the old ones, at an annual tag sale for a fraction of the price," George revealed, shaking his head and taking another sip of the delicious wine.

"My wife pretty much does the same thing." Don Spencer contributed his two cents on the subject. "Only she buys linens, dolls, collectables of all sorts. It's a great arrangement, when you think about it. What goes around, comes around."

"We visit plenty of tag and yard sales ourselves," put in Carrie, and Judith nodded. "So, it all evens out, in the end. You men should start coming with us sometime. You can't even believe the fantastic things people sell, especially the rich. Most of what we find, is still brand new! One man's trash, is another man's treasure, as they always say."

Terri and Angie couldn't agree more. They had both furnished their apartments from tag and yard sales. Terri checked the newspaper every week, when the season started. One could never have enough book cases, books to go in them, or extra pillows and quilts. Also, since Terri and Brianna had set up their shop, they had managed to find many great buys to fill out their kitchen with utensils, pots, and pans, cutting boards, hot pads, you name it! Why buy everything brand new? It was more fun to find bargains.

As they were finishing their soup, Lauren was clearing and asking for opinions. "Did you all enjoy the French Onion soup?"

Everyone agreed. The soup had been *absolutely* wonderful. None of them had ever tasted anything like it. As she smiled with satisfaction, Lauren also cleared the first set of wine glasses and placed salad in front of them.

The salad was light, consisting of field greens with a white Truffle oil vinaigrette. To go with the salad, Lauren poured a dry German Riesling, into another shimmering glass in front of their plates.

They all enjoyed the crisp greens with slivers of fresh, bright carrot, paper thin slices of radish and perfectly sliced rings, of sweet red onion. Conversation was light and enjoyable. Terri couldn't remember the last time she had felt so calm and comfortable. Her cold was pretty much gone, and it was so nice to be in such good company. She took a small sip of her wine and met Rico's eyes. He flashed her such a dazzling smile that she felt her stomach lurch. He then reached for her hand and gave it a tight squeeze. Terri hoped it was a good sign. Perhaps soon, they could have that long overdue talk and put all their cards on the table, as it were. She hoped to convince him there was another person in this world for him so he could move on. It would be even better if he could figure it out for himself. Yeah, *that would be nice and tidy.* Why does everything always have to be so *damn* complicated? Terri was wondering this, as Lauren began to remove their salad plates and wine glasses.

Cynthia then came into the dining room with small sundae glasses of passion fruit sorbet. "At large formal dinners in France," she explained, "sorbets with an alcoholic base are served between the main courses, taking the place of liqueurs. Isn't this pretty? Fortunately, we have *only one* main course or we would be here all night." They all laughed at that. "This will help clear your palates before we serve it." They all admired the light refreshment, as she placed small, shiny spoons next to each glass. "Please catch your breath, settle your stomachs, and stretch your legs if you wish. It will be about half an hour, before we continue the meal."

They all slowly enjoyed small scoops of the cool, sweet, fruity, and *indeed,* refreshing sorbet. Then everyone moved away from the table to, as Cynthia had suggested, stretch their legs. Angie and Terri went to Judith's lovely dressing room, which was conveniently connected with a private bathroom. They conversed between the rooms as they attended to necessities.

"I saw that look between you and Rico," Angie said, in her best catty junior high school voice. "Are things *finally* moving along in that weird relationship you guys are carrying on? I never saw two people hedge so much, on whether they like each other or not. Geez! I mean, for crying out loud. You're the first girl, Rico has shown any interest in since I've known him. Get on with it already!" Angie was running a comb through her, at the moment, medium length, straight black hair, as Terri came out of the bathroom and shot back at her friend.

"Hey, *you* were the one, who told *me* in the first place, that Rico might have some issues! So now *you're* wondering, why things aren't, as you put it, *moving along?* Define that, by the way." Terri checked her own make-up and realized she had been thinking *exactly* the same thing. Consequently, she didn't know what to tell Angie. Until she and Rico had finally talked everything out, she had no answers, for herself or for her friend.

"Moving along, as in, you're officially *a couple*," Angie said decidedly, using her fingers to make *the dreaded finger quotes.* "You act like a couple, holding hands, calling each other everyday, making plans for the future, that kind of stuff."

Terri knew Angie was being *very* careful not to suggest that she and Rico start sleeping together. Terri did not need to say it. She fully intended to wait until she was married and Angie knew this. They had discussed it many times and agreed completely on the subject. If it wasn't Rico, then she would just have to move on with her life, until, *or if,* someone else came along. It wasn't just, *the old-fashioned thing* to do anymore. There were too many risks, physically, emotionally, mentally. Certainly, no one knew this better than Angie. What she had been through with 'Jeff the Jerk,' was always in the back of their minds.

Terri sighed and put down the small brush she was using to fluff her hair. She didn't accomplish much. It pretty much looked the same. She sprayed it lightly, with a small bottle of hairspray, Judith kept on the vanity for that purpose.

"Let's just wait and see, O.K. Ang? I can't define our relationship right now. If anything happens though, you will be the first to know. How about that?" Terri grinned and Angie eyed her suspiciously. Terri hadn't told *anyone* about 'the kiss' and she usually had a pretty tough time hiding anything from her best friend.

"I'll be the first to know, huh? Yeah, well I have a feeling, you are already holding out on me. I......" Before Angie could go on, however, their conversation was interrupted by Judith informing them that it was time for the main course. "Saved by the bell....uh, sort of!" Angie said, as Terri gave her another wicked grin.

"I'm afraid you'll just have to wait," Terri said to her impatient friend, as they moved back to the dining room.

"I hate waiting," Angie said with a little laugh, "but obviously you are giving me no choice."

Fresh wine glasses were on the table in front of their dinner plates. Tall water glasses, filled with clear sparkling ice cubes and fresh water with lemon slices, were next to the wine glasses. Their napkins had been replaced with clean ones. Two pretty, gold baskets had been put on the table containing several warm breads. Delicate crystal bowls, filled with whipped truffle butter, were passed with the bread. Butter knives were placed across bread plates. The dinner guests buttered warm, fresh rolls of sourdough, garlic-rosemary, sesame seed or cheddar cheese.

The main course was served with much ceremony on the part of Cynthia and Lauren and applause from the guests. Placed before them, were gold-rimmed dinner plates, each containing thick, luscious slices of Fillet of Beef Wellington, fluffy mounds of truffled mashed potatoes and tender stalks of white asparagus with a truffle vinaigrette. The fork tender beef, the highest quality tenderloin, with layers of pate de foie gras and mushrooms, covered with a flaky puff pastry, was served with Madeira and Black Truffle sauce. None of them, had ever tasted anything like this fabulous meal and more than likely, never would again. With this mouth-watering pinnacle of the dinner, Cynthia and Lauren poured a 1988 Premium California, Cabernet Sauvignon.

"I have been saving this wine for a special occasion," revealed Judith.

"Back in 1988, when I met my first husband, with apologies to George but of course, he knows the whole story," she patted his hand affectionately before she went on, "I began collecting bottles of wine from that year. Ted owned a construction company. Sadly, one day he had a heart attack and died while on the job. After awhile, I knew I could no longer hang on to all of the sentimental things that reminded me of him. Slowly, as the occasion presents itself, we have been using the bottles, twenty different vintages, for various meals. I am especially glad, as it turned out, that I was able to purchase two bottles of this particular wine. I certainly endeavored to keep it properly stored. Please, all of you, tell me if you are enjoying it with this delicious beef and I will feel much better, as a result." Judith finished her revealing story a bit dramatically but Terri could see real tears in her eyes. She hoped then, that Rico also got the point as Judith added one more thought. "One does find, after a time, one must move on. Don't you all agree?"

Terri dared not even glance at Rico as she sipped the deep red wine, a nice compliment to the Beef Wellington and everyone gave their positive opinions.

"You apparently took very good care of these bottles, Judith," Rico said, giving his positive opinion. "I do not consider myself an expert on wine. I'm more of a beer man myself but this is wonderful!" Everyone heartily agreed and laughed to break the rather awkward moment. However, Rico was not quite done with his comments, much to everyone's, especially Terri's, surprise. "I also agree with you Judith, on a very important point." He paused and it seemed difficult for him to go on. But go on he did! "It is time to move on." He said the words rather quietly but everyone heard them.

Terri looked at him and saw the expression on his face. He had finally reached this important conclusion, without anyone else saying a word, just as she had hoped he would. Rico looked into her eyes and she finally felt they had a chance, a very good chance, to make their relationship work. Angie saw the exchange and it was enough to answer all of her questions.

Terri absolutely loved beef Wellington and had tasted several different versions of it but nothing would ever equal this. Now that Rico had finally made such a huge breakthrough in his life, it was such a relief to Terri, that the food tasted even better, which didn't even seem possible at this point. Along with the tender asparagus and fluffy mashed potatoes, it was truly the highlight of this special gourmet meal. However, they still had dessert to look forward to.

With enough space and time between each of the courses, all of the dinner guests were still able to finish every, last, scrumptious bite of the fabulous beef and accompanying sides. As Lauren cleared, everyone sighed and complimented the two women for their extraordinary efforts. Cynthia and Lauren were satisfied and pleased.

"This meal has been a fantastic learning experience for us, as well," Cynthia pointed out. "I have never prepared any of these dishes before and several of our clients are starting to develop some *very* expensive tastes. Terri, however you came about the ingredients, the truffles, the pate, the caviar, and cheeses, to contribute to this fabulous repast, I also *thank you!*" She removed Terri's dinner plate and said, "Hope everyone has room for dessert!" They all moaned and groaned, *again,* as Lauren finished clearing.

"Don't worry," she said, "dessert won't be for about 20 minutes. You will love it!"

As all reflected on the delicious meal they had just been so elegantly served, there was little conversation. Terri dared not even *look* at Rico. She was astounded by his sudden decision and almost a little afraid. Where would he expect their relationship to go after this? Terri could only assume, that he and his fianceé had *not* waited until they were married, to consummate *their* relationship. That was the norm for most, *in this day and age,* as they say. As much as Terri had enjoyed this wonderful dinner, it was time for it to end. She now hoped that she and Rico would have at least have some time to talk.

Now, to finish their evening, they were first served coffee with choices of regular or decaf, of course, in preparation for dessert. No more alcoholic beverages, *thank goodness.* Terri couldn't help but wonder if Rico would be able to drive them home. It was their *set in stone rule,* after all, *not* to drive after having indulged in the various wines, not to mention the cocktails and champagne. Normally, she and Angie spent the night. Lately, Brianna, who still being under-age, did not yet drink alcohol, drove them home.

She forgot this conundrum for the moment, as Cynthia and Lauren proceeded to serve *the piece de resistance!* Several silver trays were placed on the table in front of them, as all other dishes, save water glasses and coffee cups, had been cleared.

Cynthia began with this question. "Ask yourselves, my dears. How is it possible, to live in a world, where 'truffle' can mean either chocolate or fungus? Answer? You have both!"

On the trays, were several kinds of chocolates. All were in bite size pieces, with elaborate place cards, describing which each kind was. They all gasped at the presentation and once again, began applauding.

"Everyone try a little bite of all of the selections and please give me your absolute, honest opinions. If you do not like a certain chocolate, tell me. If you love one, tell me why."

As the dinner guests selected a chocolate and tried to ascertain, which was the best or their favorite, Cynthia carefully took notes. Lauren supplied warm damp towels to keep hands clean and chocolate free.

They carefully read the cards in front of each of the chocolates before they tried them, so as to be the best judge of how they tasted by what was in them. Terri and Angie were in their element. Not many things, in their book, could top chocolate.

The chocolates were carefully labeled with pretty red and white cards, in *French Script,* no less.

Truffes au Rhumm
Chocolate Truffles flavored with dark rum.

Truffes au Cointrueau
Chocolate Truffles, flavored with Cointreau,
an orange flavored liqueur.

Truffes au Pastis
Chocolate truffles, flavored with anise seeds
and Richard Pastis or Pernod.

Truffes "Nutella"
Chocolate & Nutella Truffles, coated in
finely chopped, toasted hazelnuts.

Truffes Moka
Chocolate Mocha Truffles

Each had their favorite and no one had any complaints, to say the least. Chocolate was chocolate. It was almost impossible to go wrong. Terri, who especially loved hazel nuts, decided the Truffes Nutella was her favorite. Most of the men liked the Truffes au Pastis. Angie preferred the Truffes Moka. All were delicious, however. They finished their coffee and finally prepared to go home. This brought up the question once more of how that would be accomplished. Terri didn't ask, not wanting to second guess the Chief of Police. He had it covered however, as it soon became apparent. Suddenly, they all saw flashing lights outside of George and Judith's house.

"What in the world....?" Judith was startled at the outset, to realize that a police car was in front of her home.

"Not to be alarmed," Rico assured her, "it's our escort home." He looked at Terri and smiled. "Didn't you think I'd have it covered? I can't possibly drive. I'm much too full!"

Terri sighed with relief and everyone laughed.

"Who is our escort, by the way?" Will asked as he struggled into his coat. He and Angie had both had more than enough, *of everything*, not to mention they were all exhausted.

"Royce and Harris," Rico said, as the doorbell rang.

Officer Tom Harris was at the front door, hat in hand. "At your service, Cap'n!" He said gallantly. "Heard there was a pretty wild party at this residence this evening. Looks as if we're right on time."

"You certainly are!" Rico helped Terri into her coat and explained. "I had this all set-up ahead of time. If anyone knows the rules, not to mention the law, it had better be me! I'll ride with Royce and Tom can drive my car. Let's head out!"

Will sat in the front with Tom Harris, while Terri and Angie sank into the back seat. Terri loved Rico's Grand Prix but she had never had the occasion to sit in the back seat. Obviously, she normally sat in the front with her date.

Officer Tom Harris was one of Terri's favorites at Rico's police station. They had met at a picnic last summer and he had brought his pretty young wife and twin boys. He and his partner, Officer Jim Royce, were another pair of Boston's finest and had been looking after Will and Angie's duties, while they were still on sick leave.

Angie yawned and fell back onto the leather seat. "If I died right now," she exaggerated, as usual, "I would go ecstatically happy! Can you believe that meal? Nothing can top that, *ever!*"

Terri agreed, then quietly sat contemplating all the things that had happened in just the last five days. It seemed more like a month! Talk about emotional peaks and valleys! She also couldn't get Rico off of her mind and felt frustrated, that they would not have a chance to talk tonight after all. Under the circumstances though, with all the alcohol they had drank and the food they had eaten, both of them were probably too tired to think clearly anyway. Right now, all Terri wanted to do was change her clothes and snuggle into her cozy, warm bed. Suddenly, she could barely keep her eyes open!

Officer Harris sniffed the air in the car appreciatively. "Man, those leftovers smell good," he commented. "Jim and I are going to have to stop for supper after we get you guys home. Suddenly, I'm starving!'

It was no wonder. In the large carry bag between Terri and Angie, were enough leftovers for several meals. Cynthia had sent along the rest of the Beef Wellington, Truffled mashed potatoes, French onion soup, chocolate truffles, not to mention, whatever was still remaining of the ingredients for the dinner itself. They still had caviar, pate, cheeses, and breads. Back at the shop, the lobsters, shrimp, and yet more truffles, still needed to be used. The shrimp and lobsters of course, were frozen. The amount of food Logan had ordered, had been so vast, that this dinner had been but the tip of the iceberg. What would they do with the remains? Huge Super Bowl Party?

Terri couldn't think about that anymore either. They were finally back at the apartment. After mumbling something about getting Will home, Rico gave Terri a quick kiss and she and Angie literally stumbled up the stairs and in the door. The two cars drove off and Brianna had already been looking out the window, to see what was up.

"Well, I see you were safely chauffeured home. I had wondered about that. Usually, I'm the driver. Oooooo, what's in the bag?" Terri handed it to her excited and no doubt, famished young partner and encouraged her to help herself. "Beef Wellington!" Brianna said with surprise. "Potatoes, soup, chocolate! Wow, what a fine repast. I shall fix myself a plate." She proceeded to do so, placing an arranged meal on a dinner plate. "It's still hot, too. Yummy! I'll probably get a heartburn, eating this late but it'll be *sooooo* worth it. Wow!"

"You're too young to get a heartburn. If you do, though, there are Tums in the bathroom cabinet," Terri said with a huge yawn. "I know you will enjoy it. The beef is unbelievable. Have some soup, too. Then can you put everything away,

Sweetie? I'm so tired, I can't see straight!" With another enormous yawn, Terri headed to her room to get into her P.J.s. Angie was already yanking blankets and pillows back out of the closet, to make her bed on the sofa. Terri threw an over-sized Red Sox t-shirt at her equally tired friend, as she made her way to the bathroom.

Angie snuggled into the sofa with Louie. Brianna, assuring Terri she would put everything away, *no problem*, sat on the other end of the sofa, eating and making satisfied yummy noises. 'Saturday Night Live' was on, the guest host, doing the usual timely opening of the show. No one would ever have thought a week ago, that they would be in the middle of a disturbing murder mystery. The whole incident had reached a dead stop, as far as Terri was concerned. Needing sleep as much as she did, she could do nothing right now, however. Terri crawled in between the puffy covers of her comfy warm bed and Maria jumped up to join her.

"You miss Jenni, don't you?" Terri asked the purring cat. Maria answered back with half growl, half meow, making Terri believe the cat knew *exactly* what she was talking about. "I do too. I just wish there was something we could do to clear this mess up. I'm missing something else, though, Maria. I mean about this case. There's something getting past us. Something we haven't thought of. Some weird angle to all of this. What do you think, mmmm?"

Maria made another musical noise in her throat, giving away nothing, as she settled down next to Terri. Too bad cats could talk but they just chose not to! Maria couldn't help her mistress with this one. Terri needed to think it through but for now, she was quickly dead to the world!

Chapter Twenty-Two

erri woke-up suddenly to the phone ringing, *again!* It was the land-line, the business phone, so she didn't move. Her bedroom door was open just enough so she could hear it and be disturbed from slumber. The answering machine kicked in and after hearing her own voice, Terri heard the caller and the words that made her jump up and run to it.

Angie, awake on the sofa, stopped Terri from picking up the phone. "Don't answer it, Terri. Let her talk," Angie hissed. "We need to get as much on the machine as possible!"

"Terri, this is Nadia!" The message had started. "I need to talk with you, as soon as possible. There are things you must know. Alex *did not* shoot Logan. She….." Suddenly Nadia was interrupted and they heard her struggling with someone. "Romero, no!" Nadia's voice was frightened and then they heard what sounded like a sharp slap. "I must do this. You don't understand!"

Terri couldn't handle it anymore. She rushed to the phone and grabbed it.

"Nadia! Nadia!" Terri urgently yelled into the phone. "Nadia, are you there?" But she had hung up. Or someone had hung up for her. "Damn it!"

Terri slammed the offending instrument, back into it's stand and jumped up and down in frustration.

"Angie, for God's sake! I could have made contact with her. What the hell?" Tears were coming out of Terri's eyes thinking about Nadia and this bastard Romero, whoever he was, harming her. What would they do if this man injured her or *worse*? She had seemed to be on the brink of some sort of a confession.

Brianna came running out of her room followed by Louie, who as usual, was poofed up at being abruptly disturbed from his cozy bed. Maria came sauntering out of the kitchen and growled at her brother. They touched noses and Louie calmed down.

"Not again!" Brianna, as unsettled as the cats, complained. "What is it with all these weird phone calls?"

"I'm sorry, Terri," Angie was already by the phone to play the message back. "Who knew this poor girl was on the verge of being assaulted? Why don't people be more careful? Nadia should have made sure there was no one on her tail, if she was going to make such an important phone call. Obviously, that doesn't help us much right now but let's run this." Angie pushed the button and they heard Nadia's frightened voice.

"Oh, my God!" Brianna said. "She just said right out, that Alex *did not* kill Logan. Can you *believe* she would call and say that, over the phone no less? Man, do we need coffee or what?" She headed to the kitchen and proceeded to grind French Roast coffee beans. She set them to brew, filling the apartment with the enticing aroma of fresh coffee.

"Not only can I not believe Nadia would call me to start with," Terri, who was completely stunned said, "I also can't believe she speaks English."

"That should not surprise you, Terri," Angie said calmly. "Most of these people can speak English. They can speak English fluently. They protect themselves, however, by not revealing that fact." She pushed the button and listened to Nadia's voice again. She also checked the caller I.D. "Shit!" Angie said, disappointed.

"What now?" Terri asked, as Brianna came in with a tray of coffee and all the fixings. She filled three mugs as Angie went on.

"You have got to be kidding me! She called from a damn pay phone! Where did she find a *stupid pay* phone? I didn't think there were any out there anymore. Shit!" She grabbed her coffee and stirred in cream and sugar. "That pretty much gets us no where! What the hell did this Romero do, anyway? Follow the poor girl?" She sipped the hot brew and snorted with anger.

"Apparently," said Terri and then sadly added. "The asshole obviously smacked her around for it! Why do men do that? Why do they think they can pick on defenseless women? There are a few pay phones around yet, by the way, Angie. People do still use them once in awhile. Especially if they don't want anyone to know where they are. Crap!" She sipped her coffee and tried to think. "How do you know it's a pay phone, anyway?"

"Because it says 'pay phone' over the top of the number. See?" Angie handed Terri the phone.

"Oh, brother! Well, can we find out where this phone is and see if they are anywhere around that area?" Terri knew this was one hell of a long shot but she had to ask.

"Do the words, 'looking for a needle in a haystack' mean anything to you?" Angie was typically disgusted and disappointed, at the same time.

"We don't know if Nadia was on foot, or if she had driven somewhere. We obviously know she was followed by this Romero creep!"

Her musings were interrupted, this time by Terri's cell phone ringing.

"I do not know this number," she said cautiously answering. "Hello?"

"Terri, this is Alex Buckley," came the reply.

"Oh, Alex, hi," Terri was relieved and got questioning looks from her friends. "I looked at the number and didn't recognize it. We just......" She looked at Angie and saw her shaking her head, *No! 'Do not* tell him, that Nadia just called here!' Terri's eyes widened and she nodded, O.K.

"We were just having coffee," Terri said then. "How are Jenni and Benjamin? It's only been a couple of days but we miss them very much." This she said most sincerely. It had been a little crowded but they had enjoyed having them anyway.

"Well, that's sort of what I called about, actually," Alex said, sounding a little apologetic. "First of all, I got your cell number from Nick Guerrero. Is that alright?"

"Of course, Alex!" Terri had no problem at all with this. "Anytime that you need to call me about the children or anything, I would want you to be able to reach me. Can we help you now, in some way?"

"Um, yes," Alex sounded a little uncomfortable and Terri waited for him to go on. "Having been, uh, incapacitated for the last few days, I have several meetings to go to with my board of directors. Yes, even though it is Sunday. You can't believe what a mess this has been. I was wondering if….." Terri stopped him and answered before he asked.

"Alex, would you like to drop Jenni and Benjamin off for the afternoon? We would love to have them!" Terri told him warmly and Brianna was nodding *yes,* in the background.

Alex Buckley breathed a sigh of relief. "Thank you, so much, Terri. You can't imagine how anxious I am about my children. I can't even think about leaving them with anyone else. Would 1:00 be alright?"

"That would be fine and tell them to bring their outdoor clothes. We have more snow to play in!" Terri pushed end on her phone and looked at her friends. "Oh, Kaaayy. We've been up, for what, like about 20 minutes? Anyone have any comments? Angie, why can't I tell Alex about Nadia's phone call?"

"This has to be reported to the police, *first.* All we can do with this, is hope Nadia somehow manages to call back." Angie sipped her coffee and Terri nodded in reluctant agreement.

"Hey, the kids are coming over!" Brianna was happy. "What shall we do, besides play in the snow, I mean?"

The first thing on the agenda was breakfast. After last night's big dinner, no one felt like a huge meal. They would have lunch ready for Jenni and Benjamin when they got to the apartment. Terri quickly called Alex back to let him know. He gratefully acknowledged that would be much better for them, as opposed to a trip through the drive-through.

The girls decided on fresh fruit, cereal, and toast for breakfast. Lunch would be barbecue beef sandwiches, with chips, pickles, and cookies. Speaking of cookies, Terri and Brianna needed to make several batches of, 'The Best Chocolate Chip Cookies in the World!,' for dinners for the week. This would have to be done down in the shop, to use the large cookie sheets and confection ovens. Using the small kitchen, in the apartment, would take forever because of the bulk they needed. Making the cookies, would also provide entertainment for the kids. Also, it being Sunday afternoon, the shop would be closed, of course, so they would be undisturbed by customers and delivery people, walking in and out.

Angie had wanted to call Rico right away but Terri begged her to let him and Will sleep. Rico had a rare Sunday off. Let them both get some rest. There wasn't anything they could do about Nadia's phone call today. Also, it was not even the case of Angie and Rico's precinct. They had no idea what detectives were assigned to the case either. They finally settled the immediate problem by deciding to contact Guerrero. Terri called his cell and left a message on his voice mail, assuming he and his family were probably at church.

The three friends spent the morning, basically being lazy. They read the Sunday paper and Angie even went back to sleep for awhile. Terri washed a couple of loads of laundry and then took her shower. Brianna double checked the orders for Super Bowl sandwiches making sure, *one more time*, that they would have all the necessary supplies on hand. It was one week away and they were pretty much set. They hadn't even planned their own party yet. The death of Logan had changed everything. They had gone from their usual schedule and care free plans, to making adjustments in just about everything they normally did every day.

Brianna also checked their inventory, to make sure they had all they needed to make the cookies. Brown and white sugars, Crisco shortening, eggs, flour, etc. were all in abundant supply, down in the shop. They were all set with cookie supplies, so Brianna went to the kitchen and started browning ground beef for the sandwiches for lunch. Angie finally came out of her morning stupor and took a shower. Terri helped Brianna finish making lunch and then got out stew meat, to make a slow-cooker beef stew for supper, while Brianna took *her* shower. This particular stew, called for a quart of Terri's canned tomatoes and they made it often in the cold weather. It would cook all afternoon while they were making cookies down at the shop. Later, they would curl up all comfy, in their pajamas and have bowls of the savory stew with saltine crackers and cheeses.

Just before 1:00, Jenni and Benjamin were knocking on the door. Terri opened it, and they waved good-bye to their father.

"Terri!" Jenni jumped into Terri's arms for a huge hug. Terri squeezed her and smelled the cold in her hair and on her coat.

"Have you grown since the last time I saw you?" Terri asked, teasing the little girl.

Jenni looked at her and laughed. "We just saw you the day before yesterday, Terri." Then she thought about it a second and answered back. "Maybe a little."

Benjamin didn't say much but he looked glad to be back. The kids took off their winter clothes. Jenni hugged Brianna and Angie, finally getting to Maria, who didn't really appreciate human hugs. She got one anyway and tolerated it admirably. She wriggled out of Jenni's grasp rather quickly, however, and ran behind the sofa to play her usual game of hide and seek. Louie tore after her and then everyone started talking at the same time.

"What's it like to live in a hotel?" Brianna's question got an immediate response from both of the children.

"Awful!" Jenni said passionately. "I like it here better."

"I don't like it much either," Benjamin said. "But I don't want to complain. We are with our dad, Jen. You should be more grateful. At least Daddy is not in jail anymore." Benjamin scolded his sister but Jenni tossed her head.

"Of course I'm glad to be with Daddy, Beanie," Jenni said back at her brother. "But the hotel is too big. The people are too busy to play with us and the food is not as good as Terri's is." She ran to the sofa and looked down at Maria and Louie.

"Don't call me Beanie," Benjamin started after his sister and Terri jumped in to get control.

"O.K., you two! Let's just be glad we have this afternoon together. Are you going to school tomorrow, by the way?" Terri asked and nodded at Brianna to put lunch on. Angie, watching the whole drama with amusement, followed Brianna to the kitchen. Sustenance first and foremost.

"No, we *are not* going to school tomorrow," Benjamin answered, sounding disappointed and frustrated. Boy, there was a lot of *both* those emotions to go around lately! Terri decided not to pursue the reasons, why Alex Buckley still felt it necessary to *not* send his children to school.

They sat down to lunch, Jenni and Benjamin at the counter, Terri, Brianna and Angie, at the table.

"This meat is really good, Terri," Benjamin said, as he put down his sandwich and grabbed a napkin. "Kind of messy, though. What is it?"

Benjamin and Jenni had never had barbecue beef sandwiches! It had always been a staple for Terri's family, as it was economical and easy. How would they have managed without ground beef? Ground beef and a lot of chicken, along with fresh seafood of course, had been on the Springe table, as she and her siblings were growing up. They had always had a garden, too. That was the one thing, Terri wished she could have in the city. She had to settle for the Farmer's Market, however, and that was pretty close to the real thing.

"It's an old family recipe," Terri came back. "I'm glad you guys like it. Eat up now. We have lots of work to do!"

"Work, Terri? On Sunday?" Jenni sounded shocked at the sacrilege.

Terri laughed and Brianna started clearing plates and tossing napkins. "Oh, you guys will like this kind of work," Angie said. "You'll even be able to *eat* your work."

Jenni and Benjamin looked puzzled and then quickly raced each other to the bathroom to wash up.

An hour later, they were taste testing, 'The Best Chocolate Chip Cookies in the World!,' and licking melting chocolate, off of their fingers. They each had tall glasses of cold milk, and flour and sugar all over their clothes. Terri laughed out loud, for *like the millionth time* today, at the sight of them and everyone was having an amazing good time.

"Whoever thought work could taste this good?" Benjamin asked, as he grabbed another cookie. Jenni nodded and took a huge gulp of ice cold milk.

"I've never tasted anything like these, Terri," Jenni said, agreeing enthusiastically with her brother, *for once.*

"You never will again either," Brianna put in her expert opinion and took a bite of a warm cookie. "Barbecues and Terri's chocolate chip cookies in one day. You two are certainly getting a good food education on this visit."

"I think I've gained about 10 pounds this week-end!" Angie complained, as she took a bite of her third cookie. "I won't be able to fit into my uniform, by the time they let me go back to work."

"Have a *diet* cookie, Ang," Terri teased, as she pulled another warm sheet of cookies out of the oven.

"What's a diet cookie?" Benjamin asked, perplexed by the thought.

"One cookie!" Angie said forlornly. "Who can eat, only *one* of these though? It's impossible!"

It took most of the afternoon, to get the cookies all baked, cooled, and packed into plastic containers, with wax paper in between the layers. They made enough cookies, some with walnuts, some without, for Terri and Brianna's regular customers, for people going in and out of the shop and for Jenni and Benjamin to take back to the hotel. Despite their protests, the two tired youngsters were happy to see their father when he picked them up at 6:00. They never did get out to play in the snow. Oh well, maybe next time.

Terri, Brianna, and Angie, settled down later with hot bowls of beef stew. The tender chunks of beef, with carrots, potatoes, onions, celery, and spices, in the tomato broth, warmed them up and filled them up. Along with crackers and cheese and hot tea, of course, it made for the perfect winter evening supper.

They watched, "The Three Musketeers," with a gorgeous, young, Keifer Sutherland, a very sexy, hot, Charlie Sheen, and the lovable Oliver Platt.

It had quickly become one of Brianna's favorites after she and Terri and Angie, had become fast friends. "All for one and one for all!" They said it often and meant it. The three women would do anything for each other. It meant a lot to Brianna, as she had grown-up with so few friends and very little emotional security. Despite her wealth, with the ability to have pretty much *anything, anyone* could want in this material world, Brianna loved her life with Terri and Angie.

Terri watched her snuggling on the couch with Maria and still couldn't believe how fortunate she was, to have Brianna in her life. She took another bite of stew, looked at her phone and saw that it was 8:30.

"I wonder why Nick hasn't gotten back to me yet," she said just as her phone chirped! "Sheez," Terri said then. "I hate when that happens! Yeah, it's Nick." They talked for a few minutes, Terri explaining the phone call from Nadia the best she could and then saying good-night.

"Yeah, he's coming tomorrow," Terri said, as she put down her phone.

"Of course he is," Brianna wasn't surprised as she got up and started to clear their supper dishes. "Did you expect anything less? I told you he's the best."

"The best and then some," Terri agreed, as she finished her stew and helped Brianna clean up the dishes. Angie yawned and started getting her blankets and pillows settled again for the night. She would still be off work, for at least another week. That being the case, she was happy to stick around and help Terri and Brianna get meals ready tomorrow for their weekly clients.

The movie was over, back in it's case, the T.V. shut off once more. Angie was ensconced on the comfy couch. Everyone had taken their turn in the bathroom and they all settled in for the night. Louie and Maria, cuddled together, at Angie's feet. Brianna and Terri retired to their rooms.

Terri looked outside at the street light peeking through her window and could see it was snowing again. Please call me back, Nadia, she said to herself, hoping to send brain waves to the girl somehow. Please be all right, Nadia. *Please be all right.* Terri could feel herself choking up. All this time, she had seen Nadia, in the back ground. She never spoke to anyone. She never let on that she even existed, with a word or a gesture. Terri realized that now. No one knew, that all the while Nadia had been doing her job, she had basically been invisible to the clueless Logan. While her nasty boss had assumed she didn't even speak English, who knew what Nadia had seen and heard? She obviously *did* know what had happened. She was trying to find a way to get to Terri, to clear this up. Would they be able to clear this up without her? Terri didn't see how. Alex was out of jail, for the moment. However, unless it could be proved, beyond a shadow of a doubt that he was innocent, Alex Buckley could still end up standing trial for the murder of his wife.

Please Nadia, call me back, *please.* Maybe if she thought it enough, it would actually happen. Terri was tired but she kept thinking it, watching the snow falling softly and keeping it in her thoughts, as she went to sleep. Please call Nadia, *please.*

Chapter Twenty-Three

Monday morning was a busy one. Terri tried not to think about Nadia too much. They *all* tried not to. But every time the business phone rang, everyone jumped just the same.

Nick showed up at about 10:30 that morning. Terri was browning, yet more ground beef, to make a basic 'Hamburger Macaroni Casserole,' for one of their client meals. They had changed their presentation of the meals, quite a lot since Terri had first started making them on her own. After preparing a large quantity of casserole in a huge baking pan, they scooped family sized portions into aluminum containers and covered them with plastic covers. Home makers were able to slip these containers, after removing the plastic covers, of course, into the oven and warm them up for a family-style supper. Brianna was cutting up cooked chicken breast, to put into a wonderful, Chicken-Rice Mushroom Soup. With the soup, Terri would include chicken and ham salad, to put on bread or fresh rolls. The girls would have this soup for *their* supper tonight, with chicken salad sandwiches. Terri still made the Twin Pines chicken and ham salad, potato salad and cole slaw. Nothing could beat these recipes, she had been given permission to take away from her old job. Angie was browning boneless pork chops, to go with a savory mushroom gravy, mashed potatoes and colorful veggies. Succulent, thick pieces of boneless, snow-white haddock, with butter, would be the fourth meal. Paired with the fish, would be twice baked potatoes, with bacon bits, broccoli, and sour cream. Tucked in with this meal, would be pretty lemon slices and extra butter. The potatoes were delicious and a client favorite. They made enough to have with a meal themselves, later in the week.

Nick Guerrero sniffed the air appreciatively, as he sat down and opened his brief case. Terri put a piping hot mug of coffee and a plate of chocolate chip cookies in front of him and he nodded gratefully.

"When did you girls have time to bake these cookies?" Nick took a bite and a look of pure ecstasy came to his face. "Oh, my God, how did I live without ever tasting these? Holy Moses! Terri, you have got to give me the recipe for these, for my wife to try. These are fantastic!"

"Well, first of all, we baked them yesterday afternoon and Jenni and Benjamin helped. What do you think of that?" Terri watched Nick with satisfaction, as he picked up another cookie.

"Jenni and Benjamin were here? Oh, yeah, I suppose that makes sense. I certainly know where Alex was yesterday. I was with him. Not my normal relaxing Sunday but the last week or so, has been anything but normal, I'm afraid." He took another sip of coffee and Brianna topped off his cup.

"I was thinking the exact same thing myself, last night," Terri said, as she sat down at the table with him. "Ever since Logan called last Monday, with that ridiculous food order, nothing has seemed the least bit normal." She looked at Nick and sighed. "Want to hear Nadia's phone call or what? Maybe you'd rather sit here and eat cookies all morning instead."

"That would be great but I guess I'd better listen to the phone call." Nick sighed too and took out his note book. "Let's get on with it then."

Before Terri pushed the button, to let Nadia's voice float out into the room, she looked outside to make sure no one was anywhere near the shop.

Angie and Brianna said nothing. Brianna put a cover on the huge soup pot, to allow it to simmer and thicken, and then continued browning the ground beef, with onions, salt and pepper. Angie slipped the browned pork chops into one of the big ovens and waited.

Terri looked down the street, first left, then right. Something about a vehicle down the block looked more than a bit familiar, however.

"Oh, no," she groaned.

"What?" Brianna, Angie, and Nick all asked, at exactly the same time.

Terri looked at them as if she had seen an apparition. "It's Davis and Johannsen. They're parked down the block. I can't see the car that well but I'm almost positive it's them."

Nick got up and looked down the block where Terri saw the car parked.

"Oh, yeah, that's them alright. What are they up to now? If they were going to case this joint again, they should have at least commandeered a different vehicle. Not too smart, if you ask me," he commented with disgust.

"Commandeered?" Brianna asked. "You mean, like, as in, 'with every intention of bringing it back?'" Angie elbowed her and they both started giggling like teenagers.

"Alright, you two!" Terri tried to scold them, as she started laughing too.

"O.K., maybe just borrowed," Nick said with a grin at the girls, as he thought the problem through. "Although, that might depend on who you're *borrowing* it from." More giggles came from Brianna and Angie, after this remark.

"Well......, so what do we do?" Terri asked, glad that Nick was with them this time. Obviously, Davis and Johannsen had seen Nick arrive, so they weren't going to come into the shop as long as he was there.

"Nothing," Nick said firmly. "Absolutely nothing. I'll talk to them before I leave and tell them to lay off. Now, let's hear that message."

Everyone sobered and quieted down while Terri played Nadia's message, and Nick listened carefully. He listened to it several times, taking careful notes. Terri's nerves were completely frayed by the time he was done. Hearing Nadia's pleading voice over and over was spooky, to say the least. Terri only hoped that she was still alive. She *prayed* the poor girl was still alive. Another dead body, would be more than any of them could handle right now. They had to find her alive and well, *somehow.*

"Don't let anything happen to that message," Nick said, as he prepared to leave. "How nice it would be to have answering machines, that still had those tiny little tapes in them. I could take it with me. Obviously, I'll have to leave it in the care of you ladies."

"Thanks, Nick," Brianna gave him a brief hug. "Oh, don't forget about the two thugs down the street, K?"

"Don't worry about those two. I will dispatch them for you. Whatever is going on in this investigation, those two watching your shop is out of line. Leave it to me. I'll call you later." He patted Brianna's head and lightly kissed her shinny hair. Then he was gone.

Terri watched as Nick got into his car and headed down the street. He stopped briefly, *very briefly*, to speak to Davis and Johannsen. Whatever he said, certainly was effective. The car took off and sped by, without so much as it occupants giving the shop a glance.

"Whew! What next?" Angie finally spoke up. "I'm just about ready to scream. What about you guys?"

"Ditto," said Brianna, as she opened jars of canned tomatoes and starting adding them to the ground beef. Terri cut and stirred in fresh mushrooms, along with oregano and garlic salt. She mixed in large cans of tomatoe sauce, evenly blending the ingredients, and slipped the big pan of casserole into a hot oven. She also answered Angie's question, only with a lot more words.

"Yeah, I'm getting there. Freak city. Hanging on by my fingernails. Anyway you wanna put it, I'm getting there,"

Terri said, washing her hands and looking around. "What do we have to do yet? The fish and the twice bakes. O.K. Let's finish up." Terri felt more jittery then ever. Keep calm, she tried to tell herself. Keep calm.

They kept busy the rest of the morning, still jumped every time the phone rang and just waited for the next thing to happen. But what would that be? At 12:15, Rico called Terri's cell and said that he was dropping Will off at 1:00. He and Angie could spend the afternoon, resting and watching movies. Terri and Brianna would deliver meals and run errands. Rico would be at the station, untill 7:00, or so, if nothing unusual came up. Terri told him that soup and sandwich would be waiting when he came back to pick up Will.

Nadia's recorded message was still under wraps, per Angie's decision. She not only thought it best to leave it in Nick Guerrero's hands, she was also still trying to protect Will. The whole situation was beginning to take shape, for the three friends. They discussed it and each filled in the gaps.

Logan had somehow set the whole thing up. She had not planned on being the one to die, *obviously.* Alex had told Terri, straight out, that Logan *wanted his children.* She wanted Jenni and Benjamin and, of course, his money. What could be a better plan, then to set up a break in and make it appear as if Alex had been killed? The 'burgler' runs off. Logan tells the police that she didn't see anything. Alex is out of the way. It was risky but it was workable. Also, being pregnant, possibly with another man's child, gave her even more reason to *need* Alex out of the way. All Logan had to do, was let the authorities assume it was her husband's child, thus getting their sympathy. She takes over complete care of Jenni and Benjamin, tells them the baby is their little brother or sister and voila!, her life is all set up *real nice like.* All she has to do is find herself another man, if not the father of the baby and enjoy herself for the rest of her life. Poor Jenni and Benjamin are none the wiser. They love Logan and trust her. Logan was counting on that too.

Nadia and Jasmine probably knew the whole plan. Nadia was trying to get to Terri, to clear it up. The big question now was, *who had shot Logan?* How did *she* end up dead instead of Alex?

The three women were completely spent. Brianna and Angie were getting their supper ready. Will was watching the news. Rico would be over in a few minutes to have the meal with them and then take Will back to his apartment. It had been snowing off and on, most of the day but now had cleared up. The apartment, was as usual, warm, cozy and cheerful. It was Monday, so almost time for the latest episode of *24.*

Terri was digging around in a pile of newspapers and magazines, with a puzzled look on her face. What had she done with her calendar? I can't get a damn thing done, without my calendar, she was thinking. Why do I always misplace that thing? Terri's calendar, along with her cell phone, was her lifeline. Everything had to be written down carefully, for each day, in each little square. She was a nut about her calendar and drove everyone else nuts because she was always misplacing it.

"Has anyone seen my calendar?" Terri asked and whined at the same time. "Where did I put that stupid thing? Crap! I'm such a bonehead!"

Angie and Brianna looked at each other with a, *not again?,* glance.

Brianna thought for a second and then remembered.

"Terri, the last time I saw it, was in the truck. Where's your huge bag? The two things are usually in the same place. Don't you normally put the calendar *inside* the bag?" They also teased Terri because for everyday use, she always carried a huge satchel.

"My purse, and by the way, I need everything in *my huge bag*, is on my bed. I must have left the calendar in the truck. I'll go down and look." Terri grabbed her *huge* bag because the truck keys were in it. "If I'm not back in five minutes, send out a posse," she said, as she grabbed her leather coat, the closest one to the door.

"If you're not back in *two* minutes, I'll send out a posse," Angie warned.

"C'mon, hurry up. Supper is almost ready. You'll probably run into Rico, before you come back up, so don't do any messing around. Both of you get back up here, a.s.a.p!" She sounded serious and Terri was too tired to argue.

"Yes, Mother!" Terri shot back, as she slipped into her coat and dug into the front pocket for the truck keys. At least she was organized enough, to have a specific place, in the purse, to put the keys. Otherwise, she would be looking for them all night. She carefully maneuvered the steps, which were covered with a fresh layer of fluffy snow. The truck was about five feet from the steps.

Terri *felt* them before she *heard* them. She had just opened the driver door and spotted her calendar on the seat. It was too late to do anything, as she was quickly pushed into her own truck. She reached for her precious calendar and the door lock of the passenger side. As soon as she unlocked the door, it opened and someone else got in. Before she could make a sound, she was trapped between two people, dressed completely in black.

"Who are you?" Terri managed to stammer, as she was squeezed in between two bodies. "What the hell are you doing? If you want my truck, just take the damn thing but please let me go," she begged.

"Si, we want your truck," a familier voice said, "but we also want you. Nadia needs to tell you some things and we will take you to her now. Don't worry, Terri. Please don't be scared. I won't let anyone hurt you but this was the only plan we could come up with." There was an accent, of course, but the English was flawless, just like Nadia's message on the phone.

Terri couldn't believe her ears or her eyes. She looked at the driver and *did not* recognize him. He started the truck easily, backed out and began driving down the street. The passenger, on her right however, was Ignacio. They were stealing her truck and for the *second time, in less than a year*, she was being kidnapped!

Chapter Twenty-Four

"Ignacio, please listen to me. This is a *very* bad idea," Terri tried to reason with him. "Kidnapping is a federal offense. If you guys aren't already in trouble, this is not going to help the situation. Please take me back, *now* and you can just keep the truck. I'll tell everyone that I just gave it to you. How about that?" She was shaking and absolutely petrified but she tried to sound casual and friendly.

"We not only *need* your truck Terri, we need time. If you are on your way to somewhere, which you must be or you wouldn't be wearing that coat and carrying such a large bag, we will use that time. We will take you to our living quarters. We will tell you the whole story. Then you can go back to your friends and tell them what happened, if you wish. No one will *ever* find us. Also, by the time we get done with your truck, no one will ever find that either. We have thought of everything. Now please, just stop talking. We will be there in a few minutes." Ignacio sounded firm and confident but he didn't sound dangerous.

So, they had the idea that Terri was on her way, to some function or other and no one would think to look for her, for at least a couple of hours? In her truck? They thought she was going somewhere, *this time of the night, in her truck?* It was fortunate that the dumb old thing even had working headlights. They never took the truck *anywhere* at night. She and Brianna had been making plans to buy a new one this summer. The truck she wouldn't miss but would they really let her go? At the moment, she had no choice but to wait and see.

They had only been driving for about 10 minutes but Terri was totally lost. The driver, who had not spoken, had taken several turns and in different directions, obviously trying to confuse her. Well, it was working! Terri had no idea, where in the hell they were. Why wasn't there a cop car on their tail? Brianna and Angie, would have been looking for her for several minutes by this time. What was going on here? The truck was gone, she was gone. They had probably missed Rico, by mere seconds. Where was everbody? Would no one come to her rescue?

"We are here." Ignacio simply said, as the truck pulled into an alley and both men opened the doors. Ignacio took Terri's arm and pulled her, none too gently, out the door. She hung on to her bag. The stupid calendar fell to the truck floor. She grabbed it and tucked it into a side pocket, where it should have been in the first place. She didn't even have her cell phone with her! It was sitting on her night stand, where she had put it down, after she had last spoken to Rico.

Terri looked around at the walls of the buildings on each side of them and saw several windows, with lights behind shades. They walked about fifteen feet down the alley and into the third door, on the right. Ignacio led Terri down a short hallway and into a warm kitchen.

"Oh, Dios mio! You did what you said. You have brought Terri, Ignacio." It was Jasmine and Terri nearly cried when she saw her. Jasmine wouldn't let anything happen to her, would she? Terri was hoping this would be the case. She had never been anything but kind and polite to all of them. Jasmine went on. "You poor child," she fussed over Terri. "They drag you here, against your will. Ignacio, Romero, this is a bad thing." So the other man *was* Romero. Where was Nadia? "Are you feeling fine, meha?" Jasmine asked. Her English wasn't quite as fluent as Ignacio's but Terri nodded.

The kitchen smelled wonderful and was sparkling clean. Terri had not only been taken against her will, she was missing her supper! She felt her stomach churning. "Where is Nadia?" She finally had gotten a hold of herself, enough to ask the most important question.

"I am here, Teresita," Nadia came in behind them, from another room. Terri turned around, at the Spanish pronunciation of her name. She had actually gotten very good grades in Spanish and had loved the class. She knew about as much as she had managed to retain. She hardly spoke Spanish well though and she felt ashamed of that fact suddenly. They knew her language but she barely knew theirs. Where was the balance here?

"Nadia," Terri went to her and they hugged each other tightly. "When you didn't call me back, I thought something terrible had happened to you." She turned and looked accusingly at Romero. "I heard him slap you," she said pointing at the other man, who still hadn't spoken. "I was afraid, that he had done you serious harm. You are alright, though?" Terri looked closely at Nadia and was surprised when the other girl began to laugh.

"That fool you see there, is my cousin Romero. He didn't slap me. I slapped him!" She laughed again. "I have been beating him up, ever since we were children. I suppose that is wrong of me but he is too ashamed to admit it." Romero glared at his cousin and Terri strained to suppress the laughter in her own throat. Amusing as that part was, they still had to straighten out this mess and Terri had many questions. That had to wait for awhile however, as Jasmine had food prepared for all of them. They got no argument from Terri, as she was told to sit down and eat with them. She couldn't help it. She was famished and everything smelled so good.

Terri didn't feel afraid in the least. She wasn't at all sure, how she would get home though. She assumed that her truck, had quickly been taken away and was being disguised for some sort of get away. What else could they want it for? For now, she needed to eat, if for no other reason, just to keep up her strength.

Jasmine and Nadia put out dish after dish of hot food, from which came many delicious smells, making Terri's stomach growl.

"You are hungry meha, yes?" Jasmine smiled at Terri.

"Yes, I guess I am," she said back. Jasmine must have heard the noises coming from her empty tummy, making Terri feel only a *little* embarrassed.

Terri tried everything they put in front of her and it was all wonderful. Pork with red beans, tomatoes, onions and celery. Rellenitos, stuffed planteens, with black beans. Tostados, with refried beans, cheese, and chicken. Tacos, with many different delicious fillings. They certainly cooked with a lot of beans! Terri wasn't sure how her stomach would react to that fact but everything tasted so good, she just kept eating. Where were the Tums when she needed them? They offered Terri soda to drink and she chose a 7-up. It would help settle her stomach. The men drank beer. Jasmine and Nadia drank coffee.

"Oh, Jasmine," Terri said enthusiastically. "Your Guatemalan dishes are absolutely wonderful! I would love to have the recipes," she added. Nadia was washing dishes, pots, and pans in a metal sink, as Terri dried them with a clean hand towel. It had been a long time, since she hadn't just stacked the dishes in a dishwasher. She kind of liked the old-fashioned way. It brought people closer together and gave them a chance to bond. It was nice.

Terri finally snapped out of it though and remembered where she was, as in, *not at home.* "I have to let my friends know where I am," she finally begged Nadia. "They will be frantic. Please, Nadia. There must be a way I can contact them."

Nadia thought for a second. "We have much to tell you, Teresita. If we give you a chance to contact your friends, will you promise to stay for awhile? Now, *I am* begging you!" Tears of fright rolled down the girl's face and Terri's heart sank.

"I promise, I will not leave until we have talked this all out," Terri said, as she finished drying a large cast iron frying pan, that she would kill to own.

Good thing, that was just a cliché! Terri would not kill, to do or have *anything*.

"Ignacio, Romero," Nadia called into the other room, where the men were watching T.V. "Come to the kitchen. It is time to tell Teresita, what happened to Mrs. Logan!" She pronounced Mrs., as *meeses*. Nadia's English, was also quite fluent but Terri loved her accent. It sounded so romantic or something. Ah, the Latin languages! Along with French, they were the most appealing and sensual. Terri then made up her mind to bone up on her Spanish, as soon as possible. She would take every class, the university had to offer next semester. Maybe, she would even try a French class for good measure, learn while she was still young.

Romero came into the room and Nadia demanded his cell phone. He sheepishly handed it over. Nadia gave it to Terri.

"Please, Teresita," she said, "make this call very short. We must not be found." Terri looked confused. "Trust me. We will tell you everything. You will understand."

Terri quickly called Angie's cell. "Terri, oh my God!" Angie's reaction was understandable. "Tell us where you are! We will come and get you. Terri, where are you?" Angie's voice had turned to complete panic, as opposed to her calm, police-like manner.

"Angie, listen to me. I haven't much time. I am fine. I am with Ignacio, Nadia, and Jasmine. They are going to tell me what happened. I'll call you back soon." Terri reluctantly shut off the phone. Whatever was happening here, she did not want to be found, or for *them* to be found. At least not yet.

They sat down at the table and it was Nadia who, somehow taking command, spoke first. She informed Terri, first of all, that she and Romero, *were not* in this country legally. Ignacio and Jasmine were. Nadia and Romero, would take Terri's truck and leave tonight. They had contacted someone, to pick them up at a check point in Virginia. From there, they would go to another check point and so on. "We cannot go back to Guatemala," Nadia said sadly. "We will get jobs in some other place, you understand?" Terri nodded, feeling a terrible pain for them.

"What happened to Logan Buckley? You must tell me now." Terri needed to know what had occurred and hope the authorities would believe it.

"Logan wanted me to kill Senor Buckley," Ignacio said, without feeling. "She was forcing me to take the gun. 'It would pay well,' she said to me. Enough to bring more family here. Get legal papers for Nadia."

"Logan knew that Nadia was here illegally?" Terri suspected as much.

"Si," Ignacio went on. "We did not, how you say, struggle with the gun, like in the movies, you understand?" Terri nodded. "The gun, it was jammed. I think that is the correct word." Terri nodded again. "She was cursing, hitting the gun, trying to put bullets into it. We were arguing. I did not want to kill Senor Buckley. He was a foolish man but he was good to us, yes?"

Terri was starting to picture it now. Logan didn't know how to load or use Alex's handgun. She must have been trying to put a shell into the chamber and wasn't handling it properly. It happened all the time but as a rule, to children. Logan had been a child herself. A foolish, foolish, *selfish* child.

"Ignacio, did the gun go off, as Logan was trying to load it? Did she foolishly hold it towards her body? It went off by accident? Is that what happened?" Terri laid out the scenario for him.

"Si, si!" Ignacio said excitedly. "The gun, it go off. She fall, to the floor and there was blood, much blood. I thought I would be sick."

"My mama and I, we are running to the hall," Nadia said then. "Mrs. Buckley, she is on the floor moaning, crying for help. The police, they were coming. We heard the noises. We heard the police cars. Senor Buckley, he come down the stairs and told us to run away. 'Go away as fast as you can,' he told us. We did what he said. Later we heard she is dead. We are very much afraid. Do you understand?"

Terri understood perfectly now. Foolish, selfish woman! Logan Adams-Buckley had shot herself. What a sad ending, to what could have been a good and decent life. She *could have* had everything she wanted. The money, Jenni and Benjamin but she didn't want to share, even with the kind, lonely, Alex Buckley. She wanted it all, *all for herself.* Foolish, foolish girl.

"I do understand," Terri said, "but I have a couple more questions. First of all, who wrecked the police car and tried to harm my friends?"

Nadia looked more stricken then ever. "Diego, my, how do you say it? Lover," she wiped away a tear. "He was very frightened for me. We were to marry. I sent him away. I could not marry someone who would do this. It was muy stupido! I was angry. He is gone. Your friends, they are fine Teresita?"

"Yes, they are going to be fine. Diego was very fortunate….. lucky, as some say, they were not hurt. There is one more thing I must tell you. Logan, Mrs. Buckley, she was going to have a child when she died." Terri looked at Ignacio and Romero. "Were either one of you possibly responsible for that?"

They didn't need to answer, however. Jasmine, Nadia, and Ignacio, all looked at Romero. Tears were fast coming out of his eyes and he just laid his head down on the table and sobbed.

Chapter Twenty-Five

Spring was coming and they were all thankful. Terri was thankful to be alive and well and with good friends. Angie was thankful she had the day off. Brianna was thankful she was passing all of her classes, with flying colors, *again!* Louie and Maria were thankful to sit by the big open bay window, to smell the spring smells and listen to the birds. They were *all thankful*, that baseball had started!

Terri sighed like she always did as she looked out the window and got a goofy look from Angie.

"So, what, may I ask, are you sighing about now?" Angie was the practical one. Terri was the dramatic one. They cancelled each other out pretty well that way.

"I was thinking about Nadia," Terri couldn't help it. "I'm really glad that she and Romero got away."

"Yes, and you aided them quite nicely by just letting them have your truck! Not to mention your lousy timing, going down to look for that dumb calendar of yours," Angie came back with. "I know, I know. You didn't give a damn about the truck but Terri c'mon! They broke an awful lot of laws, ya' gotta admit that! They could have just as easily killed you, you have to admit that, too."

"I really don't want to believe they would have hurt me." Terri just didn't want to give up her feelings. "But you just can't imagine, what they are dealing with Ang. You can't believe what it was like to see Romero cry. He really loved Logan. I could see that. He lost her and his baby. It was terrible to see that kind of grief. They never would have hurt me Angie, I know that for sure. I never felt afraid, especially when I saw Jasmine and Nadia."

"You know that Logan didn't give a shit about Romero, Terri," Brianna got on Angie's side. "She was just using him, like she used everyone else. She even used us. God, that still pisses me off!"

Terri knew her friends were right. Logan had used them all. She had placed the huge order with Terri's Table, to make it appear as if she was a loving wife to Alex. If she had been planning a large party for his family, wouldn't that make her look good and generous? She didn't realize it at the time but Alex *had* no family. Had she planned to profess ignorance about that? Who knew! She crawled all over Alex, in front of other people, as they had suspected all along to put on a show. She was just too immature to realize, that she was getting just the opposite reaction from others.

Will had taken the whole story hard, *really* hard. They were left with no choice, but to tell him the truth about the cousin he had loved so much. He had asked for a leave of absence from work. He went home and when he got back a month later, not another word came from him about it. Family was family but every family tree had it's nuts! There was nothing more to say. Angie still hadn't stopped being angry about it. She had missed her partner and her genuine feelings for Will, made it difficult for her to forgive.

When Ignacio had taken Terri to a 'drop-off point' of her own, she had stood on the street, cold and alone for nearly a half an hour. Promising to call the police, Ignacio must have run into complications. Her rescue was anything but immediate. Her *rescuer*, as it turned out, had been none other than Captain Fred Farrell! When a police car finally raced up, Terri was sure in her romantic mind, that Rico had come to find her. Imagine her surprise, when the big 'Herman Munster' captain, had unfolded himself from the driver's seat.

"Well, well," he had said in his scary booming voice when he saw Terri shivering and cowering in the corner of a store front. "If it isn't my buddy Rico Mathew's girlfriend, Terri Springe! We've been looking for you for quite awhile, young lady." Terri chose to ignore the 'young lady' part. She guessed, compared to this guy, she *was* young. "Wanna come in where it's nice and warm?" Terri nodded *yes,* very quickly and Captian Farrell opened the back door. "I'd let you ride shot-gun," he joked "but I have a partner, too."

Terri was happy to see the female officer with him. She was introduced to Officer Laura Clayton, who handed her a soft blanket and a Styrofoam cup of hot coffee. It wasn't the best coffee in the world but it was warm and comforting.

'What had taken them so long?,' she had asked. Ignacio had called the police, just like he had promised. But fear of being found, had kept the call short and the directions to where he had left Terri scanty and confusing. Boston was a big city. She still wasn't sure where she had even been. All she remembered, was that she was positive she was going to freeze to death. That hadn't happened. Captain Farrell and Officer Clayton, after reporting they had found 'Ms. Springe,' had taken her to the nearest hospital. Terri wasn't really paying attention to where they were going but much to her relief, when they got there, Rico was by the emergency ward door to greet them. He had grabbed Terri and squeezed her, until she laughed and told him to loosen his grasp! She was crying and laughing at the same time. Rico kissed her and held her and kissed her some more. For just this once, Terri didn't mind a little P.D.A!

After the doctors told them Terri was fine and nothing was frozen, Rico had taken her home. Good thing she had been wearing her fabulous leather coat! When she got home, Brianna cried, and squeezed Terri as hard as *she* could, and Angie yelled and yelled at her. This, of course, had been Angie's way of being afraid and upset and glad to see her friend safe and in one piece.

"Hey, Terri," Angie rousted her out of the rest of her thoughts. "I'm sorry. You are right about some stuff. But they should *not* have kidnapped you. Let's just let it go now, huh? We can't talk about this anymore. Let's get ready for the game, K?"

"K.," said Terri, with one last sigh, finally snapping out it. "It may be awhile before I forget about this one, though. It pretty much sapped every emotion I had and then some."

They were going to the first home game of the season, naturally. It was 9:00 in the morning and they had plenty of time but they wanted to eat lunch somewhere first. Amber and Kelli, would be going with them. Brianna, as it turned out, just happened to have a boyfriend, with tickets of his own. They all could have flipped, when she brought him home, *finally*. His name was Pete Fazio, a transplant from Brooklyn, of course. So when Brianna had introduced him, Angie's first reaction had been, "Holy Sopranos!"

"Always nice to meet the fans," Pete had immediately come back with, charming accent and all. Holy Mackerel! He was one of them! The rest, as they say, was history.

Angie headed for the shower. She had spent the night, *again* because they had gone to a late movie. It had almost seemed as if, Terri's experience had brought the three friends even closer, if that was possible.

They were right now, in the middle of turning the rooms above Terri and Brianna's shop, into one huge apartment. There would be *three* bedrooms, a big open kitchen and dining area, a luxurious bathroom, the whole works! A big bay window, had already been installed, in the front of the apartment for Louie and Maria to sit in. Since Terri and Brianna owned the building, there was no rent to pay, just utilities. The business was doing fantastic and they had hired three students, who lived in the city, to help out part-time. They were Brianna's friends, so they were hard-working, fun and reliable.

Terri still looked out the window, as Angie showered and Brianna put in laundry. Their new apartment would have a proper laundry room too. For now, Terri wondered what Jenni and Benjamin were doing. After the investigation had been closed and it had been determined that all evidence confirmed the story told to Terri, the kids had gone back to school. Alex had found an old but modest home, not far from Judith and George, which was nice. It had the back lawn Alex had talked about. He had hired a proper housekeeper, who was a lovely grandma type that Jenni and Benjamin loved to have waiting for them, when they got home. Alex came home at a proper time most nights, and the housekeeper went home to her husband. Four nights a week, Alex, Jenni, and Benjamin sat down to a proper supper, with delicious meals from Terri's Table.

Davis and Johannsen, the pesky F.B.I. guys, as it turned out, had even tried to help in Terri's rescue. They had actually been watching her apartment, the night that Ignacio and Romero had stolen her truck and taken Terri with them. Unfortunately, they had just gone to a nearby gas station to get coffee. They saw the truck go by and immediately assumed it was suspicious. Running back to the car, they had raced after them. Davis had even tossed his coffee! But Romero had been too slick for them and after a few blocks, they had lost them. Terri had never quite figured out, what the two were up to and they wouldn't say. She guessed, that was between them and Alex Buckley. She had been grateful nevertheless, that they had tried their best to help.

Everything is in order, Terri thought now. Everything is fine. Why do I still feel so anxious? She and Rico were fine. Terri had left off prying into his private life too much, for the time being. He still had issues, but who didn't? He had also become, just a touch more protective but it was O.K. with Terri, *for now*. Basically, they weren't taking it too fast *or* too slow. He had finally stopped disappearing, for the so-called, family emergencies and Terri had not yet pursued it. They were just moving at a normal pace, dating for real and looking forward to all the big movies coming out this Spring. 'The Da Vinci Code' 'X-Men Three' 'Superman Returns' Rico had gotten tickets ahead for all the movies, for the two of them and all their friends. They wanted to be the first to see each one. Terri had turned him into a movie nut, just like her and Angie. Then, of course, 'Pirates of the Caribbean: Dead Man's Chest' would be coming out in the summer. When would the third one come out? Everyone was already asking. How fickle and demanding they all were!

Terri's cell phone went off at her elbow, once again interrupting her thoughts. It was never far from her now. She kept it with her, *at all times*, no matter what. She didn't recognize the number but answered it quickly.

"Oh, my God, Courtney! Hi, Honey!" This made Brianna pay attention. Angie came out of the bathroom in her robe, just in time to hear Terri greeting her Wisconsin cousin. She and Brianna looked at each other, put up their right hands, grinned, and wiggled their thumbs. Terri waved them off and whispered, "Knock it off, you two!" They snickered in very bratty fashion but waited. Something exciting was up!

After several, 'your kiddings' and 'that's so cools' and 'I can't waits,' Terri closed her cell and looked at her two smartie pants pals.

"Well, you two dorks," Terri began, pausing and dragging it out. "It's time to take that vacation we've been talking about." Brianna and Angie looked at each other, with wide eyes but said nothing. Terri went on. "Courtney and her fiance have set the date! I am her maid-of-honor. They are getting married this fall. Prepare to pack your bags. We are going to Sister Bay, Wisconsin, in beautiful Door County!"

To be continued……..

Recipes for Double Truffle

Quik Chicken Curry Divan

This recipe, along with creamy home-made macaroni and cheese, are by all accounts and opinions, the ultimate comfort food. Terri, Angie and Brianna, make it often for themselves on cold winter nights and for 'Terri's Table' customers. For extras, add some crispy bread, and/or a salad and you're set for a delicious, warm, wholesome meal. Enjoy!

Start with:
2-3 lbs. of chicken breasts (fresh or frozen)   Leftovers from a rotissere or roasting chicken, may also be used, if you have enough.

3-4 large pieces of broccoli (Cut into smaller pieces, throw away tough ends, trim off any leaves or brown spots on stems.)

For sauce:
1 can of cream of chicken soup (Fill can with water, scraping edges with small rubber spatula, getting as much of soup as possible. Add 1tsp. of chicken broth granules to water in can.)

1 cup of mayo (Hellman's recommended or your favorite brand)
1 cup of shredded cheese (whatever you have on hand, even a couple of types combined, such as medium cheddar, Swiss, or mild brick)
1 tsp. of curry

Sprinkle on top:
½ cup of plain breadcrumbs
Paprika (for sprinkling over top to make it pretty)

Thoroughly cook chicken, if using raw of frozen, in microwave. Start cooking on high, for three-four minutes, on a micro-wave safe plate. Turn chicken pieces carefully, (will be very hot) and cook for three-four minutes more. Keep checking chicken, also carefully carving into smaller slices or pieces. Chicken must be completely cooked!

As you are preparing chicken, also have broccoli cooking in kettle on stovetop. Add a tsp. or 2 of salt to boiling water, if you wish. Be careful, not to over-cook your broccoli or it will turn to mush! Boil until pieces can be pierced with the tip of a knife, and are bright green. Drain broccoli, (careful again, do not burn yourself) and place pieces into bottom of large casserole dish, or medium sized blue oval roaster, with cover. Place cooked chicken slices and/or pieces over broccoli.

Mix ingredients for sauce. Use water and chicken broth, mixed in soup can, to add to soup, mayo, cheese and curry, (in separate bowl, of course) to thin sauce, making it easy to pour over chicken and broccoli (you may not have to use all of water in can, don't make it too soupy). Use rubber spatula, to spread sauce over all of meat and vegetables, scrapping as much as possible out of bowl. You don't want to waste even a tiny bit of this wonderful sauce! Sprinkle breadcrumbs over top of all, sprinkle Paprika, over top of breadcrumbs, just enough to make it look nice.

Place covered dish, in pre-heated 350 degree oven, for at least 45 minutes. Sauce should be bubbling, when done. This dish also smells wonderful. You will love it with your mac' n' cheese (recipe follows) which cooks right along with it!

(**Author's note:** This wonderful recipe, was given to me, many years ago, by my dear friend and 'sister,' Ruth Schlicher. The original recipe was made with left-over chicken. I revised it and normally use frozen or fresh chicken breasts.)

Home-made Macaroni and Cheese

Creamy and comforting, this recipe for mac' n cheese, can go with almost anything. For a kids meal, add cut-up hot dogs or ham cubes. Serve on the side or add meats right to casserole dish and mix. For a easy meal, prepare ahead, throw in oven for 35 to 45 minutes and then serve with chicken strips or hamburgers. Anything goes with this wonderful side dish.

Start with:

2 cups of elbow macaroni (cook according to package directions, drain). Add 1-2 tsp. salt, if desired, to cooking water.

For sauce:

3 table spoons of flour
1 stick of margarine (butter can be substituted but burns more easily)
1 ½ cups of 2% milk
1 can of cheddar cheese soup
Paprika to sprinkle on top

Prepare white sauce:

Melt margarine in medium sauce pan. Stir flour into melted margarine over medium heat, until it bubbles, carefully breaking up any lumps. Slowly add milk. Turn up heat, and stir until thickened and you have a beautiful white sauce. Remove from heat. Stir can of cheddar cheese soup into white sauce, mixing thoroughly, once again using small rubber spatula, to get as much soup out of can as possible. Pour sauce over cooked macaroni, that you have already placed into a pretty 2-quart casserole dish. Sprinkle with paprika, to make it look nice. Cook right along with chicken curry divan, at 350 degrees. This dish should also be bubbling nicely, to signal it is done.

Note: Always remember to remove labels from soup cans, rinse out cans and properly **recycle!** Terri is very big on **recycling!**

The Best Chocolate Chip Cookies in the Whole World

No one has ever beaten these chocolate chip cookies! They are to die for (so to speak) and wonderful. They can also be used as a 'diet cookie,' in the sense, that the concerned consumer, should eat one or two, as opposed to four or five. This is how you would do that and still achieve that 'fresh out of the oven' quality. They can be frozen, in a large zip-loc bag and taken out one at a time. Place on a paper towel or small micro-wave safe saucer and warm-up, for 10 or 15 seconds. Mmmm......just like fresh out of the oven! Remember, One cookie, is a diet cookie!

A half-dozen cookies, you are in trouble. Here comes the recipe!

1 cup of **CRISCO** shortening (the brand name here, **is a must**)
¾ cup of brown sugar
¾ cup of white sugar
2 large eggs
1 tsp. of vanilla
1 tbsp. of water

In a large, glass mixing bowl, blend together above ingredients, with an electric mixing, until smooth. Set aside.

Mix together following dry ingredients, in separate bowl. Make sure they are well blended. **Do not sift flour!**

2 cups of flour (Any extra flour, that you can stir into dough, without it getting too dry, will make for a softer cookie. Anywhere from a half to ¾ of a cup, will do. You can also add a little more water to dough)

1 tsp. of baking soda
1tsp. of salt

(Start pre-heating your oven to 375 degrees)

Slowly add dry ingredients, to sugar and egg mixture, stirring to blend together. When thoroughly mixed add:

One twelve ounce bag of Nestle's semi-sweet chocolate chips.

(In this case, a less expensive brand of chocolate chips can be used but I would not recommend it!)

One cup of chopped walnuts (optional, some people can not eat nuts, but you can make a couple of trays without walnuts, for them).

Spray your cookie sheets with low-fat cooking spray. This only needs to be done once. You can also, cover cookie sheets, with a thin layer of shortening, if you have no cooking spray on hand.

Place teaspoons (the ones you stir your coffee with) of cookie dough, (stop eating it, you are dealing with raw eggs!) on the cookie sheet, making four rows of three each, having each tray filled with a dozen. Take a fork, dipped in warm water and flatten the balls of dough. Place cookie sheet in oven and fill another cookie sheet, etc. Watch cookies carefully, so as not to burn. As they start to turn golden brown, remove from oven. They will even bake for another minute or two, on the hot cookie sheet. Remove cookies from cooled cookie sheet, and place on wax paper laid out on table to cool. Store in large freezer bags or plastic container with cover.

It is not unheard of, to triple or even quadruple this recipe, so many people love them! 'Terri's Table' makes them for their customers, adding a cookie two, or three, for each person, with their meal. Makes a lovely dessert. Terri and Brianna also serve them to visitors, with coffee or other hot drinks, especially in cold, winter weather. Love 'em for yourself!

Author's note: I got this recipe, from my dear friend, Kathy S. (passed down to her, from her dear mother, Beverly) and have made them, more times than I could count. They are ideal for family gatherings, picnics, parties and even for building projects, to hand out to the workers, when they are taking a short break.They are also appreciated by new Mommies, new neighbors, or anyone going through a change in their life, who needs a treat. They are the perfect gift of food. Pack in a clean box or Tupperware container, between layers of wax paper. Give generously!

Hamburger Noodle Casserole (Basic family recipe)

This is another, can't miss, winter night warmer upper. Add a salad and some good bread, for a delicious meal. Like spaghetti and chili, this casserole is also better, after a day or two, warmed up in the micro wave, for leftovers.

1 lb. of ground beef
1 medium onion, chopped

Start water boiling, for two cups of elbow macaroni, according to package directions. Add 1 or 2 tsp. of salt to water, if desired. It does stimulate the water to boil faster. Brown ground beef thoroughly, until no longer pink, with onions. Salt and pepper, to taste.

Add to browned meat:
1 quart of canned tomatoes (recipe for canning tomatoes, in <u>Spaghetti with Murder</u>)
2 tsp. of garlic salt
1 tbs. of oregano
1 4 oz. can of tomato sauce

Cook macaroni until tender, drain and lightly rinse. Dump into medium-sized blue oval roaster. Carefully, it will be very hot, add beef and tomato mixture to macaroni. Thoroughly mix together ingredients. Add a 4 oz. can of mushroom stems and pieces, if desired.

Author's note: If I want to double this recipe, I use one extra cup of macaroni and two pounds of ground beef. There is usually no need to add extra canned tomatoes, just another 4 oz. can of tomato sauce. Fresh mushrooms can also be used, if you have them. Spices to taste. Cook, at least 1 and a half hours, at 350 degrees. Let casserole set, for 15 or 20 minutes, after removing from oven, if possible, leaving the cover on to keep it hot. Warm up and enjoy!

Slow-cooker Beef Stew

Yet, another winter night warmer upper! There are just so many, I wish I could include them all. This one, however, is for the good old, <u>finally being used again</u>, slow-cooker. Prepare in the morning, supper is ready after dark. Like Terri, Angie, and Brianna, you will want to enjoy this in bowls, with lots of saltine crackers. Add anything else that you would like, cheese or a salad or fruit, bread or rolls, instead of crackers.

Brown on stove-top:
2-3 lbs. of cubed stew meat
1 medium onion, chopped

In a large frying pan, with hot oil, brown meat, sprinkling with flour, salt and pepper. (I always have a mixture of this, in a container, ready to sprinkle over meats, such as beef for Swiss steak or pork chops, as well as beef stew meat.) Mix browning meat, with flour mixture, using a wooden spoon to move pieces around the pan, to nicely brown. Add meat to bottom of slow-cooker.

Add to meat in slow-cooker:
1 quart of canned tomatoes
1 tbs. of Worcestershire sauce
1 tsp. of ground sage
1 or 2 stalks of celery (thinly sliced)
2 or 3 medium potatoes (cubed)
A couple of dozen baby carrots

This stew can cook all day, 5 to 6 hours on high. When you come home, check vegetables, turn to low if tender. The flour mixed with beef when browning, will help this stew to thicken. This recipe makes enough for three or four people. Again, warm-up and enjoy!

Aunt Kristy's Barbecue Beef

2 lbs. of lean ground beef
1 medium onion (chopped)
1 green pepper (chopped)
salt and pepper (to taste)
2 tbs. of vegetable oil

Brown ground beef, until no longer pink, in oil with onions, green pepper, salt and pepper, drain.

Add to ground beef mixture:
1 can of tomato soup
¼ cup of brown sugar
1 tsp. of brown mustard
dash of vinegar (probably about ½ tsp.)

Heat browned and drained, ground beef, with tomato soup mixture. Serve on sandwich buns or even in soft or hard taco shells. Add anything you want to the tacos, such as cheese, onions, tomatoes, lettuce, just like a regular taco. Serve with chips and pickles, like Terri did. Or, if this is the main part of your meal, add a salad, or fresh veggies, with dip. Don't forget the cookies!!

Additional recipes from DOUBLE TRUFFLE can be found at the following websites:

Find the scrambled eggs and dinner recipes at:
epicurious.com

Scrambled Eggs with Truffles
Asparagus Parmesan Pastry Rolls
Truffle-Infused French Onion Soup
Fillet of Beef Wellington
White Asparagus with Truffle Vinaigrette
Truffled Mashed Potatoes

Find the chocolate truffle recipes at:
French food.about.com

Truffes Moka
Truffes au Rhum
Truffes au Cointreau
Truffes au Pastis
Truffes Nutella

Find the Guatemalan recipes at:
foodnetwork.com

Chile Rellenos
Green Chile Stew
Plantains Glazed with Temptation Caramel
Grilled Carne Advada
Flan Mexican
….and many, many, more.

<u>Teaser</u> (from the author)

Recipes to be featured in my next book, OVER-EASY, which
will be set in Door County, Wisconsin!

The Perfect Prime Rib
Meat Balls in Beef Gravy
Grandma's Hot Turkey Sandwiches
Rocky River Bottom (cream cheese-pudding torte)
DOOR COUNTY Fish Boil (of course)
….and many, many, more!

Thanx, for reading, DOUBLE TRUFFLE!